# *Miss Wayne*
## & THE
# QUEENS OF DC

ESSENCE MAGAZINE BEST SELLING AUTHOR OF
BLACK AND UGLY AS EVER AND A HUSTLERS SON 2

# T STYLES

**PUBLISHER'S NOTE:**

Library of Congress Control Number: 2010928716
ISBN: 0-9823913-4-X
ISBN 13: 978-0-9823913-4-1
Cover Design: Davida Baldwin www.oddballdsgn.com
Editor: Advanced Editorial Services
Graphics: Davida Baldwin
www.thecartelpublications.com
First Edition

**Printed in the United States of America**

What's Up Fam!!

I can't explain how boosted I am right now! So much good shit is poppin' off for The Cartel. But first, I have to speak on this book, "Miss Wayne and the Queens of DC"! Maaaannnnnn...All I gotta say is BRAVO T. Styles! I had the pleasure and privilege, of course, to read this trailblazin' novel before it hit the press. I could not put it down! T., has weaved, literally, a novel together that is full of passion, drama, foolishness, love and lessons so great, you will be left wanting more. Where, "Black & Ugly As Ever" leaves off, "Ms. Wayne" picks up the ball, runs with it to the end zone and scores!!!" Fam, you in for a treat with this one so get ready!

Next item of business is what's next for us, MOVIES! The Cartel Publications is on to movies! The first movie out the gate to be filmed is, "Pitbulls in a Skirt". Yep, the story you fell in love with will now be put on screen. So make sure you look out for that one. It's the first of more to come, but rest assured, they are comin'!

Aight ya'll in keeping with tradition, with every novel you all know by now we shine a spotlight on an author who is either a vet or a new comer makin' their way in this literary world. In this novel, we recognize:

## " *Jessica A. Robinson* "

Jessica is a new author who has already penned two novels, "Holy Seduction" and "Pretty Skeletons". The Cartel Publications applauds Jessica for wanting to become an author and actually completing her goal. Many people want to write and may even start a novel, but it takes true dedication and determination to COMPLETE one! Congrats Jessica, you did it baby girl and we see you. Keep 'em comin'

On that note, I'ma leave ya'll to it! Go head, call out sick from work, go grab your favorite snack and get ready to read greatness!

Be easy!

Charisse "C. Wash" Washington
VP, The Cartel Publications

www.thecartelpublications.com
www.twitter.com/cartelbooks
www.facebook.com/publishercharissewashington
www.myspace.com/thecartelpublications
www.facebook.com/cartelcafeandbooks

# Acknowledgements

I acknowledge every one of my fans who stay with me, and support me as my career grows. I truly…truly do this for you.

# Dedication

I Dedicate This to A Community, Who's Culture, Style
and Influence More Often Than Not Goes without
Credit.

# *Note to Readers*

During your read of Miss Wayne & The Queens of D.C., please keep in mind that the characters often refer to themselves as women because in their heart they are. Please don't get confused during the duration of the storyline by the use of exchanging feminine to masculine references.

# *Foreword*

*In gay culture, a House is an organization led by a house mother or father. Each house is unique and each has its own identity. Some houses are active in the community and others can be dangerous and violent if tested. One thing is certain, not mentioning its existence is to deny one of the biggest vehicles of self-expression within the gay community. And I don't intend on doing that.*

*People always wanna know when I knew I was gay. What kind of fuckin' question is that? I am what I am just like they are what they are. Chile...I'm not in to answerin' questions that can't be answered. I've been Miss Wayne all my damn life! This all I know. What I would like to know though, is why didn't I get my ass on that plane when I had a chance? Why didn't I follow my instincts and leave the bullshit behind me? Oh well, it's too late to think about the what if's now. All I can do is face what's comin' my way, and hope I live to tell my story.*

*- Miss Wayne*

# Unwanted Houseguest, Unwanted Problems

## ❧THE PRESENT❧

*The taste of salty blood and metal lingered heavily inside Miss Wayne's mouth. His eyes were closed shut and every part of his body was riddled in pain. He couldn't remember how he got into the situation. All he knew was that he was in danger, grave danger. And at that moment that was all that mattered.*

*Lifting his head slightly, he tried to pull his bloody pasted eyes open. When he realized he couldn't, he dropped his head back on the floor as the smell of feces and urine wafted heavily within his breathing space.*

*"Wayne! Wayne!" The heavy whisperer called above him. "Are you still alive?"*

*Finding not the energy to answer, he felt as if the room was spinning. And as he had several times that day, he drifted out of consciousness.*

# *Mercy On Your Souls*
# *Miss Wayne*

## SOME MONTHS EARLIER

Daffany's mom looks bad.
*Really bad.*
No scratch that.

Really bad is Miss Tyrone sittin' ova here next to me lookin' a hot ass mess. Since I've known him, we've always had a love and hate type of relationship. So even though I told him he was dead wrong, he was determined to wear those black liquid legs stretch pants despite my saying that it was the worst thing to sport at a funeral. Before we continue, let me say this…in my entire life, I've never met anyone more scandalous than Tyrone. Trouble follows her around wherever she goes. So why do I keep him around? Because I know he'd never try no bullshit with me. The girl knows better.

We had only been here, at Stewarts Funeral Home in Northeast D.C, for only five minutes and Miss Tyrone had already scared the hell out of the boys choir and made the preacher forget his sermon. That's not even the worst part about this mess! On the way to her seat she knocked over Ms. Hathaway's brand new church hat and poked Miss Parade on the side of her neck with all that extra dick she's smugglin' between her legs. I don't know why she doesn't realize that twelve inches of basket crammed in stretch pants is not feminine. I don't care how far back you *try* to tuck 'em! Trust me…I know.

I swear…sometimes I know exactly why I left the DC area and other times to tell you the truth...I don't know why I left. My gay friends are different. They're over the top and sometimes they could give a fuck about who they hurt. It's all about the money to buy a designer bag, wigs, gear and sometimes a sex change. For what? To *walk* in a ball, sugar!

Before movin' to LA, I started the House of Dreams. A *house* in the gay community is like a fraternity or sorority, where membership is accepted but mainly rejected. I'm the overall Mother, which means I have to show the children of both the DC and LA chapters the way to live glamorously and get that money…but believe me when I say it's easier said than done.

The ball circuit is the best. When I was here in the DC area, if I wasn't hanging with Parade, Daffany and Sky before she was murdered, I was dressin' in drag and walkin' the walk, honey! Trust me when I say you haven't seen anything like a gay men's ball. Trophies are given and sometimes prizes awarded based on the winner for specific categories. I won many of them including the Drag Queen Realness category. Through it all I never won the one trophy I always wanted, the Legend Category. Do I feel deserving? Hell yeah! Nobody in DC has won as many balls as me, baby. So this girl is Legendary!

Oh shit, I done ran a mental marathon and forgot what I was talkin' about. Anyway, this day is for Miss Daffany's mother's funeral. We'll talk about all that other shit later. Where were we? Oh yeah! We were speakin' about Miss Tyrone's ape lookin' ass.

"Girl, put this jacket on and sit down," I tug on her silk pink shawl, which is far too thin to be wearing in the end of winter. My black insulated coat with the tiny red hearts inside the panel, swing from my hand. "You disturbin' Ms. Stan's goin' away day. Don't nobody want to see all that early this Thursday mornin'."

This is why my DC house gets a bad name. Everybody knows the DC chapter is not as grand as the one I started in LA. We get money from throwing house parties. Here Miss Tyrone is the mother of the house of DC, which is a rank under me, yet she has no class or loot.

"Girl, move!" she says pushing the coat away. "If anything I'm bringin' a little excitement to this gawd awful funeral." Miss Tyrone remains standing and clapping along to the choir's voices despite their evil stares. What she really has her eyes on is the preacher. She claims they have a thing going on and to tell you the truth, I can't call it. I don't put shit past nobody these days, even a man of the cloth.

"You know if my baby hears you down there," I say pointing at the other end of the wooden row seat we share, "I'm droppin' your ass with a left and then a right? You do understand this don't you?"

"She can't hear me," Miss Tyrone whispers. "But you know I'm tellin' the truth. That black ass thing up there don't look nothin' like her mother. Dead or livin'! What was she smokin' before she died? Kerosene?"

I hated to admit it but she was right. I guess all the years of using hard drugs, selling her body and neglecting her only daughter had finally caught up with her.

And when I look to my left, on the far end, I see Miss Daffany's face. She's saddened and her energy cuts through me like a knife. When we got on the plane to come back home for the funeral she said she could handle it. Said she knew this day would come and had prepared for this moment most of her life. I guess she underestimated the power it took to bury your mother. This scares me because it's so important to keep her stress at a minimum…any change in her emotions could cause her immune system to go out of whack and flare up her HIV.

"You okay?" Miss Parade grips Miss Daffany around the waist as they both look at the open casket in the front of the church. Miss Parade is pregnant again for the second time in three years. I swear every time that Jay boy puts his dick in her pussy, two legs and two arms comes out. They already gots twin boys with a baby girl on the way.

You should see those beautiful little boys. They look like little Indians with smooth black skin like their mother and silky black hair like their father.

"I'm fine." Miss Daffany whispers. "Just wish I was somewhere else. I don't want to go through with this."

"She's in a better place, sweetie you know that." I reach over and touch her hand.

She smiles.

I smile back.

If ever I doubt what real love feels like, when I see the way Miss Parade and Miss Daffany look at me, I know that there is a God and if he's blessed me with friends like these, then I must be worthy. I use to be able to look into my mother's eyes and get the same feeling…but I can't say that anymore. And no, I don't want to talk about it right now.

We were just about to give God the praise and the glory when an usher reaches over and taps Miss Tyrone on the shoulder. "Excuse me, sir. We're gonna have to ask you to put somethin' else around your waist or remain in your seat. We've already gotten several complaints 'bout your clothin'."

I shake my head. Oh shit! Here comes the drama!

Miss Tyrone places his hands on his hips and pivots his body around to see all the church members staring in his direction. He was acting as if he was the Messiah, wanting to see which one of his disciples turned on him.

When he didn't get the pity or the response he wanted, he gripped his collar and says, "How dare you come over here and embarrass me like this, mothafucka!"

"Hold up, Miss Tyrone...we in church!"

"Fuck that shit! This mothafucka got me all the way fucked up!" He yells. The church choir continues to sing although their voices go down a notch. "I don't recall God sendin' out an invitation talkin' about a dress code." He places his fists on his burly shiny hips. "Now since he gave me these balls," he slaps his crotch area sending a massive CLAP sound throughout the tiny church, "then if they're bulgin' a little, I must be still alright in His eyes."

The usher's dark face turns as red as the brand new Sunday morning dress I chose to wear today.

The usher was about to say something else until I say, "Honey, this is a gay man. You done already got cussed the fuck out and called everything but Susan. So unless you want a continuation of this show, co-starrin' you, I suggest you go on back there and pray he doesn't read you on the way down the aisle."

He grips his black leather bible and points it at Tyrone as if to cast out the demons.

"Trust me, them scriptures in the Good Book won't have nothin' on the words he'll give you if you don't sit on down somewhere. Go on now!"

The usher looks at Miss Tyrone's troublemaking ass, Miss Daffany, Miss Parade's nine-month-old belly and turns around to me and says, "God, have mercy on your souls!"

"Girl, I do believe he's the one who been slayin' all the drag queens in DC. Look how he tried it wit' me."

"Bitch, sit your dry ass down and respect this funeral." When he doesn't move quick enough for my taste I say, "Don't move me to perform acts on you up in here. Sit!"

Finally he does and for the first time since we got off the plane from LA, Miss Daffany laughs. We all laugh. I guess Miss Tyrone's hot ass mess antics came in handy after all. I love to see my friends happy.

Focusing back on the sermon, the preacher does his best to continue the funeral. But when he messes up a scripture I get angry. You see the bible is the one thing I know from front to back. My mother made sure of it.

What the scripture was supposed to say before he messed it up was, *"Children, obey your parents in the Lord, for this is right. Honor your father and mother— which is the first commandment with a promise – that it may go well with you and that you may have a long life. – Ephesians 6:1-3*

Yeah…he had it wrong. I know that one in particular because I was conflicted as a child. Although I loved my mother, I hated my father and found it hard to obey him. To tell you the truth, I hate him to this day.

◆ •••••••••••••••••••••••••••••••••••••••••• ◆

# Reflecting On the Younger Years
## Miss Wayne

*The hardwood floors in the old Southeast DC apartment carried a brilliant shine. Ten-year-old Wayne Peterson positioned himself in the hallway, a few feet from his bedroom door—his parent's room was in the middle and the front door was on the opposite end.*

*Wayne loved to pretend that the hallway was a runway. Then he would dance toward the door. Once at the* door, he'd pretend Prince Charming would come rushing inside to whisk him away...but he never came.

One crisp, sunny morning, he decided to open his curtains and let the sunrays shine against the hardwood floors in the hallway. He'd already placed on four pairs of his mother's brand new stockings to make up for not having dark tights. Then he tied up the back of his white t-shirt and slid on his mother's white nursing shoes, which were the only shoes resembling high heels in the house. With the shoes on, he ran to his room, pressed play on his tape player and allowed Whitney Houston's voice to boom through the speakers.

*"I'M EVERY WOMAN! IT'S ALL IN MEEEEEEE!"*

Although his mother was home sleep, suffering from multiple sclerosis—which rendered her unable to care for herself, she didn't mind the loud music one bit. In fact she loved it. In her mind she was thankful for her blessings and the Lord still seeing fit to allow her to hear despite her failing health.

*"Okay, Miss Wayne, work that runway!"* he said to himself.

Busy with his one-man show, he heard a noise. At first he thought it was his mother calling him but when he ran to his room and turned the music down for a few seconds, he heard nothing. With nothing left to do, he refocused on his trademark dance.

*Stoop and walk. Right Kick.*

*Stoop and walk. Left kick.*

*Stoop and walk. Throw arms in the air.*

*Stoop and walk. Strike a pose.*

The large white nurse shoes did not fit properly and flopped under him as he lit the hallway on fire with his moves. But the moment he reached the end of the hall, his father, Bells Peterson, who had returned home early from the war, met him with a hard jab to his tiny jaw. Wayne *hadn't seen him in over six months and this is how he chose to greet him.*

*"What I tell you about runnin' 'round here like a fuckin' girl?" He frowned down at Wayne, unmoved by the blood that fell from his mouth...dampened his white shirt and glistened against the shiny hardwood floors. "You a boy and I ain't raisin' no bitches!"*

*Although his father had warned him about what he deemed as 'actin' like a girl' he'd never...ever...hit him until that moment. His extra light-skin and eyes were just like Wayne's and before the alcohol abuse, compliments of the Gulf war, he was very handsome. But like a lot of soldiers, when times got hard, his looks took a toll.*

*"I'm sorry." Wayne whined. "I was just dancin', daddy. I didn't mean to act like a girl. Really."*

*"Sorry ain't good enough! You got my Daddy's name and you runnin' 'round here like a fuckin' sissy!" He clenched his fist again preparing to beat the life out of his only child.*

*Wayne was picking himself up off the floor and then he heard, "Now...I know that ain't my boy down there on the floor. I know that's not what I'm seein'."*

*When Bells and Wayne looked in the direction of the voice, they saw Marbel Peterson. Standing in her room's doorway might've seemed ordinary for some but for a woman who suffered with MS most of her life, this was a magnificent feat.*

*"Baby?" Bells said with slight fright in his voice. "What...I mean...how did you get up out of bed on your own?"*

*"You ain't hearin' me. Was that my chile lyin' on that floor? Please tell me you didn't place hands on my chile!"*

Even though the disease had entrapped her muscles, it didn't take away her beauty. She was still strikingly beautiful with her deer eyes and beautiful dark skin.

Bells took a deep breath, broadened his shoulders and said, "Yeah I taught him a lesson. 'Cause it's obvious that since I've been gone, things have gotten out of control 'round here! This boy act like he don't know he got balls 'tween his legs!"

"That's what you call it when you hit a chile? Teachin' him a lesson?"

"Sure I do! If he's gonna be a man, he's gonna have to act like one. A real man takes care of his family, not act all feminine so somebody can take care of him. Now I'm raisin' men 'round here! 'Specially the ones that got my dead daddy's name!"

"And I told you before he ain't actin' like no girl! He actin' like our son! Just 'cause he different don't give you no reason to hurt him."

For lack of a better argument he said, "I'm the man of this house and you'll do as I say, woman! Both of you!"

"Is that right?" she smirked.

"That's mothafuckin' right! I pay the bills in this bitch and I demand respect! Now if you can't fix it to see things my way, then there's the door!"

Marbel smiled a little. Then she pushed the strength of her body away from the doorway and further into the hallway. She was on her way to him.

"Mama, be careful!" Wayne said running by her side to offer his assistance.

"Move out the way, boy. I gots to address my husband and I gots to address him right now. And for what I'm about to say, I need to look into his eyes so he knows I'm not messin' around."

*Wayne never saw such power in his mother until that moment. Further and further she scooted down the hallway, leaning on the wall for support. When she made it to Bells, the confidence he possessed when he first came through the door had slightly diminished. He knew it took little masculinity to come into the house and hit a child, but it took courage, strength and love to move a body that refused to budge without help for over a year.*

*"Now you hear me and hear me good." She said in his face. "We ain't hittin' kids in this house and we not makin' them feel bad for who they is either. Now that's my only son," she pointed at Wayne, "and I loves him...in all his splendor. Now if you's ashame of him, go on...go back out that door yourself. But me, I'm stayin' right here." With that she reached in her cotton robe, flicked a knife and held it against his thin chin. "But you betta neva...eva...put your hands on my son again. Understood?"*

*He nodded ever so slightly to avoid the slash.*

*"Great. We understand one another." She said tucking the knife back into her pocket. "Now welcome home and help me back to bed."*

# *Mr. Husband Material*

## QUEEN TYRONE

Adrian and me are in the house chillin' and surfin' the net in the three-bedroom townhouse on Galveston Street in Southeast DC that Dayshawn rented. I didn't live here at first, until five months after he bought it, he was havin' problems payin' the rent. From then on I've been here to help him out. Although we live deep in the fuckin' hood, if you ask me, I don't want to be no place else.

Wearin' black tight shorts and a powder blue baby T, I know I'm killin' it right now. And once I shave the hair off my face, biiiiitttttcchhh, you won't be able to tell me nothin'! All I need now is some dick and some smoke and I'll be good.

Miss bitch-face Adrian over here is wearin' grey sweats and a plain white T-shirt and I laugh. Lookin' at Adrian is like lookin' at a girl. His light brown skin and soft curly hair sits stupidly on his head and I feel sorry for him. I mean…if a man wants to fuck a nigga who looks like a bitch, he'd be with a girl. I'm not hatin'. I'm just statin'.

I will give him credit for one thing, he owns more diamonds than most girls would get in their whole lives. Last time he had it appraised, it went for about ten thousand dollars, and he didn't leave the house without his diamond heart shaped necklace, bracelet and ring.

On anotha level…lately I have been havin' so much on my fuckin' mind. Shit most people don't have to worry about. I'm a gay man, in my early thirties, and the only thing I care about is getting fucked or fuckin' someone.

I'm not talkin' about sometimes either. It's an obsession with me. Like if I can't have it, I'ma die! I done fucked everybody from my son's bus driver to my wife Shannon's brother. I know it's fucked up, but it is what it is and to be truthful, I could care fuckin' less what you or anybody else thinks.

I'm a queen.

I'm a mother of the House of Dreams.

And I'm fabulous in all ways.

And while your minds' are workin' overtime, let me put them to rest...yes I did say I have a son and a wife. But she was what we gay men called a *beard.* Because being with her was like wearing a beard in public...she was someone I could pretend to be in a heterosexual relationship with for everyone else's sake.

I guess now you're wonderin' how is it possible for me to have a thirteen-year old son and be a gay man. I didn't always hate pussy. I fucked my wife and came inside of her just like the next man.

My wife and I, who I'm still married to, on paper anyway, are no longer together. When it was good it was good but after a while it just lost its flavor. She was my *first.* My first sexual experience in high school. My *first* girlfriend and the *first* person who taught me that there was nothin' more I liked, than to be fucked in my ass.

Shit, Shannon was handy with her mother's rubber dicky, which she found one day while lookin' for money in her room. Shannon's a bigger freak than me. And if her mother knew how much mileage that dildo had on it and how many times it had been in my ass, she probably would've performed an exorcism on it and burned at the stake. Yeah...back then things were simple. I was a bisexual man who loved fuckin' both men and women. That is, until one day the look of her pussy made me jealous. I remember lookin' at the way she moaned and saying to myself, 'I wish someone could make me feel like this. I wish someone could make me feel safe and hold me in his arms.' So I went out to find the real thing.

The day she discovered where my heart really lied, my son was born and I wasn't by her side. So the next day she got out of her hospital bed, left our son at the hospital nursery and came lookin' for me. It took a while but she found me, cruisin' for trade at a public park. I was faced down on wet green grass, with the trade's fingers in my mouth and his dick in my ass. Bareback...no condoms! The way I like it.

Instead of takin' that as my out of the relationship, I felt guilty and asked her to be my wife. Only to realize a week afterwards that I couldn't be married and faithful at the same time. Through it all she could never bring herself to say, 'I want a divorce', and I doubt she ever will.

While waitin' on Adrian to pull up a website, someone knocks on the front door. It wasn't a surprise because people come over this bitch uninvited all the time.

When I open the door, my friend Gary who prefers to be called Garisha is standing before me wearing a red summer dress and tennis shoes. After all this time, I still can't get over how ugly she is! This queen is uglier than two Bernie Mac's put together. Large pussy bumps 'round out her face and all I can say is that it's truly a sight to see. The worst part is, she has pushed so much silicone in her face, that she's starting to look like a lion. It's a mess.

"Bitch, I need to use your bathroom," Garisha asked busting into the door. "I just met this trade on the way over here!"

Although irritating most of the time, I fucked with him because he was the only person I knew more gutter than me. We did shit together so cruddy that I'd have to kill somebody if they ever found out. Including fuckin' this 16-year-old boy after he came home from football practice one day. He use to come 'round Galveston all the time to smoke and drink our shit up. But one day he started flirtin' and tellin' me, Garisha and Big Boody Brandy that we couldn't handle him…and how he would fuck the shit out of this and that.

As usual, we got drunk but this time decided to go to a hotel to finish the party. Big Boody Brandy had a date so she didn't go with us, but that ain't stop me and Garisha. The young boy was all game when we was suckin' his ass and lettin' him fuck us all night. But I guess he got mad when me and Garisha turned his young ass around and broke his back out. If you ask me I think he liked it but just like most 'so called straight men' who think about shit too much the next morning, he was afraid someone would find out and threatened to cry rape. When we found that shit out me and Garisha put on men's clothes and waited for him after school. The moment we caught him alone we beat him to death and buried his body at Anacostia Park. That was six months ago and they haven't found his body yet.

"Why you gotta use our bathroom, Garisha?" I frown. "I mean…what's wrong with your place? Or the street?"

"I need to freshen up! Bitch, you know I live all the way off 58th!"

"Well I'm busy right now so you can't stay long." I say closing the door. "Where ya'll goin' anyway?"

"Where you think? I'm goin' somewhere to get some dick! But I gotta douch my bussy first!" he says referring to his asshole. "And I know you not actin' all different! Wit' all the mothafuckas I let in my house for you!"

"Bitch, I don't need a history lesson Just hurry the fuck up!"

When I'm walk back to Adrian, Garisha runs to the bathroom and yells, "I need a washcloth!"

"Girrrrllll…what is you givin' right now?!" I scream. "Ain't nobody got no time for all that shit! Use a sock!"

"A sock?!" He yells walking back into the living room. "But I need it to clean my girl!"

"Bitch, either use a sock or use your hand. Your choice."

Garisha sits on the sofa, removes his tennis shoe and then his sock. Mind you I said he's wearing a summer dress. So you already know what he's givin'.

"You gonna need me for somethin' else one day! Rememba this shit!"

"Girl, bye!" I say fanning her off.

When she walks to the bathroom, I focus back on Adrian at the computer.

"Have you found his page yet?" I ask.

"Nope. I can't find it. I don't know what's wrong."

"You sure you puttin' in the right stuff?"

"Yes. I'm puttin' in the right information."

"Well why isn't his picture comin' up?" I ask lookin' down at Adrian while he supposedly keys in MrHusbandMaterial's screen name in the searchable window on the gay website, AllTheWayOpen.com.

He pauses and says, "I'm not sure. You think he blocked you? I say that only because you said he didn't think you looked like the picture you posted on the site when he met you last week."

As I look down at Adrian I grow angry. Fuck is he tryin' to say? I posted my real picture on that site, even if it was taken in the ninth grade.

"Girl just try it again! Ain't nobody tryin' to hear all that shit you drippin'!"

While I'm lookin' at the computer screen, the TV which is playin' the news is featuring The Drag Queen

Slayer story again. Apparently some fool is runnin' 'round DC killin' queens. When he's done, he usually cuts off a part of their body and eats it.

"I'm done," Garisha says walking into the living room. "Thanks for nothin'!"

I smell something so nasty lingering in the air that I can't believe it came from his body.

"Please tell me you just took a shit too." I say covering my nose.

"Girl, what are you talkin' about?" He asks rummaging through his purse.

"All I know is I smell somethin' and it don't smell like soap! And if you ain't just shit, somethin' crawled up in your ass and died."

Adrian turns his nose up and say, "Girl you do smell a little foul."

"Shut up, bitch face! Always hatin' on a grown ass woman! I'm out of here! I'll call you later, girl." He says walking out the door.

I shake my head, turn the air conditioning on to get rid of the smell and lock the front door. Garisha's ass got somethin' and she betta go get it checked out before her dick falls off!

Adrian refocuses on the news and says, "You think they gonna catch him?"

"Don't worry about all that...did you find him yet?" I pause lookin' down at him.

"Not yet. I'm gonna log in with my account though. Maybe it'll work now."

As he logs out of my account and into his, I think about some things. Like how I wished I would've stayed in school and got an education. I sucked a few dicks to get my homework done and even found ways to get my tests completed. With my smart ass, I went all the way up to the ninth grade without being able to read word *one*. If

I could, I would be keyin' in the info on the site myself. But as it stands, I can barely read my name on paper if I saw it. When a teacher found out I was illiterate in school and I couldn't bribe him with sex, I dropped out in the 9th grade. I guess you could say I haven't looked back since.

"Give me his screen name again." He says sneezing.

"Uggh! Cover your nose!!" I scream. "You know I hate snot and shit! Be careful!"

"I'm sorry."

"His screen name is MrHusbandMaterial." I frown.

The moment he searches for his name under his account, his picture comes up. I spent two months talkin' to this nigga on the phone before we finally got together. And now he wants to play me? You know what, if he don't want this bussy, fuck him! I'll get a new nigga in the morning.

"You okay?" He asks.

"Why wouldn't I be? I ain't trippin' off no trade."

"You sure?"

"Look...don't piss me off, Aid! You know how that can be. Anyway ain't nothin' wrong wit' me so I ain't hardly worryin' about one nigga. His dick was trash anyway. All I got to do is make a phone call and I'm set."

As I'm walking into the living room, I see Adrian staring at me.

"What now?!"

"Can I make a suggestion?"

"About what?" I ask with an attitude.

"You have beautiful dark skin, yet you wear make-up a little lighter than your complexion. And...sometimes you should wear a full wig until your hair grows out."

"What's wrong wit' my hair?"

"Ummm...well...I don't like when you braid your natural hair and wear it out without combing it or anything. It sticks up in the air and kinda makes you look…messy."

"You really think you got it over me don't you?"

"I'm not sayin' that…I just really care about you."

"Honey…you just do you, and I'ma do me!"

As I walk to the living room and sit down, I down the vodka on the table and pour me another glass. Since I'm not gettin' no dick I know immediately what I need is to get high.

"And call, Big Boody Brandy over here to bring me some smoke!" I tell him.

Big Boody Brandy was another queen I ran with from time to time. Everybody used her to get their drugs because she made drop offs and ran shit around Galveston. Her name is Brandon Bar but like most queens, she changed it up a little to suit the lifestyle. Brandy knew a lot of shit about me that I wish she didn't. For instance, she was the one who knew that me and Garisha was the last ones with that football player before we killed him. And to tell you the truth, I hate that she has that over me.

"I ain't got no money, Ty." Adrian tells me. "You have any to give her when she comes?"

"Ya'll ain't never got shit on the package but always wanna smoke."

"I gave the rest of my money to Chris."

"How come you stay givin' Chris money but he don't give you shit? I mean, if ya'll are so good friends he should look out for you sometimes too."

"He's my best friend, Ty. And he does looks out for me sometimes. But my cell phone is in his name and I didn't want him having to pay for it."

"Yeah…well…whatever! You just better not be tellin' him none of my business. I told you he know Shannon. So if I find out you been tellin' him any of my business and I can't see my son, I'ma be fucked up with you and you gonna know."

Even though I didn't see my son Avil a lot, I don't want no problems in case I want to.

"I wouldn't do that," he says looking all stupid and shit. "Whatever goes on in here stays in here."

"Yeah whateva. And just so you know when Big Boody Brandy brings me my shit, it's all mine. Don't ask for shit! Go ahead and call her…tell her I need a fifty bag of weed."

After she makes the call I walk into my bedroom and call Garisha for a favor.

"You still with dude?" I whisper so Adrian can't hear me.

"Just finished up. His ass couldn't last two minutes. Why?"

"You want some smoke?"

"Bitch, you know I want some! I'm on my way!"

"Girl…HOLD! You all in a hurry and the train ain't even got here yet. Is your brother home from jail yet?"

"Yeah…why?"

"Boody Brandy on her way over here to bring me a fifty bag. I want you to have your brother rob her ass."

"Ain't that's your peoples?"

"You wanna play twenty questions or get high?"

"I'm callin' him now."

"Good! And hurry up!"

As I wait for my bag I realize I'm tired of bein' broke. Some shit is gonna have to give! I'm gonna need a steady flow of cash if I'm gonna maintain a certain life-style.

Twenty minutes later while waiting on Garisha I hear a loud knock at the front door. Knowin' my smoke is here puts me in a better mood already. I just hope they covered their tracks because Big Boody can be a mess.

Things were all good until I open my door and see Garisha covered in blood.

"You alright girl?!" I ask as she drops to the floor.

"No, girl! I been stabbed!"

# *Catch A Liar By Her Wig*

## ❧MISS WAYNE❧

I thought about my mother today.

I think about her everyday even though I haven't seen her in over two years.

It's so hard to think about the current condition of our relationship when we use to be so close. It's hard to think about anything pertaining to her at all. And although I know I should face her I hated her after the last time we spoke. And if you knew how close we were, you could never imagine how that could be.

Sigh.

Anyway, I just dropped Parade and Daffany off at the Embassy Suites hotel in DC so they could get some rest. Although the funeral was the day before yesterday, they were both still mentally drained.

Once in the black Honda Accord rental, I called Day-shawn back to find out what she had to tell me earlier that was so urgent.

"Girl, I can't even say it on the phone. All I know is Big Boody Brandy stabbed Ugly Garisha and they sayin' Tyrone mixed all the way in this mess! I'm scared, Miss Wayne!"

"For somebody who don't wanna say nothin' on the phone, you sure sayin' a lot."

"Well it's true."

"Where it happen?" I ask.

"'Round here."

"You were there?"

"Naw…I was pulling up when that shit happened. So I backed up and went the other way."

23

"Sneaky Day…always weaseling out of shit." He got that name because whenever some shit went down, he always managed to get away undetected.

"Just hurry, girl! I think shit 'bout to get out of hand 'round Galveston!"

When I hang up with her, I stop by the liquor store to grab me a bottle of Kettle One and some cranberry juice. Then I play Mariah Carey's CD, "The Emancipation of Mimi" to relax my mind. The shit ain't workin'. You don't understand, Miss Tyrone is my girl, but sometimes she got a lot of shit with her. And if you're on her wrong side, she can be your worst enemy. She changes how she feels about you with the blow of the wind.

I arrived at Day's place thirty minutes later. The moment I walk inside I can't believe the scene. I ain't been here in over two years and everything inside the house is the exact same. They got the same old pathetic lookin' black leather sofa pushed up against the wall. And a wooden coffee table sits in the middle of the floor and is covered with worn out gay men magazines. Who knows what kind of mess is dried up on 'em.

When you go to Day's you know to bring your own chair or you'll be sittin' on the floor. Like now, somebody brought a Redskin's portable chair and a couple of grey metal ones too. The only other furniture in the living room is a computer station, which sits in the corner . A wobbly office chair sits in front of it.

Dayshawn's place use to be real nice. But they'd been robbed so many times, that he stopped fixin' shit up. You never knew what would happen at any given time 'round here. These bitches always got somethin' goin' on! If somebody ain't gettin' stabbed, they're gettin' shot or killed. And that shit happens on the good days.

"What's the blast?" I ask walking into the house. The usual suspects, Tyrone, Adrian and Marlo who preferred to be called Marlene, were all in the living room smoking weed.

Dayshawn locks the door behind me and the iron bat they call 'The long arm of the law', falls on the floor. He picks it back up and places it in the corner next to the door. It was supposed to defend them if someone tried to come in. Personally I never known a mothafucka to be scared of a bat when they got a gun…have you?

"Thanks for comin', girl," Dayshawn says kissing me on each of my cheeks. "Too much shit is goin' on today."

"Let me get you some ice and cranberry juice, Mother. For your drink." Adrian says to me.

I hand him the bag and say, "Thanks, darling." Then I sit on the sofa next to Tyrone. "Now, Tyrone, do tell! What the fuck happened? Why Garisha get stabbed last night? And why your name ringin' bells?"

She readjusts in her seat and I already know she's 'bout to make some shit up.

"Girl…I don't even know where to start."

The moment she's about to give me the T, someone knocks at the door. Adrian returns with my drink and I notice that the Vodka bottle doesn't come back with him. Shit makes it in this house but it never goes out.

When Dayshawn opens the door Big Boody Brandy comes barging in running up to Tyrone. She's carrying a black teacup Yorkie that is barking at the top of its lungs. Big Boody never went anywhere without that dog and I always wondered how she got shit done on the block with it. She even showered with that yip-yapper.

And then there's Day! Please tell me who opens the door without lookin' through the peephole first when you know you got beef? They live in the mothafuckin' hood for gay sake!

On guard, Marlene and me immediately stand up and Adrian runs into the kitchen to grab a knife.

Big Boody Brandy fucked with a few of the hustler's around the way and had a reputation for her violence. And although she's mad now, I still had to give the girl props. She looked real cute in the tight fitted black dress she was wearing and her red Prada pumps. She also was one of the few queens who could sport a boy cut and still look pretty. And she has an ass so fat, you know it was manufactured.

"Bitch, you tried to set me up didn't you?!" She yells in Tyrone's face, the dog barking too.

"Brandy...what got you on fire, honey? 'Cause I know you know betta than to be runnin' up in Day's place wit' all this drama." I ask.

"Miss Wayne, this bitch tried to have me robbed! And I know she guilty 'cause she never answers the phone when I call!"

"You're on ten and I'ma need you at a five. We can hear you fine without all the yellin'."

She lowers her voice a little because everybody in this bitch know they don't want me rockin' out in this mothafucka. What fucked me up was that the dog stopped barking too.

She takes a deep breath and say, "I been callin' here to see if she had a part in Garisha's ugly ass robbin' me and every time I call, she's supposedly never home!"

"I'm tryin' to figure out why you think Tyrone is involved when ya'll cool?" Dayshawn asks.

"This bitch know what the fuck happened," she says placing her finger in Tyrone's face. "Open that fucked up grill and speak the truth bitch!"

"Brandy, I don't mean you no harm...but if you don't sit the fuck down I'ma get all up in this business right here! And then you won't need to worry about Tyrone because your problem will be wit' me. And I know you don't want that."

# *Miss Wayne* & THE QUEENS OF DC

Big Boody Brandy takes a look at me and everybody else. Then she plops down in the Redskin chair, wiggles her pump and lights a cigarette. The dogs curls up in her lap and I think it goes to sleep. What the fuck?

When smoke swirls around in the air she says, "Adrian calls me yesterday for a fifty bag of smoke. When I got out of my car to bring it up the steps, Garisha's brother, Detroit pops up behind me with a fake ass gun and says, 'You know what time it is.'"

"When I look at his arm, I see his name tattoed on it and know it's him. His dumbness didn't even have enough sense to put on a long sleeve shirt. Anyway, I ask him has he lost his mind tryin' to rob me? He tried to get all rough and jam that fake gun into my lower back even harder. He scared my baby Maxie right here so much that she shitted in my hand," she continues petting her dog. "I was so mad I didn't care if he shot me or not so I turned around and pulled out my nine. I carry my shit everywhere I go on account of that Drag Queen Slayer running around DC and shit. Any who, that nigga Detroit took off runnin' and my feet was already hurtin' in my shoes so I couldn't catch his ass! He betta be glad too because although his gun was empty, mine was not."

"That still don't mean Tyrone was involved." Dayshawn says.

"I'm not finished. I see Garisha's monkey lookin' ass in that beat up white Chrysler Plymouth she be drivin' a block over from ya'll house. Do you know that bitch tried to drive off when she saw me runnin' toward her? But the Gods were with me and her car wouldn't start up! So I stuffed Maxie in my shirt, put my nine back in my pocket, pulled that fish out of the car and beat her for all she was worth. But instead of fighting queen to queen, she bit my arm! So I stabs her back in hers. The whole time she screamin' Tyrone had everything to do with it," she continues pointing her cigarette in Tyrone's direction. "So I brought Garisha to your doorstep and left the bitch right there. Now I'm here to find out if you crossed me or not, Tyrone."

"Brandy, that bitch lyin'! I wouldn't do no shit like that to you. You my sister!"

When the dog starts yapping like crazy Big Boody says, "Easy, Maxie. Be easy." Then he says, "Bitch, everybody 'round the way know you shiesty! I heard about you runnin' 'round DC raping niggas and shit! And I also know about Anacostia park bitch!" she continues. "I smelled your shit a long time ago! I just ain't think you would be stupid enough to do no cruddy shit to me." She says standing up her dog yapping again. "But I guess you just that fuckin' dumb."

*Did she say raping niggas?* I know I've been gone from DC for a minute but I ain't hear none of that shit before.

When she gets up I say, "You gotta go, Brandy. Sounds to me like Garisha is the one you got beef wit', not Tyrone."

When she doesn't walk out, Dayshawn, Marlene and even Adrian walk up to her. And I say, "The door, Brandy."

Brandy struts to the door and says, "You betta not let me catch you on the street, Tyrone." Then she looks at us and says, "Ya'll crazy for trustin' this sneaky bitch. If she stabbed me in the back, she'll do it to ya'll too. But it's cool, Tyrone. You gonna see me again."

When she leaves, five minutes later, gunshots fire into the front windows of the house. Glass shatters everywhere and we hit the floor. Did she really just shoot at this house with that dog in her hands? That bitch is crazy!

When I raise my head, my heart thumps out of my chest when I see the front of Adrian's shirt is red.

"Oh my God! He's been hit!"

# *Thug Lovin' Times Two*

## ❧QUEEN TYRONE❧

Adrian and me just finished puttin' plastic over the windows to cover the bullet holes somebody fired in here yesterday. Miss Wayne and Dayshawn asked Big Boody Brandy did she do it but of course she denied doin' anything of the sort. It's cool with me though. I'll find another way to get back at her ass.

Although the black Hefty trash bags over the windows looked super ghetto, I knew we wouldn't be gettin' them fixed anytime soon so it would have to do. Any money we had 'round here was used for drinkin' and druggin'.

When we were done, I plopped down on the sofa and rubbed my feet.

"Where the fuck is Dayshawn? He got us in here doin' all the work."

"Wit' Miss Wayne. You know they gettin' the stuff for the cookout tomorrow."

"Oh yeah." I say sitting on the floor. I didn't feel comfortable sitting on chairs because Big Boody Brandy let it be known 'round Galveston that she was still after me. And I didn't want to risk the chance of the next bullet goin' in my head.

Yesterday got out of fuckin' hand. First someone shoots up our windows and then Marlene passes out thinkin' Adrian was shot. Turns out he fell in the cranberry juice from Wayne's cup when it spilled on the floor.

"Where you goin'?" I say seeing Adrian running back and forth into the bathroom to style his naturally curly hair.

"I'm supposed to be hanging with some friends tonight. You wanna come?"

"What am I...a charity case?" I say with my hands on my hips.

"No...I just don't want you to be alone tonight. With all that shit goin' on with Big Boody Brandy."

"Who are you hangin' with anyway?" I ask. "I thought you were tryin' to hook up with your best friend Chris to *fake* not be interested in wantin' him no more."

"We cool," he says in a low voice. "But it's not workin' between us."

"Really?" I smile happy the little princess doesn't get her way *all* the time.

"Yeah...and he has made it clear that he wants to be with his baby's mother. He not even paying my rent no more at my apartment so I had to give it up and since I ain't got no job, I don't know what I'm gonna do. You think Day will let me stay here until I get on my feet?"

"Day?" I say. "You need to be worryin' about me. I'm the one who pays the bills around here."

"Well...you think you can let me stay here?"

"Maybe...'pends on how much fun I have tonight...what's they names anyway?"

"Levi and Corey. I met Levi on the site and Corey is his friend. Both of them are thug cute." He brags.

"People say that shit all the time," I say wavin' my hand. "And they turn out to be a hot ass mess."

"I'm serious. Levi and me hooked up before so it's all good. I know what he looks like. We may go to the movies or somethin'."

"The movies?"

"Yeah...unless they can come here."

"They can come over," I tell him trying to think of something cute to wear. "What you wearin'?"

"I'm not sure."

"Well don't dress fem, Aid. You look too much like a girl when you do that and it defeats the purpose of them wantin' to be wit' a man. I'm not hatin' I'm just statin'."

"I guess you're right," he says reluctantly.

I needed a head start if I was going to shine and I didn't want him tryin' to look more beautiful than me. And because everyone always raved about how pretty Adrian was, I decided to put on my tight red leather skirt, my black and white tiger pumps and my black top. Then I grabbed my blond wig with the Chinese bang cut in the front to really set things off. It always looked right against my chocolate skin.

When they finally got there, Adrian opens the door wearing white pants, a white shirt with a few buttons opened at the top and his white Louis Vuitton leather shoes. He looked a little butch and it's just what I wanted.

When they walk fully inside, I was shocked to see two fine ass men standin' before me. Adrian was right! They *both* were just my type.

One of them grips Adrian tightly around the waist and kisses him softly on the lips. "This is Levi," Adrian says holdin' his hand, lettin' it be known that she had the best of the two.

Levi has light skin with grey eyes and he chose to wear blue jeans and a red t-shirt. He reminds me of Miss Wayne, if he was butch and I want him. So I look deeply into his eyes and give him the look that says, *'I'm ready when you are'*.

The other one, who I figured was Corey, has a smooth brown complexion and braids. He had a real 'thug look' goin' on wit' some swag to boot! Lookin' ever so relaxed in a black V-neck cashmere sweater, blue jeans and Nike boots, I know he's my speed.

"Stop being rude, Adrian," I say as I walk toward them switching my hips from left and right. Adrian has nothing on me when it comes to my flirt game. "Offer them a seat."

They sit down on the sofa and we sit on each side of them.

"What's up with the plastic on the windows?" Levi asks.

"It's a long story," Adrian tells them looking at me.

"Oookkaaaay." He says looking suspiciously at the windows. "So…what's up tonight? What are ya'll tryna do?"

"I don't know…a movie maybe?" Adrian adds.

They look at each other and smile. I know then that they have no intentions of puttin' us on their arm in public.

"I was thinkin' we'd just chill here," Levi says. "But we do wanna know what kind of stuff ya'll like to do for future reference."

I cross my legs and lick my lips. "Don't ask a question you're not ready for."

"Why is that?"

I giggle and give him the 'fuck me now' look. "Well your question can be taken a lot of different ways." I reply.

"Well, take it in the best way that works for you." He says lickin' his lips.

"Mother Tyrone, can I talk to you for a second?" Adrian asks standin' up.

"Not now, darlin'. Mother is entertainin' guests."

"Okay…uh…well, Corey," he says tapping him on the leg, "tell Tyrone a little about yourself, since you're here to meet him."

When he opens his mouth, it blows the hell out of me that he has a serious stutter problem. "Wa...wa...what you wanna know...know....know...about...about...me?"

I laugh and say, "For starters I wonder how long it would take you to ask another question?"

He looks at Adrian and then at his friend. "I...I...I'm working...working..."

"You know what, honey, how about you just smile. Talkin' really isn't your thing."

"Mother, you being rude," Adrian says.

"Remember where you are and who I am," I remind her. "For somebody who ain't got a pot to piss in or a window to throw it out of you need to relax before you find yourself out on the street. This my house." I shut her ass down, smile and say, "Anyway...Corey knows I'm just playin' with him. Don't you, honey?"

He nods and I'm thankful he's not tryin' to speak again.

"Are you guys hungry? I'm thinkin' of makin' my famous fried chicken, candy yams, rice, greens and 7-Up Cake. What ya'll think?"

"Wow," Levi says, "I think I don't believe you gonna make all of that for us."

"Then you don't know me *yet*," I smile. "Besides, cooking is how I express love." I say placin' my hand on my chest. "Well...one of the ways anyway."

He chuckles.

"Th...Th...Th...That sounds...," Corey stutters.

"Good. That sounds good," I say finishin' the sentence for 'Stutterin' Stanley'. "Now relax yourself before you pass out. Let me cater to you." I turn to Adrian and say, "Adrian take their shoes off while I prep the meal."

Eager at a chance to show my sexy, I take my shoes off too and show my tiny cute size thirteen feet. Then I rinse the chicken, put the yams in the pan and begin to clean and wash my greens before placin' them in the pot. Lastly, I place a troth of grease into a fryin' pan and wait for it to bubble. Then I look behind me, and when I'm sure no one is comin', I remove flour from the cabinet and push it deeply to the bottom of the trashcan. When the preppin' *and* fakin' is done, I decide that I'm ready to perform.

"Oh my God!" I cry out lookin' frantically through opened cabinets.

"What mother?" Adrian asks runnin' into the kitchen. "Are you okay?"

"I don't have any flower. I can't believe it. There was an entire pack here yesterday."

"You want us to get some?" Levi asks enterin' the kitchen too. His show of affection and concern makes me want to fuck him even more.

"No, you guys are comfortable." I say to him. "Your shoes are off, you're listenin' to music...I wouldn't feel right askin' either of you to run out here to no store." Luckily when I look into his and Corey's eyes, I can tell that runnin' around town looking for flour is the last thing on their minds. But I'm not surprised. In the process of perfectin' my plan, I waited for them to get good and comfortable before fakin' like I didn't have flour.

"I can go get it," Adrian says reluctantly.

"You sure?" I ask him.

"Yeah. It'll take me thirty minutes to get there and back."

In my mind, I'm thinkin' thirty minutes is plenty. "Works for me."

Adrian gets himself together and walks out the door, the moment the door closes I say, "Well, while she's gettin' the flour, I figure you guys could enjoy some hors d'oeuvres."

Levi smiles and Corey stands up.

"What did you have in mind?" Levi asks.

Let's just say by the time a minute passes, I was standing in the middle of the floor with Corey's dick in my ass and Levi's dick in my mouth.

"Damn you feel good as shit!" Corey says, no stutter. It's amazin' what good boo-gina can do for a speech impediment.

I was puttin' the slob down on Levi's dick and I smile when I look up and see his eyes roll to the back of his head. The funny thing is, I didn't put the entire stick in my mouth yet. When I do, trust me, it will be a wrap.

"Mmmmm," Levi moans, "damn you suckin' that shit good, nigga. Keep that shit right there," he says pawning the back of my head pushin' his dick to the back of my throat. Irritated my wig is movin', he throws it to the floor and says, "Fuck that shit. I want to feel your head, nigga." He continues pushin' deeper. "Open that mouth wide and suck this shit!"

I know he wants to choke me, but it ain't happenin'. I perfected the art of suckin' dick before I knew how to walk on my father and uncle. So I don't care how far back you push, or how big your dick is, I can open my throat wider.

Doing a quick time check by lookin' at the clock on the wall, I can see we have ten minutes left before spoiled little princess comes in here and discovers we started the party without her. So if I want to please them both and get my shit off too, I was gonna have to reach deep to pull out my inner freak.

So I found my rhythm. First I pulled Levi closer toward me, so that the entire shaft of his dick remained in my mouth, then I wound my hips and squeezed the walls of my boogina so that Corey was right where he needed to be. Next I jerked my dick repeatedly not missin' a beat.

When I felt my body shiver, I knew I was about to cum. And right on point, I felt Levi's creamy load fill my throat, Corey's oil slide down my ass and my own wetness fill my hands.

We were done *and* we didn't get caught. All we had to do was hurry up and get dressed before softy came back. We were almost in the clear until Adrian walks through the door and sees me adjustin' my skirt, Levi zippenin' his pants and Corey wipin' the cum off of his jeans.

We stop what we are doin' and stare at him in the doorway. And to think, the clock says we had two minutes left.

Damn.

# Missing DC

## ❦MISS WAYNE❦

Me, Parade, Daffany, Dayshawn and Tyrone are out on Miss Dayshawn's deck. The temperature dropped a little so it was a little chilly but we were okay. So many people were in this backyard earlier in the day that we were happy that now it was just us.

My body is here but my mind is focused on the call I got earlier from the person who is caring for my mother. They say she's gettin' worse and that I should go and see her before it's too late. But right now, I just can't. How do you lose the person who has been your rock most of your life? I don't know.

"Where's Adrian?" I ask Tyrone.

"Somewhere actin' like a bitch. She mad because the two thugs she brought over here last night wanted me instead of her."

"Wait a minute, how come that don't even sound right?" I ask.

"'Cause ya'll stay thinkin' twinkie sexier than me when she's not. I'm not hatin', I'm just statin'."

"Girl you can feed Parade and Daffany that bullshit if you want to, but I already know the deal. 'Cause ain't nobody in their right mind choosin' you over no twinkie. Unless you offered them some dick first."

We all laugh but Tyrone looks at me strangely. Normally he can take my jokes but tonight there's something behind his stare that makes me think otherwise.

"You alright?" I ask him. "'Cause you lookin' mighty hard."

"Oh...yeah...I was just thinkin' about somethin'."

My mind wanders as Miss Tyrone proceeds in tellin' her stories again, as if we didn't just have that uncomfortable moment.

I step to the side and smoke my cigarette. A habit I picked back up recently. Something was bothering me and I wasn't sure what it was. All I know is that the moment I got off the plane the feeling was worse.

As I continue to smoke my square, I glance over at Parade. She's laughin' so hard at Tyrone it looks likes she's about to shit herself. And Miss Daffany is damn near on the floor reliving Miss Tyrone's antics as he talks about the usher at the funeral.

"I think he wanted to fuck me. I mean, why else would he come for me about sitting down? Maybe he was the one lookin' instead of everybody else and couldn't help himself."

"You always makin' somethin' to be what it ain't." I tell him.

"Don't act like I ain't fuck the preacher at the funeral before."

"Here we go again with your Hollywood Chronicles."

Just then Adrian walks up the back steps with Marlene holding him up. Adrian's pissy drunk.

"Was that Tyrone talkin'?" he says with slurred speech. "Because if it was I wanna tell ya'll somethin'. Don't ever leave your man 'round him."

Marlene sits Adrian in one of the chairs on the deck and says, "I been through hell with twinkie today. He drank a whole bottle of Kettle One by himself. Now I need me a drink after that shit," he continues walking to the table full of half empty liquor bottles. "Ya'll got any-thing left?"

"You aight, honey?" I ask Adrian ignoring Marlene.

"I'll be fine. Just wish I had more real friends like you."

"Girl, are you still talkin' 'bout the shit that happened last night? 'Cause if you are you need to know them nig-gas wanted to fuck me the moment they got there. Don't hate me...hate the game."

"Girl, leave Twink alone and finish your story," I say, hoping they miss me with all the other bullshit.

"Anyway," Miss Tyrone starts rolling his eyes at Adrian, "one day the preacher asked me to go along to visit his grandmother at this nursin' home. I was one of his regular members and use to play the organ for his church sometimes. For real, I don't even know how he knew I was in the life because I was a butch queen back then."

"Bitch, you use to wear two gold hoop earrings and red lip gloss." I remind her. "Just 'cause you dressed it up with slacks and a button down shirt don't make it no dif-ferent."

"And don't you forget I have a son and a wife, motha Wayne. So trust me, he was not suspectin' me for no queen."

I shake my head.

"I remember that shit with the preacher." Miss Day-shawn adds. "He use to call the house sometimes. Sayin' he was callin' to pray over you and save your soul."

"Mercy, that's a mess." Marlene says grabbing a drink. She always eating and drinking without puttin' in on shit.

"That's fucked up that you lumpin' all preachers to-gether because all of them not the same." Miss Day says.

"Fuck all of 'em...they the biggest pimps in the world." Miss Tyrone disrespects. "So I don't care how you try to clean it up. They pimp their congregation just like they on the stroll. Anyway, we couldn't fuck in a hotel or nothin', cause someone would recognize us. So I use to go with him to the nursin' home to visit his peeps.

"His dear sweet grandma ma was half blind, deaf and stupid so we use to take her out of the bed and push her up to the window to look out of it, that way the bed was free." He laughs. "As long as her face felt the warmth of the sun on her cheeks, she ain't know nothin' 'bout her grandson the preacher partin' the black cheeks behind her back."

"Bitch, you goin' to hell!" Miss Dayshawn says.

"I don't think they'll have him there either." Marlene adds, pouring some more liquor in her cup.

"What is your point with this story, Tyrone?" Miss Dayshawn laughs. "'Cause right now all I can say is that you crazy for this shit right here."

He looks up for a minute and says, "Oh, shit! I forgot. What the fuck were we talkin' about again?"

We all burst into laughter.

Having enough of Miss Tyrone, I turn my attention to Miss Daffany. She appears to be doin' well but I can tell she is taking the burial harder than she thought.

When Miss Daffany suddenly stands and leaves Miss Tyrone's conversation, I know immediately somethin' else is on her mind. She sits on a lawn chair and I sit next to her.

Smiling she says, "What are you looking at, Miss Wayne?"

"Did I ever tell you how proud I am of you? It's like you're a new person now. I've never seen you glow so much in your life."

"You mean it's been a long time since you've seen me clean for so long."

"That too. But also you're takin' care of yourself now and got a new boo." Her new friend is HIV positive and loves the ground Miss Daffany walks on. She met him at a support group for people with the virus.

She waves me off and says, "Miss Wayne, don't start being mushy."

"Bitch, I'm bein' real. I'm not tellin' you nothin' that ain't true. You know that's not the ole girl's style."

"It's still tough hearing it." She lowers her head. "Nobody ever really told me that they were proud of me, in my entire life."

"Well maybe now you deserve it."

"I don't know where I would be without you." She looks down at her hands. "You didn't give up on me. Even when I treated you like shit, you fought for my life. I never knew that kind of love existed. Mama was so selfish." She pauses. "I remember when your mama use to buy me clothes," a smile spreads across her face, "and she found out my mamma was selling them for drugs. She busted up in my house and told mamma that she wouldn't get in the way of her killing herself, but she'd be damn if she was gonna stand by and watch her take what was mine and kill me too. Mama never took my clothes again...none your mother bought for me anyway."

When she mentions my mama, I grow sad.

"Have you talked to her yet? Or gone to see her?"

"Miss Daffany, I keep tellin' you I don't wanna talk about it."

"Okay...okay," she smiles. "I see you still not ready."

"Daffany, please."

"It's dropped." She smiles. "Do you know we've been through so much together, Wayne? First when Sky was murdered," she utters softly looking around to see if anyone was listening. Speaking of Sky's death is still taboo and we hardly ever talk about that night, "and then with Parade and Smokes tryin' to kill her...not to mention you saving my life by coming in that drug house to rescue me. I took you through a lot, we both did, but you never left our side."

"I'M SICK OF LOOKIN' AT YA'LL RIGHT NOW! I NEED SOME DICK!"

"Bitch, calm your ass down!" I say to Tyrone.

Miss Tyrone waves me off and proceeds in running his mouth. That is one funny fish.

Out of nowhere Miss Daffany says, "You miss DC don't you?"

I drop my head before lookin' back into her eyes. "I don't know if I would say *miss*...but there's somethin' that makes me want to be here." I cross my sexy legs and wiggle my blue sequin pump, which matches my blue sequin top. My True Religion jeans hug my curves.

"Well do you miss your friends?"

I pause and say, "I do but I don't. You know I have my gay friends back home, too. But here, there's a lot of backstabbing, lying and other shit I can't tell you about right now." I didn't want to give all the details of the shoot out the other night because I knew she'd just worry.

"Then maybe you wanna stay, to be closer to your mother. You know, to bring closure to your relationship?"

"Miss Daffany, please!"

"Miss Wayne you have to deal with it. You help everybody else with their problems but don't want nobody helpin' you with yours. Please tell me what's goin' on with your mother? Why don't you talk about her any-more?"

"Not now, Daffany."

"I hope ya'll not over here being mushy." Miss Parade says leavin' the loud ass queens to themselves. She sits in an available seat next to me interrupting the conversation and I'm happy.

"BITCH, I'M TRYIN' TO TELL YOU! MISTER HAD ME FUCKED UP! HOOOONNNNEY, THE OLE GIRL DON'T PLAY!" Miss Tyrone continues stompin' around in his black stretch jeans, no shoes and a white t-shirt. His five o'clock shadow showin' against his dark skin and his hair sticks straight up in the air.

"We can hear you fine without the bullhorn!" He was drunk and really feeling himself.

"Just 'cause you lesbians want to exclude yourselves from our conversation, don't try to rock...(one snap)...my...(two snaps) boat!"

And then she strikes a pose.

I fan the air.

"Gone with you!" I tell her before redirectin' my attention to my friends. "We weren't talkin' about nothin', Miss Parade."

"Yeah. Nothin'." Miss Daffany says rubbing Parade's swollen belly. "Just want to know if Miss Wayne's gonna leave us."

"Are you?" Miss Parade questions leanin' in toward me. She looks cute wearing the one-piece jean jumper that I brought her last month. "What about my kids? What about Daffany's baby? What are we going to do if you gone?"

"Hold up!" I say placin' my hand against my chest. "First off the ole girl ain't say she was leavin' either of you." I point, waving my finger between them. "Second of all, I don't recall bein' either one of your baby's daddies."

They laugh.

"Well if you're not thinking about leaving, why she say that?" Miss Parade asks.

When my phone vibrates I pull it out and check the number. It was Jay, Parade's pressed ass husband. Don't get me wrong, I like him, but we needed those few extra days we stayed here so that Daffany could feel closer to her mother's spirit. But here he was callin' Miss Parade every second of the day. And every time she got off the phone with him, she'd be upset. So tonight, I was having none of it.

"'Cuse me, darlin's." I stand up and walk to the far end of the deck for privacy.

"Who's that?" Miss Parade questions.

"Your husband," I joke.

"Stop playing," she says waving me off, not believing me.

Well I tried. I shrug.

"Yes?" I say into my phone with my hands on my hips.

"Wayne, where's my wife?" Jay yells, my God-kids playin' loudly in the background. "She don't need to be runnin' 'round DC when she carryin' my seed."

"Jay, please! That nut you deposited ain't been a seed in nine months. Anyway, we're still here and she's okay. She'll be on a plane tomorrow but I don't want you upsettin' her. So unless you calm down, I'm not givin' her the phone."

"Are you fuckin' crazy or just stupid?"

"Are you gonna calm down?"

"Fuck no! I wanna speak to my wife!"

"Sorry I can't do that. Bye, bye," I hit the end key and when he calls back, I turns the phone off altogether.

I'm so happy she left her phone at the hotel I don't know what to do. Just 'cause you're married don't mean you're a slave. She needs to breathe.

Just when I was about to rejoin them, through the glass door I see Miss Tyrone tusslin' in the kitchen with Miss Paul. Paul stayed competing against me in the ball circuit. Knowing every category I tried for, 'cept for the Lengendary category, I won. That rusty bitch never won shit!

"Unlock my door, bitch!" Miss Dayshawn yells through the glass tryin' to slide the door open. Apparently Paul has locked us out on the deck.

"Fuck is happenin' now?" I ask him.

"He's gettin' beat!" Miss Dayshawn says.

"I know that but why?"

In the corner of my eye I see Miss Parade and Miss Daffany moving toward the door.

"Stay over there," I instruct them with my hands. I don't need them being anywhere near this drama. Who knows if Miss Paul is packin' heat.

"Miss Tyrone ain't been payin' the bills and I ain't know." Miss Dayshawn says to me. "Now Queen Paul wants us out of here tonight. Where we gonna go at the last minute?"

"First off why you lettin' Miss Tyrone handle the bills? You know she ain't good with responsibility."

"I know but his wife use to give us money for the rent."

"You mean to tell me Shannon still carryin' his ass and paying his bills?"

"Sometimes."

"Well what about the credit cards? You not gettin' them no more?"

"I didn't want to tell you, Wayne, but I lost the connect I had at M&T bank. He got fired for givin' me cus-

tomer credit information. They tryin' to prosecute him
now and everything. I still have an inside connect but
he's acting scared and barely answers his calls. It's just a
matter of time before he stops helping us too."

Miss Dayshawn's connect at the credit card company
was how I ran my credit card schemes on the side. Thank
goodness I had the legit business because I don't know
what I would've done.

"That's heavy, Miss Day. You should've told me!"

With the news he was bringin' me, I forgot Miss Tyrone was gettin' kicked around like a NFL football. Just
as I look inside, we see Miss Tyrone's entire bare ass being smushed against the sliding glass. Paul has ripped the
old fish clothes' right off her body.

"YUCK!" We all say lookin' at the crustiness that is
her behind. A small circle of fog forms around it.

"Damn it! That bitch is beatin' Miss Tyrone's ass for
POINTS!" I say.

"Somebody go help her!" Miss Adrian screams cove-
rin' his mouth. Miss Adrian is so pretty and so feminine,
that sometimes you forget she's a boy even though he
doesn't dress in drag *all* the time. "It's gonna kill her!"

"Ain't nobody gonna kill nobody!"

I take off my shoes and hop down the stairs. Then I
walk around to the front of the house, take the plastic off
the window next to the door and unlock the door. Once
inside, and without wastin' time, I grab Paul's barracuda
lookin' ass by the shop-mart weave she's wearin' and
punch her so hard in the face, she smiles.

"Listen, I don't know what's goin' on, but you picked
the wrong time to pull some shit like this!" I maintain my
hold on her hair and she's bent at my feet.

"Yeah, bitch!" Miss Tyrone screams jumpin' around,
naked from the waist down. "What you gonna do now?"

"Miss Tyrone, be a queen and go put somethin' on! Your pussy is showin' and you scarin' the fuck out of everybody outside."

"Oh," he says in a feminine tone as she covers her penis and runs in the room...her entire ass out for all to see. "I'll be back."

"This is my house and all ya'll gots to go!" Paul continues. "Look at my fuckin' windows! Big Boody Brandy told me 'bout all the shit ya'll got goin' on 'round here!"

"Did Big Boody tell you she was the one who shot up the house?"

"All I know is I want ya'll out of here!"

"And if we don't leave? Just what the fuck are you gonna do about it?" I grab her weave tighter.

"Wayne you ain't got a whole lot to do with this now...'course all that could change if you want it to."

This bitch tries it so I release her, drop my voice three octaves and approach.

"Fuck you say?" I ask in my natural male tenor.

She looks at me, and then everyone else and says, "So ya'll gonna jump me now?"

"If I needed their help I would've unlocked the balcony door a long time ago."

"You always have been jealous of me." She says sweat pouring down her face.

"And then you woke up," I smirk.

"Ain't no free rides in my house." She picks up a few pieces of her hairball from the floor and says, "Jealous bitches." Then she grabs her purse and moves toward the door, knockin' a porcelin object to the floor in the process.

"Jealous? Not with that Target outfit on we ain't," I say looking her up and down.

"And that ain't even a real Gucci!" Miss Adrian yells from the patio.

Paul looks back at us and says, "Out tomorrow! And I'm bringing the cops with me to make sure you're gone too!"

When she slams the door, I unlock the patio and everyone piles inside. Some of them recant the recent events but Miss Dayshawn picks up the pieces of a broken black porcelain panther from the floor.

"What is this?" I ask helping her while everyone else finds a seat inside, maintaining their idle chatter.

"Dell bought it for me...right before he left me and moved to Atlanta."

Dell was good to her but Miss Dayshawn all of a sudden acted as if she didn't want the relationship. That man wanted to marry her and trust when I tell you it's hard in the gay community to find someone who wants to be with you for life.

All Dell wanted was for her to make a commitment and move with him. He had a great job lined up and it wasn't like Miss Dayshawn was working. Why he didn't go with him is still a mystery to me and to this day she never saw or heard from Dell again.

"It'll be okay," I tell her softly. She looks at me and smiles.

"I hope so."

I pat her on the back and we finish cleaning up the mess. I know how good it feels to get a gift you cherish from someone you love and I know even more how bad it feels to have it taken away.

# Reflecting On The Younger Years
## Miss Wayne

Wayne had a rough day in school when he came running into his quiet home. He didn't understand why kids teased him. So what he talked and walked feminine. He never bothered anybody and didn't understand why others bothered him.

"You're too big to be actin' like that!" one kid would say. "And you a boy!"

"My mother told me not to play with punks!" another would say.

He was just tired of being persecuted for something he didn't understand. He wasn't trying to act like a girl. He was just trying to be himself.

"Hey, son," Marbel said walking up to him as he sat quietly on the large flower sofa with turquoise trims in the living room. She'd been doing much better with the Multiple Sclerosis and the moment Wayne saw her Hershey kissed skin, he smiled.

"Hey, Mama. I see you're doin' betta today." She sat down and he scooted closer to her, flinging his pink Barbie book bag on the floor. "You want or need anything?"

"Yes I do, but he's here now." Wayne rested his head on her shoulder.

"Mama...how come you doin' betta now? Is the medicine finally workin'?"

"Why you ask, Wayne? You not happy I'm doing better?" she joked looking down at him.

"I am. I just don't understand what happened. Last month you couldn't walk, now you walk by yourself."

"Son, there's something about love that just does it for you. I mean, when I saw you the day your father hit you, on the floor, all helpless," she stared out into her living room, "I saw what life would be like for you without me. It's too early for me to leave and I gots so much to teach you. So much I want you to learn."

A tear fell from Wayne's face. "I hate, daddy! He hate me and I hate him too!"

Marbel separated herself from her Wayne and said, "Son, don't ever let me hear you say something like that again. Understood?" she lowered her chin. When he nodded yes she pulled him back to rest on her shoulder. "Your father loves you. He do. He's just worried that's all. It's gonna be tough being the Queen you are." They both laughed. "But," her voice got deeper, "it's tougher than anything not being yourself. And no matter what you do son, live your whole life loving people and yourself, for what they really are. In the end, it's all you got."

"I love you, ma."

"I love you too. And I'm already proud of your future and you ain't even grown yet."

"Why you say that?"

"'Cause, you're gonna be a great friend. People will be drawn to you like a magnet. But you're gonna have to watch the people you surround yourself wit' too, Wayne. Everyone who wants your friendship ain't fittin' to be in your presence. Remember that."

He smiled thinking of the future because as it stood, he didn't have a friend in the world.

"Hold up. I almost forgot that I have somethin' for you." Marbel pushed herself up and walked into the room, returning with a red shoebox. "Open it."

Wayne's eyes lit up as he accepted the box. And when he removed the lid and saw his first pair of red glitter pumps, he squeezed his mother so hard he almost hurt her.

*"Thank you, mama! They look like Dorothy's slip-pers from the Wizard of Oz."*

*"I got them from a Toy store."*

Wayne placed his feet into the shoes and although all of his toes were lying on top of one another inside of them because they didn't fit, he strutted around the living room like a model on a runway.

*"How do I look, mama?"*

*"Happy. You look happy, son."*

The next day, he had another rough time at school. This time it didn't bother him as much because he knew he'd get a chance to wear his shoes when he got home and mentally escape. He could pretend he was a star, had lots of friends and everyone liked him. But when he pulled the box from underneath his bed and removed the lid, the red shoes were gone.

In an instant, his world was crushed. With his head hung low and his spirit weakened, he walked into the hallway with the empty box in his hands. He stopped short when he saw his father's silhouette in the doorway.

Bells was just about to leave when he turned around and looked at his son. And when Wayne saw him, he knew instantly that he'd taken his shoes.

*"Why, dad?"*

Bells looked at him with a smirk on his face and walked out the door.

# *A Decision To Be Made*

## ❦MISS WAYNE❧

The car ride to the Baltimore Washington Airport was very quiet until Miss Tyrone decides to blast Lil Wayne's Carter 3 album.

*They can't stop me!*
*Even if they stopped me!*
*Yeah!*
*I'm on it! I'm so on it.*

He looked ridiculous tryin' to be tough while waggin' his extra long pink fingernails with rhinestones on them back and forth in the air. His body bounced around in the passenger seat in his hot pink short set as Adrian drove us down the road.

"Bitch, shut your dumb ass up." I yell at her. "We need peace and quiet back here. Miss Daffany's sleep!"

Miss Tyrone adjusts the rearview mirror and looks back at me, Miss Parade and then Miss Daffany.

"Wayne, just because you three lesbians are sad don't mean I gots to be too. Hell, if you that sad about leavin' DC, why you goin'?"

Afterwards he continues to sing to the CD. I look to my left and Miss Daffany is still asleep resting comfortably on my shoulder. But when I look to my right, Miss Parade is lookin' directly at me with grief in her eyes.

"You're scaring me. You don't seem like yourself. What's wrong, Miss Wayne? What's going on with you?"

"I'm fine," I lie holding her hand.

"Be honest. We're always honest with one another."

"We're here!" Miss Tyrone interrupts and I'm happy for the diversion. 'Cause truth is, I don't know what's wrong wit' me.

When Miss Adrian parks, Miss Tyrone walks outside and grabs one of our bags. Then he hands it to Adrian. Adrian's cute but as strong as an ox. And then I see somethin' on her face that bothers me. A bruise.

"Miss Adrian, what happened to your face?"

"It's nothing. I went to see Chris last night after I left the house and it didn't end too well," he says grabbing one of the suitcases and rushing toward the ticketing counter.

When he leaves I quickly ask Miss Tyrone. "What's going on with Chris? He hittin' her?"

"Yep. He's fine when they're having sex but in the mornin' he always hits her. You know how it is."

I shake my head and try to push Miss Adrian's troubles out of my mind.

While we all move closer to the Ticketing Counter, my heart races and I realize now that I don't want to go home.

"This why I don't fly," Miss Tyrone says looking at the tons of passengers in line. "I can't stand lines."

"You don't fly cause you ain't never got no money," I say.

"I use to go places all the time! I just don't get a chance to go anywhere no more 'cause I stay busy."

We wait five minutes in the line and the beat in my heart pounds harder. And then I hear the agent say, "Can I help whose next?"

The three of us approach the agent and she requests our ID's and ticket information. Miss Tyrone and Miss Adrian stay close behind.

"How many tickets?" the pretty black clerk asks.

"Three," Miss Parade says as if sayin' the number aloud will prevent me from stayin'.

"Two tickets." I correct her. "Just two."

Miss Daffany turns around, looks at me, smiles and says, "I knew you were staying. And I miss you already but...I understand. I want you to be happy, Miss Wayne. You take care of us so much that you forgot to have a life of your own."

I hug her tightly.

"Thanks. You don't know what this means to me. I really don't want to leave you but I need some time to see what's holdin' me back. I'll probably only stay a few months."

"Be happy, Miss Wayne. We'll be okay."

"What are you guys goin' to do?" the agent asks irritated. "There are people waiting behind you."

Miss Daffany hands the agent her identification and I slowly turn to face Miss Parade. She's angry, her eyes are red and tears fill the wells of her eyes. As the agent works on Daffany's plane ticket, I try to find the right words to say to deal with her. Right before I address her, my phone rings. I remove it from my pocket and see it's Jay.

"Hello."

"Wayne, where's my fuckin' wife, nigga!"

"She's right here." I say as I hand her the phone.

I'm rescued by Jay's nagging' ass! Yes!

Miss Parade holds the phone to her ear briefly and I hear him ask, "Baby, what's going on?! You can't be out there like that! You're due any day now!" Then she allows the phone to drop whilst Jay continues to scream from the handset.

She just looks at me and cries. And I wonder...what does Miss Parade want from me? What does she need?

"Ms., you're next. Can I have your ID?" The ticket agent says to Miss Parade.

Silence.

She doesn't move.

"Parade," Daffany interjects, taking the ID that dangles from her free hand. "We have to go. Miss Wayne, will be home soon." She hands the ID to the agent. "Let him go. Please…I'll still be with you."

"I'm so mad at you," she mumbles through a clogged nasal passage. "Why? You know I need you. You know I can't fuckin' do this by myself! You know I'm not strong enough!"

"Miss Parade, you have to let me go." I place my hands on her shoulders. "And you have to allow yourself the happiness you deserve. I can't give those things to you. I can't. But it doesn't mean I don't love you."

"But why?" She says phone still in her hand. "Why right now!"

"Baby, you have a husband who loves you and two beautiful kids. You'll never be alone again, in your life."

I know that although Miss Parade dresses fly, she still has a lot of work to do on her soul. She's tormented still…but why?

"Don't leave!"

"Miss Parade, please calm down."

"I'm pissed at you, Miss Wayne!"

I stare at her until I feel wetness trickle onto my high heel red Christian Lou pumps.

"Miss Parade, I know you're pissed at me but this is ridiculous!"

"Oh…oh…no! My water broke! I'm going into labor." She says holding the bottom of her belly.

"JESUS!" Miss Tyrone screams out.

"Not right here, baby," I say placing my hands on her shoulder knowing all the while that there was no way to stop nature from taking its course. "That man of yours is goin' to kill me if you have your baby here."

"OH, GAWD! OH, GAWD! OH GAWD!" Miss Tyrone screams.

"Girl shut yo big toe ass up and go find me a wheel chair!" I tell him as Miss Parade topples over in pain. "And tell everybody you see we need an ambulance!"

"Does she need any help?" the ticket agent asks. "No but I need two shots of bourbon and a miracle! And yeah…call the ambulance while you at it!"

People are staring and I knew I needed to take her somewhere private. When Miss Tyrone returns with the wheel chair, Miss Parade gladly takes a seat as I push her toward the restroom.

"It's comin! The baby's comin!" she cries holding her belly. "I don't want to have my baby at no airport!"

If you would've seen the sight of three gay men, two in high heels, pushin' a pregnant woman toward the woman's bathroom in the airport while Daffany helplessly tags along, you still wouldn't believe your eyes.

When we make it to the restroom I open the door and yell, "EVERYBODY OUT!"

"What…what's goin' on?"

"Leave now!" I tell a woman who is in the mirror doing nothin' that would help the ugliness that is her face disappear. "A BABY IS ON THE WAY!"

"But I don't understand," the woman says.

"Bitch, is you deaf?! The girl said everybody out! You beat that face enough and it's still there! So Go!" Miss Tyrone screams pointin' to an exit.

When she scurries away, I instruct my friends to take off their shirts and jackets so that we can place them on the floor. And when I realize everything me and my friends are wearin', outside of Daffany's sweater, clings to our bodies… I nix that idea. I never delivered a baby but I knew the delivery had to be done by me unless the ambulance hurried.

The bathroom was in a frenzy. Miss Parade holds her stomach with her legs wide open. Miss Daffany paces back and forth. Miss Tyrone opens the zipper on his tight jeans because he can't breathe and Miss Adrian seems to be frozen in place with his hands on his face.

"IT'S COMIN! AHHHHHHHHH!!!!!!!!" Miss Parade screams.

"AHHHHHHHHHH!!!!! AAAAAAHHHHHH!" Miss Adrian screams pressin' his face cheeks harder.

"Okay everybody calm down!" Realizing Miss Parade has a right to be on edge I correct myself. "Everybody but you, baby," Directin' my attention to the others I say, "Now, this is what we're going to do. Miss Tyrone, you go find some sheets, clean water and some towels."

"Some sheets? We in an aiport!"

"Exactly…and they pass out sheets all the time on the plane. So make use of yourself."

"I don't want my baby born in this bathroom." Parade says again.

"Honey, I promise you, you don't have a choice." I tell her.

"Miss Daffany, you go over to the sink, and get some paper towels for now. Dampen a few of them for Miss Parade's forehead."

"Okay…okay, is…is…is….is….is….," she was so nervous she can't complete a sentence.

"Miss Daffany, why don't you find somethin' you can do instead of talkin'. Start by gettin' me the fresh paper towels like I asked you."

She nods and walks toward the paper towel dispenser by the sink.

"AAAAAAAHHHHHHHHHHHH!" Miss Parade screams again. "I can't…I can't…take it!"

"AAAAHHHHHHHHH!        AAAAAAAHHHHH!
AAAAAAHHHH!" Miss Adrian screams.

"Miss Adrian, we already have someone doing the screamin' 'round here. So why don't you sashay, shontay, on out the door and find out where my ambulance is."

Without hesitation he does what's asked. God bless Miss Adrian with his tender hearted self.

I thoroughly wash my hands. "How are you doing, honey?!" I ask Miss Parade from the sink.

"Not so good. I…I…feel the baby's coming. I'm so scared."

"Everything's gonna be okay." I dry my hands and walk over to her. "You're no rookie at this remember? You got two at home so you'll be just fine."

"How many paper towels do I need?" Miss Daffany asks.

When I look at her, she's holding a pile so big, it looks like a load of clothes.

"I think that'll be enough, precious."

On the way over to us, Miss Daffany screams out in pain.

"You okay?" I ask.

"Yeah. I cut my hand on the paper towel dispenser." She examines her finger and continues to grab at the towels.

"Well come on over here. I need you. I don't think the baby is gonna wait for an ambulance. She's ready to be the star of the show right now. Just like her beautiful Godmother."

With that said, I get in front of Miss Parade, stoop down and raise her dress. Then I help her up and place a heap of paper towels under her lap. She maintains the hold of her belly and sits on the pile. Next I remove her panties and ask her to scoot toward the edge so that her butt is halfway on the chair and halfway off. And I place a heap of paper towels on the floor right below her.

"Good. Now listen." I look up at her. "This baby wanna come out now, Miss Parade. So when you feel the contractions comin' on, I need you to bear down onto the chair and push."

Not realizing she had the cell phone with her all this time, it drops out of her hand and I kick it away. Miss Daffany wipes her forehead with the wet paper towels trying to keep her cool.

"I need you to hold my hand!" She says to me, inhalin' and exhalin' quickly out of her mouth.

"Honey, we don't want the baby pussy poppin' on a hand stand. So I'ma need my hands free and I'ma need you to push."

"PPPPLEEEEASSSSE! HOLD MY HAND!" She screams.

I can't win. She wants what she wants so I switch plans a little.

"Okay…Miss Daffany, I need you to catch the kid." I stand next to Miss Parade and hold her hand.

"No…No…," she says shaking her head. "I don't know what I'm doin'. I never delivered a baby before."

"Neither have I. But you have had one and nature has made it very easy. When you see a head, get ready to catch it 'cause it's on its way."

"I…I can't do it. I'm scared."

"Okay," I kick my pumps off 'cause a girl does her best work shoeless and calmly say, "Miss Daffany," then I pick it up a notch, "Get ya ass down there and get that fuckin' baby!"

She hustles to her knees eyeing Miss Parade's box as she waits for the baby's arrival.

"Good." I say pattin' Miss Parade's forehead with a damp towel. "Now when you feel contractions, push, honey."

"Okay...okay," she says lookin' up at me with frightened eyes. "I'll try. Ahhhhhhh.....," Miss Parade exerts.

"Good. You're doing good." Her grip is firm on my hand.

"Ahhhhhhhhhhh!" she screams again.

"That's my girl. Keep pushin', Miss Parade!"

"It hurts!"

"I'm sure it does, honey, but the baby is comin' regardless. Now push!"

"Ahhhhhhhhhhh! Ahhhhhhhhh!"

"The head is peakin out," Miss Daffany alerts lookin' into Miss Parade's snatch like somethin's evil is gonna jump out and bite her.

"Good. But...but...let me know when...," My sentence is cut short by what I see and my voice temporarily cannot produce a sound. Fear washes over me.

"Miss Daffany, why don't you go wash your hands, and let me get the baby." When she doesn't move I say, "And please...DON'T...TOUCH...ANYTHING!!!!!"

"No!!! I need you holding my hand." Miss Parade interrupts.

"Baby, Miss Daffany is gonna hold your hand *after* she comes back from the sink and I'm gonna get the baby."

"I'm okay," Miss Daffany says. "I can do this. I want to."

"You can't." I say eyeing her hand so that she follows my stare. "You CAN'T do this, Miss Daffany. Now move and go to the sink."

When she looks at her fingers, she sees blood oozin' from her right hand. I'm thankful that Miss Parade is in too much pain to notice. The cut from the dispenser is worse than she thought. With Miss Daffany bein' HIV positive, this is more than just dangerous. Both Miss Parade and the baby are in a perilous situation.

Daffany stands and I move in position to catch the baby. "Let me go...wash my hands." She says hurriedly.

"Ahhhhhhhhh!!!!! Ahhhhhhhh!!!!!" Miss Parade continues.

"It's almost here! It's almost here!" I smile seeing the head crown.

Miss Daffany doesn't come back from the sink. She just stares into the mirror, shakin' her head and cryin'. I want to console her but there's no time and I know she's scared that she almost put Miss Parade and the baby's life in danger.

"Ahhhhhhhhhhhh!"

"Good! One more, honey! Just one more push!"

She pushes one last time and I help the baby out. I place the baby into my left arm, umbilical cord still attached and smile. Just then, Miss Tyrone burst through the door with Southwest Airlines blankets in her hand and Miss Adrian follows with the ambulance. With a crowd of people before us, I notice my phone is on the floor with the lid wide open. The minutes counting, shows that Jay has been on the phone the entire time.

Picking the handset up I say, "Congratulations, Jay! It's a girl!"

"Nigga, I'ma kill you when I see your ass!" He screams.

Let's just say he wasn't too happy about the way his first daughter was born. And I can't say that I blame him. It didn't matter that had it not been for the hissy fit his wife threw in the airport, just seconds before she boarded the plane, that she could've had the baby in the air instead. He wanted her home, but she needed me to be there for her. I know how important it is to have someone you love there for you no matter what.

◆ •••••••••••••••••••••••••••••••••••••••••••••• ◆

## *Reflecting On The Younger Years*

### *Miss Wayne*

*"Thanks for meeting with me, Mrs. Peterson."*

Mrs. Peterson smiled lightly and said, *"No...thank you for meetin' me."* She pointed to herself. *"I was surprised you called, but I figured Wayne is doin' well in school so it can't be nothin' too bad."*

*"No...no,"* Dora Brook, the school's white principle assured her, shaking her head from left to right. *"Wayne is a model student!"*

Mrs. Peterson smiled proudly and gripped her brown leather purse closer, which sat in her lap. *"That's good. He was so excited after winnin' the Spelling Bee for the second time in a row for the school. He really wanted to make you proud. He's been dancin' around with the trophy ever since he got it. I can't take the thing from the chile if I tried. Even sleeps with it."*

*"Dancing, huh?"* There was a condescending tone aback of the principal's response.

*"Yes. He's a happy boy."*

*"Mrs. Peterson, I want to be frank with you."* She sat up straight in her seat and placed her folded hands on the desk...her salmon colored fingernails overlapping one another.

*"I wouldn't want it any other way."*

*"Great, because we're concerned about Wayne here at the school."*

*"Why is that?"*

*"Well...he's not like other boys. In fact, he's not like any of them."*

*"Well we should embrace our differences shouldn't we?"*

*"Yes. But...well...uh, we've gotten a complaint from a student in gym. He said Wayne touched him inappropriately."*

*The smile on Mrs. Peterson's face was removed. "What you tryin' to say?"*

*"I'm saying that one of the kids made a complaint against Wayne. And because of the terrible accusation, I have to follow up with you...the parent. I really am sorry."*

*"Touched him where, how and when?"*

*"It was last week. Tuesday I believe."*

*"A day before the Spelling Bee?"*

*"Oh," she said looking through the large desk calendar before her. "I guess it was. I hadn't noticed."*

*"So you're tellin' me that Wayne supposedly touched a chile a day before he won the championship for your school? Yet you allowed him to participate anyway? How convenient."*

*Mrs. Brook's face turned red. "Like I said, I hadn't noticed that it was a day before the championship."*

*"Sure you didn't. What exactly happened?"*

*"I've been told that the kids were playing a game of Tag. Our gym teacher Mr. Barry Cornheart facilitated the game. I'm told Wayne was "It" and he tagged another student inappropriately on his body."*

*"Where on his body?"*

*"On the shoulder."*

*Mrs. Peterson sat up straight and eased forward, "He tagged another student inappropriately on the shoulder? Since when is touchin' on the shoulder inappropriate behavior?"*

*"Well the student said it lasted longer than it should have. He felt very uncomfortable and was in the nurse's office for the entire day after the incident. And because I'm the Principal, I have to speak with you."*

*"You've already said you had to speak to me. So what does this mean for my chile?"*

*"It means that we are suggesting that you seek a counselor for Wayne."*

*"My boy don't need no shrink gettin' in his head makin' him feel imperfect!"*

*"Mrs. Peterson, your son is....well...gay. And he needs counseling."*

*"Counselin', huh?"*

*"Yes, Marbel."*

Mrs. Peterson shot daggers with her eyes. And suddenly, she presented a kind smile across her face. It was like she had two personalities and the principal wondered what was behind the look in her eyes.

*"Mrs. Brook, would you mind if I make two phone calls?"*

*"Sure go right ahead,"* she said thinking Marbel was eager to take her up on her advice to find Wayne a counselor. She pushed the black phone across the desk. *"Dial 9 first and then the number."*

Mrs. Peterson moved the hair away from her ears, picked up the handset and dialed her first number. It rang twice. When the caller answered she hit the speaker button and placed the handset down.

*"First National Bank, how may I help you?"* the kind voice said from the speakers.

*"Oh yes, I'd like to check the availability of my checking account balance please."*

*"Sure. What is your account number and name?"*

Mrs. Brook looked at Marbel with a confused glare. She thought it strange considering the nature of their conversation. I mean, why would she choose now to check the availability of funds in her bank account? It was as if she'd forgotten all about the meeting and remembered something else more important.

"185558766." She said providing her name and information directly afterward.

"Oh yes! I have your account right here. Your balance if $46,000. Anything else?"

"No. That will be all. Thank you." She ended the call.

The look on Mrs. Brook face showed her surprise. She hadn't expected the woman to have saved so much money. Besides, it was $45,000 more than she had in her account on a principal's salary. What she didn't know was that Marbel had been saving for Wayne's college fund most of her life.

"One last call, please." Marbel said rousing Mrs. Brook from her thoughts.

Mrs. Brook nodded as she dialed another number.

"Thank you for calling the law offices of Scott Weinstein. How may I help you?" a woman's voice bellowed.

Now Mrs. Brook understood Marbel Peterson and she understood her very well.

"Yes. May I speak with Scott Weinstein? This is his client Marbel Peterson."

"Sure. Let me see if he's available."

It was a brief moment before he answered.

"Yes, Marbel. What can I do for you?"

"I know you are paid by the hour so I'ma get right to the point. I'm at my son's school and the principal has suggested that I seek counsel. So, here we are. Can you help me?"

"Sure...go right ahead. The clock is tickin'," he joked.

Marbel smiled at the principal who was flushed. "Great. So what were you sayin', about my son Mrs. Brook?"

"Uh...I...uh." She was speechless.

"Oh you're at a loss for words. So let me remind you. You were harrasin' my chile and tryin' to make me believe that somethin' is wrong with him because he's different."

"No I wasn't. I was just suggesting..."

"Listen and listen good, Mrs. Brook. I been savin' all my life for my son's future. All my life! That boy has a good heart and I'm sick of people not seein' him for who he really is. Now I had planned to use the money for his college fund but if you bother my son again, I won't hesitate to spend every damn dime on suin' you and this fuckin' school. 'Cause as far as I'm concerned, his future starts right here and right now! So what you wanna do?"

Silence.

"I'm afraid there's been a mistake." The principal said into the phone's speaker. "Wayne isn't any trouble at all. And I'm sorry to have wasted your time."

"That's what the fuck I thought." Said Marbel smiling from ear to ear.

# House of Dolls

## ⊛QUEEN PAUL⊛

It was four in the morning at Paul's five-bedroom home in Landover Maryland. He sat behind his meticulous detailed mahogany framed desk pissed the fuck off. The golden accented desk lamp lit the dark room as he rocks back and forth in his brown leather chair.

"What the hell you doin', girl?" Kevin asks walking into the office door behind him. His voice heavier than the softer tone he used during regular hours. "Why you up so early?"

When he sees five lines of coke sitting on a mirror next to a pile of unorganized papers, his mouth waters.

"The question is, what you doin' up?!" Paul says looking up at him. Then he takes a small nose pipe and inhales a line of coke. "I thought you were the Drag Queen Slayer or somethin'." His large feet sit on top of the pink furry slippers under his desk as he tugs at the sides of his black nightgown, which is much too small for his muscular build.

"Man...that Drag Queen Slayer shit is crazy ain't it? I really hope they catch whoever's doin' that shit."

"Me too," says Paul. He inhales another line hoping Kevin doesn't ask for one.

"Can I do one?"

Paul reluctantly pushes the mirror toward him and hands him the pipe. He inhales without so much as a thank you.

"You sure it ain't you?" Kevin jokes wiping his nose. "Half of the queens dyin' you got beef with."

"Don't even joke like that. I'm just as scared about this shit as you are."

Kevin giggles and sits down in his office. "Have you been in here all night?"

Paul faces his paperwork and throws his hands on top of the mound in frustration.

"I'm so sick of Tyrone and Dayshawn's bitch asses! They don't pay rent and now they fuckin' up the house. What kind of shit is that?"

"Put 'em out!" Kevin offers as he adjusts his surgically enhanced breasts under the white mini t-shirt he wears. The extra tight pair of grey gym shorts hugs his small legs. "We hate them anyway!"

"Look, bitch! I don't need to hear all that. What I *need* is help gettin' these fuckas out of my house!"

"I ain't mean to make you mad. I just hate the House of Dreams."

"Me too but cash is cash! Plus you already got work done!" He points jealously at his breasts. "I want work done on my body too. All I need is twenty thousand more and I'll be able to get my surgery. I'm tired of being a woman trapped in a man's body."

"And I'm not?" Kevin asks.

"I don't know if you are or not. I'm talkin' 'bout me. You seem to be okay with whatever you had done already! But I'm not fuckin' wit' that silicone injection bullshit you be doin'."

"You got to go to the right people. That's all."

"Everybody I know do that shit in their basement! So how can they possibly be the right people? Think about how many friends we had die from that shit. All because some queen makin' money without knowin' what she doin'." He says shaking his head. "Naw...that ain't wor-kin' for me."

"Well what about the house of Stars Legendary ball in a couple of months? If our house wins the grand prize we'll make twenty five thousand dollars!"

"That will help but I still gotta divide it with ya'll."

"It's better than nothin'."

"You stay cheerin' for a couple of dollars," he says picking up a clipped out magazine article of Janet Jackson from his desk. "But I need *real* money if I'm gonna go to a doctor to look like her."

Kevin looks at the picture that he'd seen twenty times and keeps his comments to himself. He wanted to tell Paul that it was impossible for him to look like Janet Jackson. Number one, he was six feet tall and she barely made it over five foot three. Secondly his body frame was very muscular and hers was small and lean. But more importantly he remembered the last time he told him how he felt about the matter. Paul threw him out on his ass with the quickness. It took two months of begging and Kevin giving him the black Kim Kardashian wig he wore when he won a ball a while back, for Paul to let him back in the house.

"You could've been had it if you start trickin' wit' us. Everything cost, even Bussy," he says slapping his ass.

"I'm not a whore, Kevin. Besides, that's why I got you. But I can tell you what will help. Shit will be all right if you start payin' your rent 'round here. On time!"

Kevin was shut down with all the shit he was bring-ing.

"I'm on your side," he responds in the soft feminine voice he trained since he was a little boy. He knew he was into Paul for five hundred dollars of late rent and didn't have much to say. "But what do we do now to get them out your house?"

"Well I tried it the right way. I went through the courts and they said I'd have to wait on a fuckin' eviction approval and that can take anotha 30 days. If we go another route, I can have 'em out sooner. But before I give you the details, why is Wayne back in town?"

"Redbone Wayne? From the House of Dreams?" Kevin asks giving him a quizzical stare.

"Yeah."

"I'm not sure...but I hope it's not for the ball."

"Why? You don't think we can win if the House of Dreams participates?"

"Uh...yeah. He ain't got nothin' on your house." He lies. "But I did hear his LA chapter is like that. But we can still beat them wretched queens hands down."

Paul's house, which he called the House of Dolls, had five members. Paul was the leader and his members were Toni, Kevin, Shawn and Michael. In their eyes they were built to perfection, hence the name, House of Dolls. But behind their backs they were known as the House of Moos. The only thing they did to look like women was alter their bodies, not including their faces. But the House of Dolls was ruthless. They did whatever they could to maintain their house, buy drugs and win balls. Including robbery and murder.

"Can he be a problem for us? Wayne?" Paul questions.

"It depends on the issue you have with him."

"Meaning?"

"Well...you know back in the day he use to slice mothafuckas faces up if they got him wrong. But when he moved to LA, it seemed like he fell off the scene and off the face of the earth. Why?"

Paul wouldn't dare tell him that just days earlier, he'd gotten his ass kicked in the house his mother raised him in. Wayne beat him so badly that he had bruises in places he hadn't thought he touched.

Instead of the truth Paul says, "I'm hearin' a lot about him lately. And he was in my house when I went over there."

"Oh no!" Kevin says grabbing his t-shirt. "Is he the one who beat you?"

"Why in the fuck would you ask me some bullshit like that?"

"Cause you came in here beat down harder than Ms. Rhianna in Chris Brown's car, baby. That's why."

"I told you I tripped over Ma-Ma's foot and hit my face on her cement elephant when I was at her house!" he responds in defense. "So stop makin' shit out to be more than it is."

Kevin not believing his bullshit drops his head and says, "Oh...so...now what?"

"Later on I want you to call Big Boody Brandy. Tell her I got a job for her and I want to see bodies dropped."

# *What's Cookin'*

## ⚜MISS WAYNE⚜

"Is he sleep?" Miss Tyrone asks me as I take a seat at the green table in their yellow kitchen. Us gay men love colors and Miss Tyrone and Miss Dayshawn are no exception.

"Now he is. I kept asking him what's wrong but he doesn't want to talk to me. Somethin' else is goin' on."

"Wayne, you know you always look more into things than you should. I mean, I wouldn't worry about Aid's problems if I were you. If he wants to stay with Chris, he's gettin' exactly what he deserves."

"Well, at least he finally dosed off. But I think he drank a half of bottle of vodka and took two Tylenol PM to do it." I say watching Tyrone cook on the stove, his yellow curly wig bouncing with his every move. I swear he doesn't realize that although black is beautiful, some colors just don't mesh on darker skin. And a yellow wig is one of them.

"I got some dick comin' over lata on." He says out of the blue. "So you gonna have to keep yourself company."

I look at him and say, "I sure hope a dick ain't really comin' through that door. Please say a head will be attached to it."

He laughs and says, "You know what I mean, Wayne. And speakin' of dick, when was the last time you've been fucked? Seriously?"

As mad as I was by the question, I didn't know. I hadn't had dick since dick had me.

"It's been a minute but I'm not thinkin' 'bout that right now."

"Oooo girl! I don't see how you do it. A gay man not havin' sex is just unnatural!"

"When the right person comes I'll know it."

"Fuck the right person! What about Mr. Right now?!"

"My focus is on my friends and my business. And your mind should be too. You lettin' the DC Chapter for the House of Dreams go to shit! I heard ya'll don't do balls no more or nothin'. Just smoke and get high! People also sayin' that whenever ya'll hit the scene, somebody fightin'."

"They just jealous 'cause we do us and we do us well. Trust me, Wayne, I got this."

"Oh really? Well do you got the money for your rent? 'Cause you know come Monday, Paul's throwin' ya'll the fuck out."

"I'll get his little itty-bitty change."

"How much you into him for?"

"Four thousand dollars!"

"Girl! Have you ever paid shit around here?"

"Hell yeah! I'm the only one! But shit got backed up. Why? You wanna move in to help out?"

"Naw…but I am thinkin' about rentin' a little cottage in DC somewhere if I stay." I say crossing my legs.

Miss Tyrone laughs and says, "Good luck findin' a cottage in DC anywhere!"

"You right about that shit." Just when we were enjoying each other's conversation, the house phone rings on the kitchen wall and he hesitates on answering it. I wonder why.

"You not gonna get the phone?"

He hesitantly walks over and picks up the handset. "Hello."

Silence.

"Look! Stop callin' my fuckin' house and leave me the fuck alone!" Tyrone screams into the phone before hanging up.

"Who was that?"

"N...nobody." He says obviously shaken up.

When the phone rings again he grabs it and yells, "Look...whateva you gonna do just do it!"

He was being extra but what I notice right away is the change of his facial expression.

"What? When did this happen?" he says on the phone.

Silence.

"Wayne...turn on channel 7 news!" he says anxiously hanging up.

My heart races as I wait to see what got him so riled up. When I turn on the TV, I'm thankful channel 7 is already on. A male newscaster is holding a microphone in front of a lady who's crying her eyes out.

*"Marlo, ain't did nothin' to nobody! He was a good person! Took his grandmother to church and everything every Sunday! What kind of person would kill him and cut his head off? How we 'spose to give him a proper funeral?"*

When Marlo who likes to be called Marlene, picture appears across the television, my mouth drops. The newscaster takes the microphone from Marlo's mother and commentates.

*"The LGBT community has been rocked by this crime spree and it seems as if there's no relief in sight. Police say they're doing all they can to find the man known as, The Drag Queen Slayer. But are they? What leads are they following? And will the LGBT community ever recuperate? Those are the questions we all want answers to. Back to you, Joan."*

"I can't believe that shit!" Tyrone cries. "What the fuck is goin' on in DC?"

"This is ridiculous! Not Marlene!" I say in disbelief.

We spend the next fifteen minutes going over the hows and the whys. And in the end all we know is that the murders have finally hit home. We've lost someone we have known personally. I'm so sick of death I feel like dying just to get away from it sometimes.

I decide that we shouldn't tell Adrian right now, since he has enough on his mind as is. But I did go downstairs in the basement to check on him to make sure he's okay.

"You left the bedroom door unlocked right? Where Adrian is sleeping?" Miss Tyrone asks.

"I made sure it was unlocked when I came upstairs but who knows if he'll get up and lock it back." I pause. "He's livin' here now?"

"Yeah...he lost his apartment and ain't got nowhere to go. When you really think about it, had it not been for me, he wouldn't have a place to live or friends. His family left him a long time ago because he's gay."

"Mother Theresa, any other time I'd tell you where to go, but this thing with Marlene has got me fucked up." I say rubbing my throbbing temples."

"Me too...but as far as Aid is concerned, I just hope he doesn't cut himself again."

I look at him in horror. "He's doin' that shit again? I thought he stopped."

"It's not as bad as it use to be, but yes, he still does. Look at his thighs if you get a chance. They're a mess... ripped to shreds. His stomach too. Dayshawn took him to the hospital a couple of months back because one time he cut himself so deep, he punctured his small intestine." I cover my mouth. "He gotta learn, Wayne. This is the life.

But Adrian's so stupid that he thinks everyone he meet loves him."

"Stop callin' that chile stupid!"

"I'm serious. It's sad."

As I think about Miss Tyrone's words, my cell phone rings.

"I guess your lesbian lover is callin' again." He says.

"Jealous, bitch," I say answerin' the phone.

"Miss Wayne, can you bring me some water?!" I hear Adrian yell from downstairs.

"I got it," Miss Tyrone says quickly taking a cool bottle of water from the refrigerator. "You take your call."

*That was nice of Tyrone.* I thought.

"What's up, Parade?"

She's on the phone for five minutes and already she's worked herself into a frenzy and my nerves right along with it. With the news of Marlene, I really wasn't up for the foolishness.

Miss Tyrone returns from downstairs and I watch him put too much salt on the box macaroni and cheese he claims is worthy of awards. I don't see one bag of real cheese in sight.

Sitting at the table, with my legs crossed, I hold the phone to my ear and listen to Miss Parade's rants and raves.

"You know I just had the baby, Miss Wayne. You said you would be here for me."

I sigh before sayin' anything else. And although I take into consideration that she's probably sufferin' from post partum depression, I also realize that lately she's been like this a lot. Something's really going on with her and she won't tell me what it is. And suddenly for some reason I don't care. What about me? What about my feelin's? So...I lose it.

"You know what…I'm sick and fuckin' tired of you and your whinin'! I'm not your mother nor do I choose to be. I have my own damn life to worry about! And if you can't understand it, fuck off!"

Afterwards I slam my phone shut and look up at Miss Tyrone who's starin' at me like he's lost his mind, his yellow wig on the floor in the kitchen next to his high heel shoes.

"It's about time you handled that, Wayne." He says. "Don't make no sense how you let her talk to you sometimes."

"Stay out of it, Miss Tyrone. She's family."

"Yeah, but you not helpin' her none by babyin' her either." He kicks off his shoes and when I notice he's doing a weird dance, I wonder why. "You got to cut the cord and let her go."

The more he says the worse I feel. Miss Parade *is* family. *My* family. As I prepare myself to call her back, I smell something else cookin' over Miss Tyrone's fake ass meal.

"Somebody's tryin' to out cook you, girl," I tell him.

"Yeah. Don't smell like nothin' to me," he says as he opens the oven and looks inside. "My corn muffins are almost done."

"They need to be, I'm ready to eat, even if it is a hot ass mess." Then I observe him dancing harder. "Go pee, Tyrone! I'm tired of watchin' you hop around lookin' all uncomfortable and shit."

I hear a banging in the house and I wonder where it's coming from.

"Who's that?"

"Girl you know these DC row houses are made of paper! We can hear anything Tabitha and them be doin' next door. From fuckin' to beatin' the shit out of her eight kids."

I shake my head and say, "Only in Southeast."

Then I take my shoes off, and feel that the floor is hot. "Why is the floor so hot?"

"It's 'cause the oven is on. When I cut it off, it'll cool off."

As my toes remain planted on the floor, I notice the heat is greater and the banging noise it louder. It's impossible for the floor to be this hot just because the oven is on. Something's up!

Suddenly I look around and see smoke comin' from a vent near the bottom of the floor. "Miss Tyrone, where does that vent lead to?" I point.

"Downstairs...why?" he says slowly seein' the smoke rise.

We rush toward the basement door where Adrian is and turn the knob. The moment we do, a ball of heat blows us backward. A cloud of smoke so thick appears from the door that we can barely see in front of us. Flames are everywhere. We cough profusely as we back away from the fire. I run into the kitchen and dial 911. The smell of the smoke is suffocatin' and is already inhibitin' my breathin'.

"911 what's your emergency?"

"We need help! Hurry the fuck up!" I say hangin' up.

"Adrian," I yell, hacking crazily. "Adrian can you hear me down there?!"

"We have to go, Wayne! Now!" Miss Tyrone yells as he pulls me out the front door and into the yard. He's stronger than normal and for some reason, I see a flash in my mind of him on top of me...but I can't recall the event.

"We can't leave him! We have to go back!" I wrestle with him to go back inside.

"Wayne, look at the house!" he says as my feet nestle in the damp green grass in the front lawn. "It's goin' up in flames. He's gone! Adrian's gone."

I cry.

I cry harder.

The fire trucks approach the house and park out front. As they grab their hoses and began spraying the house with water, I pray God takes mercy on Adrian.

The next door neighbor comes running outside with her eight kids. She's but ass naked with a big hobo style Gucci purse in her hand. This bitch had time to grab her purse but not a shirt? Shake my head.

"Is anyone inside?" a tall light-skin fireman with a ponytail asks me.

"Yes! Yes! My friend Adrian. He's inside. He needs your help."

There's somethin' about the way he looks at me that makes me uncomfortable.

"I'll see what I can do, but he's probably gone. You people should be more careful when you use your hot combs and curling irons around the house."

"Fuck you just say to me?!" I ask walking closer to him.

He smirks and runs into the house.

I run behind him and Tyrone grabs me back. "Just let him go, Miss Wayne. And let's hope for the best."

"I'm 'bout to push all ten of my knuckles into his eye sockets! He got me fucked up!"

"I know…but let it go."

The fireman is inside for only three minutes before he runs back out.

"I can't get inside," he tells us. "There's too much smoke."

"Well go back in! It's your fuckin' job!" I say grippin' him by his uniform forcefully.

"Look, I don't have time for this shit!" he says grabbing my wrists. "I tried! Okay?!" He throws my wrists down. "And if you ever see my face in the future, don't ever put your fuckin' hands on me again."

"You don't care! You don't fuckin' care if my friend dies or not!"

"I did all I could." He says as he spits on the ground by my feet, looks at Miss Tyrone and storms away.

I break down in tears and Miss Tyrone holds me as we both witness the chaos surrounding the house. Adrian is so helpless, so young and all alone. Soon I shake him off and run toward the house but another fireman stops me.

"What are you doing?" He's taller than me and his brown eyes are comforting.

"My friend is in that house and he won't help us!" I point at the other fireman. "But I will not stand by and allow my friend to die."

"Look," he says lookin' at his fellow fireman quizzically. "I'll see what I can do. Where exactly is he in the house?"

"In the basement...but I have to show you."

He grabs me firmly on my shoulders and says, "Let me do my job. Okay? Trust me."

I nod and he rushes inside of the house. I'm nervous but there's something about his presence that relaxes me.

We look at the house that continues to burn away before our eyes. Within seconds, the remaining windows shatter and fire shoots out of them under the night sky. All I wanted was to get away for a few weeks and already it seemed as if trouble decided to greet me. I rub my arms briskly and feel overcome with worry.

Within minutes of the thought of Adrian being gone enterin' my mind, I see the fireman rush out carrying him in his arms. The other firemen rush to him and lift Adrian

out of his arms, taking him to a gurney where the paramedics work diligently on his twenty-something year old
body.

"Oh my, Gawd! Are you okay, Adrian?" I ask rushin'
behind the paramedics trying to get a look at him.

There are too many of them and they push me out of
the way. "You can't be over here," a white paramedic
with blonde hair says. "He needs air!"

"This is my family and I'm goin' with him!" I say as
they place an oxygen mask over his nose and mouth. His
eyes open and I feel relief but his body is covered with
black soot.

"Sir you can't be over here! Now move!" the paramedic persists.

And when I turn behind me to thank the man who
saved his life, I hear him yellin' at the firefighter who spit
at my feet.

"Look, if you *don't* want to do your job than *don't* do
it somewhere else!"

"Come on, chief. He's…a fuckin' faggot."

I gasp.

"What if I would've gotten the AIDS or something?"
the fireman continues.

"This is the second time something like this has happened with you. When we get back to the station, you're
suspended until further notice!"

The fireman takes off his yellow hat, looks at me and
storms in the direction of the fire truck. And then for
some reason, the man I now know as the chief looks at
me kindly. Could he…be…gay?

Naw.

With my attention back on Adrian, I'm able to walk
up to him and he reaches for me.

"What, honey?" I say holding his hand. "What do
you need?"

He pulls me closer to him and removes his oxygen mask. "You shoulda let me die."

I was stunned and ask, "Why, baby?"

"The fire...the fire was..."

"Sir, I'm not going to tell you again! Unless you're blood related, you aren't going to be able to go with us."

Then they rush him into the ambulance and I watch them drive him away.

Through everything that was going on, I never once considered that he didn't want to live. Not once. But how could I? I've been a rescuer all my life and dying even if you wanted to was never an option. For me anyway.

◆••••••••••••••••••••••••••••••••••••••••••••••••••••◆

## *Reflecting On The Younger Years*

## *Miss Wayne*

*"You shoulda minded your own business!" a pretty 13-year old girl said with two long black pigtails as she was screaming in Parade's face. They all stood in the schoolyard afterhours. "Cuz nobody was even talkin' to you!"*

*Parade stood her ground with clenched fists. She didn't care that the four girls encasing her in a circle, meant her extreme harm. Not even the fall breeze could cool off the angry children. But Parade made a decision to defend the new girl Sky and so she had to deal with the beef that came along with her choice. Her white t-shirt was dirty beyond belief due to tussling with them in the damp grass and the hand-me-down blue jeans she wore were mucky.*

*"Look at your ugly face!" one of the girls teased.*

*Parade's heart ached as she wiped away some of the dirt that crept onto her skin during the first part of their battle. The small scratches on her dark chocolate skin bled slightly.*

*"She ain't nothin' but a black ugly bitch!"*

*Wayne seeing the altercation from a far, ran up to the girls on the small patch of grass. For some reason, he was born with the superhero syndrome. If he couldn't save someone, he'd die trying.*

*"I know ya'll not jumpin' her," he said standing in front of her. His pink backpack hugged his back like the acid wash tight jeans and colorful converse he designed himself. He threw the bag on the ground, placed his hands on his hips and stared them down.*

*He was certainly one of the flyer kids in school with his flamboyant fashions and colors. He went from being unpopular at his last school to rock-star status in two days at the new elementary school.*

*"Who the fuck are you anyway?" one of them asked.*

*"Don't worry 'bout all that, cause it ain't gonna be no jump or I'm jumpin' in."*

*At first everyone was silent when Wayne approached. Parade had never seen the boy before and Sky who was several feet behind Parade stood in incredulity. She couldn't believe the boldness that was Wayne.*

*And to think, it all started over a boy. Diamond was mad with Sky for taking her boyfriend but she pretty much predicted the entire event. She knew the moment she saw Sky with her long beautiful hair, flawless smooth light skin and expensive clothes, that her boyfriend, One, would want Sky instead. She was right.*

*"Uggh...," Diamond, the tallest of the girls said pointing at Wayne. "You ggaaayy!"*

*Wayne smacked her so hard in the face, her lips trembled like cymbals on a drum set. She dropped to the ground.*

*"Bitch, you don't know me so don't act like you do!"*

*Diamond on the ground, cried her eyes out. Her three friends walked closer to Wayne in anger and Parade stood by his side. Needless to say, Sky remained where she was, in the background.*

*Seeing their friend lying on the ground, the girls begin swinging wild arms toward Wayne and Parade. Parade who fought almost every day of her young life, landed traumatic blow after blow to the girls' faces. Together, she and Wayne beat the dog shit out of the girls sending them running on their way.*

*Something in Parade's eyes wouldn't let it rest. She caught Diamond a few feet out and stomped her like she stole something. At first Wayne and Sky were laughing until they saw the rage in Parade's eyes. She looked dejected and angry all at once. She had something on her mind...that much was evident. She felt no one cared about her and she wanted to make someone, anyone, suffer because of it. She also harbored a secret so great, she could never tell a soul.*

*Wayne ran up to Parade and pulled her away from the girl. Diamond lifted her beaten body from the moist grass and ran as fast as she could.*

*"You aight?" he asked putting one arm around Parade.*

*"Get the fuck off me! You don't know me!" Parade yelled in his face. "I didn't need no help! I had them bitches straight up!" She ran off the field and toward her house.*

*Although his first time meeting the girl who would one day be one of his closest friends was unpleasant, there was something about her he liked and he made a decision to find out more about her, even if she didn't want him too.*

# *Finger Licking Good*

## ✺MISS WAYNE✺

"I'm so sick of Popeye's!" Dayshawn says as we all strut through the restaurant's door. He's wearing black slacks, a plain hot pink t-shirt and he looks so cute. Dayshawn is what we gays consider an Abercrombie Bitch because he usually wears casual clothing with not a lot of spice. "Plus I just had a pickled egg and cheese sunflower seeds. I'm not even all that hungry."

"Me either. After seeing Miss Adrian in that hospital today, I think I lost my appetite. He looks so sad." I say feeling my phone vibrate in my purse. "Plus until I can call the bank to find out what's wrong with my bank card I can't buy shit anyway. I'm just glad it started actin' up *after* we got the hotel room."

"Well ain't nothin' wrong with my appetite. I can eat all day!" Miss Tyrone says rubbing his hands over the back of his tight ass blue jeans. His white t-shirt tied up in a knot in the back as usual. He loves showing off when he gets around men. "'Cause you know my sexy ass gotta stay nice and plump!" he continues smacking his lips and acting like a sissy. He gives queens like me a bad rep!

Since she's being loud, I walk a few feet over and say, "Hello."

"Girl, I can't believe you're on the phone again. Damn!" Tyrone says.

"Mind your fuckin' business and get what you brought your rusty ass in here for. Always worryin' 'bout what the queen is doin'!"

"Miss Wayne, where were you? I've been tryin' to reach you all day!" Parade screams into the phone.

"Parade, more shit is goin' on in DC than you know. But I'm here now so what's up?" Although she is mad now, I know she'll be exited when she hears I'm coming home later this week.

"You're being audited by the IRS." She says.

"Audited? What you talkin' about?"

"It doesn't look good, Miss Wayne. IRS agents came into ya'll boutique yesterday snatching up papers and shit. It was terrible! Then they froze you and Daffany's bank accounts! Daffany is so scared right now and I am too!"

I stop in my steps and look out before me. I put sixty thousand dollars of my money in the bank and now I don't have access to it? That would explain why my card stopped working.

"I don't understand…why? What happened?" I asked gripping the phone so tightly, I keep mashing the keys, interrupting our call.

"Daffany said the taxes weren't being paid. And since me and Jay are co-owners of ya'll business, they're investigating us too."

The smell of the food was makin' my stomach churn after hearing this shit. I had been doin' things illegal for so long, that I never thought about what it took to run a legal operation. Plus I assumed Daffany would make sure things were okay since we co-owned *All Girls* Boutique together. And now that I think about it, I was being ridiculous. She has her hands full as it is with Shantay.

"Where is Daffany now?"

"In our house but she hasn't left the guestroom. Just been in there crying all day. You gotta come home, Miss Wayne. Please."

Wow...I was just getting ready to tell her I was on the next plan to LA. But with the IRS snooping around there, I needed to stay as far away from home as possible. I had to think of a way to come up on some cash quick.

"Parade, what is Daffany gonna do about her HIV cocktail? If the accounts are frozen how she gonna pay for her meds?"

"For now me and Jay got it. But you know we have a few rental properties that are vacant and we aren't making profit. So we're covering the mortgages there plus our own. And with the new baby...and the twins, it's just too hectic. You got any money lyin' around you can help her with?"

"Chic, you sure you not gonna eat?" Tyrone laughs. "You standin' over there like a baby shittin' in a pamper. Ease up girl, why so tense?"

I couldn't even curse his ashy ass out. I needed to sit down and think.

"I got some cash in a box under my bed at my apartment. It's about twenty thousand dollars. Use your key to get in. When you get it, give ten thousand dollars to Daffany and send me the rest through FEDEX. I'ma call you back when I get the address. And don't worry, I'll think of somethin'."

When she hangs up I place the phone in my black Gucci purse. My mind is workin' overtime because the words BROKE BITCH and Miss Wayne just don't mix! Not to mention Daffany needed my help more than anything if she was going to stay healthy. Since we were paying for our own healthcare, shit was expensive. We spend a couple thousand dollars on Miss Daffany's medicine alone each month.

"Give me a three piece white, red beans and rice. Oh...and don't forget my biscuit." Miss Tyrone says to the cashier. "And a fruit punch soda too." He turns to look at me with an attitude and says, "Mother Wayne, do you want somethin' or not?"

"Uh…no, I'm good. But hurry up. I'm not feelin' too fabulous right now. Where is Dayshawn?"

"Over there talkin' to Dell." She says handing the cashier her money. "Apparently his cornball ass is back in town. And as usual Day runnin' behind his ass."

When I look behind me, I see Dayshawn standing by a table and Dell sitting down. Then I see a pretty transvestite walk over to Dell, kiss him on his cheek and sit down in the available seat across from him. She smiles at Dayshawn and offers her hand to shake. But Miss Dayshawn looks at them both and storms out of the restaurant.

Tyrone rolls her eyes up in that big ass forehead of hers and says, "I knew that nigga wasn't no good! That's why I told her to leave him alone. I'm not hatin' I'm just statin'!"

"You know a whole lot, Oprah! And as far as I know, there's nothin' written that you can't date somebody else after a relationship is over. So stop wit' all the judgmental bullshit because I'm tired of hearin' it."

She looks at me and says, "I be glad when you feel better. Ever since you been back from LA, you been actin' different."

"Bitch, what are you talkin' about? The house burned down, Miss Adrian wants to kill herself, Marlene was murdered by the fuckin' Drag Queen Slayer, the IRS has attached themselves to my money and now one of my best friends just had her feelings hurt by her ex-boyfriend! I know you a selfish bitch but can you really be that fuckin' insensitive?

"Excuse me, mam…I mean sir…are you in line?" asks a pesty little white woman behind me.

"Do you see the back of my ass?"

"Uh…yes."

"Then I'm in line." I say turnin' back around to look at Miss Tyrone.

I hear the old bitch sayin' something under her breath but I don't even care. Too much is happening too quick!

"Here's your change, cutie," the average looking male cashier says to Miss Tyrone, givin' him *the eye*.

I don't care where in the world you are, if you a gay man, you know how to give *the eye*. And *the eye* means one thing and one thing only…I wanna fuck you and I wanna fuck you right now. Personally he couldn't get my ass wet but Miss Tyrone has zero standards.

"Cutie huh?" Tyrone grins.

"That's what I said."

"Well how about sayin' that in my ear a little later? Maybe you can show me how cute you think I really am." He says leaning on the counter.

The cashier who is butch, licks his black-smoked-out lips and says, "Look, the white meat gonna be a few minutes, and I got a break comin' up in a sec, so let me holla at you before you leave right quick."

Miss Tyrone turns around and grins at me like she just nailed Trey Songz.

"I'ma go check on Dayshawn," I say. "But don't be all day runnin' your mouth. I got a lot of shit on my mind and I need to go to the hotel to think things through."

When I turn to leave, the little lady behind me pushes her way to the front so I trip her. Don't worry, she ain't fall. Just stares at me and walks her cotton ball head ass to the front of the line.

"I'll be out in a minute, mother Wayne. Tell Dayshawn I love him." He says being as fake as Gucci spelled with an O.

The more I hang around Tyrone, the more I'm starting to hate him.

Once at the car I see Dayshawn leaning against it, smoking a cigarette. You can tell she's been crying because she keeps wiping her tears.

"You got one for me?" I ask.

He gives me one and I fire it up and lean on the car next to him. A little dirt creeps onto my black jeans and I wipe it away.

"What happened? That's his new bitch or somethin'? 'Cause if it is, he needs to take her ass to the salon to get her lace front touched up. That shit look like somebody came on her forehead and let it dry up."

He smiles but more tears roll down his face. She wipes them away. See the thing about Miss Dayshawn is this...whenever she's upset, she can never let herself cry. She'll just change her facial expression and rock back and forth in place. You have to figure out what she means based on that.

"Look, if it's meant to be it will be. But until then, you gotta do you. Anyway she ain't got nothin' over you, Day. You know that."

When he drops his cigarette and smashes it on the ground he hugs me. I know he's feeling a little better, for now anyway.

We're in the car for thirty minutes and I was on my way inside to gut punch Miss Tyrone's freak ass, when she comes out smiling from ear to ear. The Popeye's bag in her hand is half crumbled and holey.

"I'm Ready!" she sings moving into the passenger seat adjusting her blue Chinese cut wig. "You alright, Day?"

"Fuck all that! What took you so long?" I ask.

"What you think?" she grins tugging at her jeans.

"I know you didn't do what I think you just did."

"And what was that?"

"Let that nigga get his ashy dick wet."

"And what if I did?"

"What the fuck is wrong with you? 'Cause I know you ain't got no condom on you to be servin' niggas today."

"He don't look like he got nothin'. Plus ain't nothin' gonna happen to me. Hell, with all the niggas I fucked in my life and I still ain't got that shit? Trust me, I'm good."

I heard about Miss Tyrone being a Bug Chaser, someone who had raw sex so they could catch HIV. I never believed it back then, but I'm starting to believe it now.

"Look how you sound!"

"I sound real."

"Oh really… well does Miss Daffany look positive?"

For the first time since seeing Dell with another woman Miss Dayshawn speaks. "Daffany's HIV positive?!"

I was sorry the moment the words left my mouth. Miss Daffany's secret was kept under wraps until now. And with Miss Tyrone knowing about her condition, I was sure the whole neighborhood would find out before long, it was just a matter of time.

"Daffany sick?" Tyrone asks.

"What, you didn't know?" I ask sarcastically. "Since you seem to believe you can tell who got what just by lookin' at 'em."

Miss Tyrone stares out ahead and says, "Well I think he was safe. I'm not too good with guessin' when it comes to fish since I don't fuck 'em no more. I had fun with him and he could fuck. After it was over, he gave me my money back plus my chicken dinner *with* biscuits!"

"So you fuckin' for chicken now?" I pause. "And you don't think that's stupid? You ain't even got a place to stay right now, Tyrone. I'm the one comin' out of my pockets for a hotel because I don't want to see my friends out on the street."

Miss Tyrone fans me away and says, "I 'preciate what you doin' and I told you that already. But we are gay men, Wayne. This is what we do. This is the life for us. Right, Dayshawn?"

Dayshawn remains quiet but nods in favor of his bullshit.

"All gay men don't act like this! Hell I'm gay and I know everybody's first and last name I fuck! Can you say the same? What was the Chicken King's last name you just fucked, Ty?"

"Look, that's you. Not me."

"I guess so because if I'm gonna give a nigga a piece of this crystal, he betta damn sure be worthy. Givin' me fried chicken with extra biscuits just won't do."

"Like I said, that's you," he says shruggin' his shoulders. "But most of us carry it like the way I just did. Me, Dayshawn and Adrian included. If you can't get with it then I understand, but that's your thing not ours and you shouldn't knock us for it. I fuck what I want, when I want and where I want. It's as simple as that. I'm grown, Wayne."

Sad ain't it? And as much as I'd love to argue, she's tellin' the truth. Sex between gay men is unlike anythin' that can be explained. It's more passionate, it's more addictive and it's more competitive.

I know competition may be a strong word for people who don't live this life to understand but it's true. Fuckin' as many men as you can in some ways makes you believe you're more desirable...more wanted. Not to mention you can bust a nut at the same time. And in a world that rejects you on a daily basis, to some men sex is everything.

But after hearing this, I had an idea. Since she's a whore anyway, I decided it would no longer be for free. I had plans to tax that action and that goes for the rest of my crew too.

When my phone rings I take it out of my purse and say, "Hello?"

Silence.

"Hello? Who the fuck is this?" I yell louder.

Miss Tyrone and Miss Dayshawn stop what they are doing and look my way.

"You betta mind the company you keep." The caller says…and then he hangs up.

I wonder who that was and my gut tells me its Big Boody Brandy. But if I've learned anything in life, it's that it's usually the person you least expect.

# The Meet

## QUEEN PAUL

Queen Paul and four of his crew members stood in front of his incinerated house waiting on Big Boody Brandy. Money had exchanged hands but Tyrone, Dayshawn and Wayne were still walking around breathing and Paul needed that to stop.

Paul just finished meeting with a shift investigator from the fire department and an insurance agent at the property. Through it all, he couldn't believe the house he'd been raised in most of his life, was burned to the ground. His mother gave him the house on his eighteenth birthday and it meant a lot to him. But if things went his way, he may get compensated for more than it was worth when the investigation was over.

All of the queens were dressed in drag and at first look, you'd think they were a bunch of linebackers playing a joke on Halloween. All of them wore stringy wigs, run over shoes and fake purses. They were definitely hard on the eyes.

"I hope she hurry up!" Kevin says to Paul. "My cousin who's doin' security at the private poker party I was telling you about said the game is goin' down tonight. So we gotta hurry up if we gonna hit it."

"There her truck goes right there." Paul points.

Big Boody Brandy parks his black Toyota Tundra at the curb and grabs her Teacup Yorkie to approach Paul. Four queens open their car doors and follow. Now the crew Big Boody ran with was official. They spent money to have work done on their breasts, lips and hips. And the clothing they wore was always from a designer label. With one look you could tell who was getting real money between the two houses and who wasn't.

Big Boody Brandy ran with a drag house she called The House of Diamonds and she was the overall mother. And one thing she didn't play was having members in her crew who didn't *look the part*...especially out in public.

"I ain't know you were bringin' nobody. I thought this meeting was private." Paul says looking at his crew and then his dog.

"I can't tell...you brought all your rag stars...I mean...rock stars with you." She smirks. "Besides, if it ain't no problems between us, it shouldn't matter who's here. We got a problem, Paul?"

Paul grins and says, "I don't think so."

Big Boody takes a look at the burned house and says, "Damn, I ain't know the shit went down like that. You know what happened yet?"

"Naw...but I do know Tyrone, Wayne and Day are still walkin' 'round. And since you got my money I'm wonderin' how that's the case."

"I got plans for them that are already in motion. And just so you know, I almost took care of them for free when I blasted in the house that night, but shit didn't work to my favor or yours."

"So you did shoot out the windows."

"What you think?" She laughs. "But like I told you over the phone, too much shit happened including this fire for me to do anything else right now. Plus Betty Badge been everywhere because of this Drag Queen Slayer bullshit. But I'ma take care of that for you when shit cools off."

"When?!" Paul yells. Maxie raises his head and barks wildly in Paul's face and he and his scared ass crew jump backwards.

Big Boody laughs and says, "Look, Paul. I know you probably use to queens just runnin' around town suckin' dick, since I hear that's all you and your crew do, but that's not my thing. I run everything around here and I need to make sure my supplier and my customers are happy. Murder is just my hobby. Now I'ma take care of that for you like I said, but you can't make me do shit. Do we mesh?"

Embarrassed by his comment Paul says, "I don't care if you suck dick or fuck your mother," all the queens gasp hearing that comment, "if you don't do what I paid you for, there's going to be problems."

Big Boody Brandy looks at her girls and then back at Paul. They all laugh.

"Bitch, you got me all the way fucked up. So I'ma tell you what I'm gonna do. I'ma take your money and let you live long enough to get out of my face. Got it?"

Paul's crew moved toward Big Boody and in turn Brandy's crew moved in sync. If someone even breathes the wrong word at this point, a fight would kick off.

Big Boody says, "Stop girls…ain't no need in gettin' ourselves all messy today." Then Big Boody turns to Paul and says, "I was gonna take care of your little problem for you since Tyrone set me up and got me mixed up in some shit. But since you bein' campy, you can consider yourself five thousand short. And if you wanna see me, you know where I be."

When Big Boody walks away, Paul looks at Kevin and says, "Don't worry…I got somethin' for that bitch, believe that!"

"What about Wayne and them?" one of his other queens asks.

"I got somethin' for them too. But I want Brandy first."

# *Trash Talk*

## ❦MISS WAYNE❦

"Tyrone! Tyrone! Open this damn door!" I yell with my hands on my hips, the red silk gown I'm wearing sweeps the floor. I would not have known he was breaking house rules if the bed in his room wasn't banging up against my wall.

Since I rented this house from Miss Rick two weeks earlier, Tyrone has turned completely reckless. And I wonder even more, if whoever called me in the car at Popeye's, was talking specifically about him.

"I know you're in there, bitch! Open this fuckin' door!" I bang. "You got one nigga in the bed and anotha nigga out here on the couch rollin' up a blunt!"

I take a look at the Mr. Thug trade sitting on our new red leather sofa wearin' nothin' but pink boxers and butter colored Timberland boots. He licks the sides of the blunt and runs a fire under it. The thing is, he appears totally unmoved by my irritation with him. His nonchalance ain't doin' nothin' but pissin' me off even more!

"Who the fuck are you anyway?" I ask him.

"Doctor, sweetheart. And why you actin' all mean? If you want, I got somethin' right here that'll make you feel good."

"You ain't got shit for me, Sharpie! And I'm mean because you in my damn house."

Just then Adrian opens his bedroom door and slides into the hallway wearing a pink silk gown and pink furry slippers. His hands and neck are still covered in white gauze to protect the second-degree burns he sustained from the fire.

"What's wrong, Miss Wayne?" He asks rubbing his eyes. "What, Tyrone do now?"

"Don't worry about that. You supposed to be in bed. It's only been two weeks since you been back from the hospital and you still haven't gotten your strength back."

"I'm tired of bein' alone," he says with sad eyes.

"So I take it that you still haven't heard from Chris yet."

"He calls… I don't answer the phone. But Miss Wayne, I'm finally ready to talk to you about what's been going on with me."

"I already know what's goin' on."

"You do?" He asks surprised.

"Yeah…Tyrone told me everything."

He holds his head down and says, "Okay. I just didn't want to keep anything from you that's all."

I want to help him more but my irritation with Miss Tyrone's manly lookin' ass won't allow me to at the moment.

"On another note," I continue pointing to the living room. "Tyrone continues to break the rules around here and I'm tired of it. So we gonna have a meetin' this mornin'."

Adrian peeks into our living room and when he does, he smiles when he sees the thug on the sofa with his feet propped up on the glass table. The man looks at him, winks, and smokes his blunt.

"Oh my gawd! He's…beautiful!"

"Not hardly."

And then I notice something that drives me mad! This homothug must've jerked his dick off waitin' on Tyrone because his boxers are stained with white shit.

"You just couldn't wait could you?" I ask pointing at the mess.

He smiles and says, "No."

I'm not even worried...because in fifteen minutes, his ass is out of here.

"Well...well...well," Dayshawn says slyly, walking through the front door. He places a grocery bag full of food on the table in the kitchen and looks long and lustfully at the man on the sofa. "What do we have here?! Tyrone stay with the eye candy."

Then he joins us in the hallway. "It's not funny and ya'll need not encourage this type of behavior!" I yell at him.

"Well I can take him in my room if you want. Trust me, it's not a problem," Dayshawn continues as he looks at him again.

When Tyrone finally opens the door, a man wearing a blue hoodie pushes past us, drops some money on the breakfast nook by the kitchen, and walks out the front door. Miss Tyrone places his hands over his face and laughs but ain't shit funny.

"He was soooo good." He smiles. "I haven't been fucked like that since the twelfth grade."

"I know you lyin' now because you ain't make it past the ninth!" I tell him.

"You still got energy for me?" the stranger on the sofa asks standing up.

We all look at him.

"The only thing that's ready for you is the front door!" I say walking toward it, opening it wide.

He looks at Tyrone who covers his mouth in embarrassment. Grabbing his pants, he angrily places them on before snatching his shirt off the floor.

"Call me when you're serious," He tells Tyrone before leaving.

I slam the door behind him and say, "This is it, Tyrone! It's time for a meetin' in the lady's room 'cause I see ya'll think I'm playin'."

When someone knocks at the door again, Tyrone goes to answer it. Then he looks at us and says, "Give me a second." And steps outside.

I figure that dude called him outside and that pisses me off. I can't wait to put Tyrone's ass in her place. Five minutes later she comes back inside and for some reason, she looks scared. I don't know what happened but I never saw him like that before. Be that as it may, that ain't got shit to do with me.

"I'm glad you're finish, Tyrone. 'Cause I'm sick of ya'll."

"Ya'll?" Miss Dayshawn says. His hair is neatly cut and his brown face glows brightly...which lets me know that he must've recently treated himself to a boy's day at the spa without helping out with the rent around here. Who do they think I am? Mr. Drummond? "I ain't done shit."

"And what did I do?" Tyrone adds.

"For starters we've only been here for two weeks and you've had more men in here than a federal prison! Not to mention the fact that you ain't bringin' in no revenue. And you Miss Day stay at the nail salon! Where you gettin' the money from? And you, Adrian...when was the last time you brought some money in here?"

Tyrone walks up to me, pulls his satin blue robe together and says, "I don't know 'bout them but I'm makin' money. And as far as I can tell I'm the only one."

"Fuck is that supposed to mean?" I ask.

"Dayshawn ain't trickin' because she's still in love with Dell and Adrian too busy not bein' in love with Chris. I feel like we're on that old ass show *Heart to Heart* around here!"

Miss Adrian gasps. "I don't mind trickin' but I don't want just anybody."

"What about you, Tyrone?" I ask.

"Yeah...you claim you're makin' money but I don't see shit but weed and cheap liquor. So let's see how much you made today," Miss Dayshawn adds.

I walk up to the table, pick up the money the stranger dropped and count ten dollars.

"You call this gettin' money?" I ask holding the money tightly.

He tries to snatch it away but you must be more than just quick to take something from my clasp.

"You need one dollar before you can make a million." He tells me.

"Yeah well you got a long fuckin' way to go!"

When I look at them I believe I've made a big fuckin' mistake. After all, I had Miss Parade FED-EX *all the money* I had left in the world, to Miss Rick's house, where I stayed for two days until it arrived. Tyrone Adrian and Day slept in Adrian's car because Miss Rick doesn't trust Tyrone and didn't want him in his house. And after hearing the rumors of the recent rape shit along with all the drama she's been involved in since I've been back in DC, I don't blame him. Tyrone just isn't the person I thought he was.

The day the money came from FED EX, I put two thousand dollars on Miss Rick's five-bedroom rental house off of 28th place in Southeast DC. That only paid us up for two months. Then I bought an old Honda Civic to get me around town. The rest I spent on groceries for the house. But I know Miss Rick, if I don't come up with the rest of his cash when the rent is due, friend or foe, he's gonna put a queen out on the street. And I can't have that. But these cunts don't seem to give a fuck!

Don't get it twisted…the two thousand dollars I spent on this house was an investment. I knew that if there were two things in the world they liked, fuckin' and party-tin' was it. So I came up with the idea to throw private weekend parties for gay and closet queens. Our parties provided them with a place to go where they wouldn't be judged. In translation I'm running a whorehouse, girl! The fee? $100 at the door. No pay no play.

Charging that kind of money and getting it was another story. First, I had to convince my loose boody crew to entertain our guests *first* and negotiate fees for other services later. They needed to be personable and sexy so the guests would come back. They needed to take care of their clothes, make sure their faces were beat and their bodies and feet were cute. But if you saw Miss Tyrone's feet, which look like DC's battered streets after a snowstorm, you wouldn't think it was possible. So trust me when I say I have my work cut out for me!

All I know is that Miss Daffany needs me. And if my plan works, I'll be able to send her money weekly for her healthcare and legal expenses. Our attorney alone who is helping us get access to our funds again, costs me eighteen hundred dollars a month. And yes she could get on Medicare to save us money on healthcare expenses but I need the best of the best doctors working on her. Because of her doctor now, Daffany's CD4 T-Cell count stays over 360.

Some of ya'll may think I'm wrong for pimpin' my friends out. And you probably think that as the overall mother, I should teach them the game and the right way to live the gay life. But my question to you would be, *ain't that what I'm doin'?*

"Tyrone, I expect you to earn real money if you wanna stay here." I say. "If you don't want to, you have an option to get your own place. But if anyone comes in here outside of the four of us in this room right now, they must pay the mistress of ceremonies."

"You got this all together," Miss Tyrone pauses. "It's like you've been plannin' this forever."

"We beyond that, honey. You know what it's giving now!" I say with a wave of my arm and snap of my finger. "You have to render to Caesar."

"Wayne, stop being so melodramatic," Miss Tyrone says as he puts up the groceries Miss Dayshawn brought with my money. "We all know you fronted us the money to get this place. There's no need to remind us over and over again."

"I didn't front you shit! I paid for everything."

"And I get that but when I do find somebody serious," he says pointing at himself, "I don't expect him to be charged for comin' over here."

"Whatever happened to all the shit you said about, Adrian? And Dayshawn? And how they stupid for falling in love?" I say pointing at him. "And now you want me to give you a hypothetical answer to a question in the event you *may* get a man? Let me make it easy, sweetheart, if they come through them doors, they payin'. That includes any so-called nigga you get for a man in the distant future. Because let's be clear, my name is the only one on this lease."

"I know we talked about them payin' one hundred at the door. But can we still earn a little on the side?" Asks Dayshawn. "I wanna save too."

"You get nothing, *unless* you put out. That means if trade wants to fuck, you gotta get up. If you don't, you won't. But the door fee is mine...what you earn in the bedroom minus ten percent, is all yours."

"Fuck this shit!" Miss Tyrone screams. "I'm outta here."

"Don't leave, Tyrone," Miss Adrian whines. He turns around to me and says, "Please don't let him leave."

"Sorry, hun but in the words of Patti Labelle, '*He's on his own!*'"

"Yes I am...and ain't nobody, includin' you gonna tell me what to do wit' my boody. And if I want to give it away free then that's what the fuck I'm gonna do!"

"Bitch, you doin' stunts and shows." I tell her. "The door is behind you...use it."

He spends thirty minutes slamming his bedroom door back and forth while collecting his shit. It should've taken him less than five minutes to move, since the sissy got only ten pair of pants and ten shirts and five tired ass dresses to her name.

"Remember that you are the one who ended our friendship, not me," Tyrone says.

"Your comment is noted. Goodbye."

He slams the door and I laugh.

# *Pussy On Your Sideburns*

## ❦QUEEN TYRONE❦

"Avil, put your mother on the phone. I need to talk to her for a minute," Tyrone says to his thirteen-year old son after he answers the phone.

"Hey, dad. Everything cool?"

"It depends on what your mother says," he says holding the black duffel with all his clothes firmly in his hand, one bare foot on the cold dirty ground and the other in his white pump. He was standing in a phone booth outside with no place left to go.

"What's wrong now, Tyrone?" Shannon says with irritation in her voice.

"Uh…I know I haven't been over to check on you or Avil in awhile, but you know I been tryin' to keep my head up. So much shit goin' on around me, Shannon. I just needed to be by myself."

"And you tellin' me that because?"

"Because I need your help."

"What's new, Tyrone? You always need my help. When you gonna give me what I need? And what I want? When somebody gonna love me best? You out there bein' weird, your son actin' all feminine and I'm sittin' here tryin' to find out what the fuck I did wrong to be all alone and playin' with my pussy every night."

"You know I wouldn't stay away from you if I could help it. Shannon, I didn't want to tell you this because I didn't want you to worry but the house I lived in burned down and I almost died in it." He lied. "I'm just gettin' back from the hospital right now. Everything I own is in my bag."

"What?! Are you okay?"

"Yeah…I just need somewhere to lie down."

"What about Dayshawn?" she says with hope in her voice, "Is he hurt?"

Always an amazing liar he says, "He died. It's just me out here now."

"Wow…I didn't know all that was happenin'." She says although it's obvious that she's pleased to learn of Dayshawn's death. She didn't like Dayshawn the moment she met him in high school because she hated that Tyrone as she called it, *'had someone to be gay with'*. "If I let you stay here though, I need to know how long you plan on stayin'? I mean, can you at least hang around a little longer this time to spend time with your family? Real time?"

"Of course, Shannon. That's why I'm callin' now."

Silence.

"No runnin' the streets and hookin' up with men?"

He had to think long and hard before he answered that question. He soon realized it was impossible for him to leave the streets. What he'd have to do was find a way to hide his activities behind her back.

"No men. Just me and my family."

"Fine, you can come home."

"Thanks, Shannon."

"Wait…before you come I need you to look like a…well…father and husband. My mother is here and you know she still believes you raped my brother Nathan. And since he been in that mental institution ever since, it's even harder for her to believe you didn't."

"You still think I did?"

"I know you didn't and she's tryin' to blame you for her shortcomings as a mother. I just don't want the problems tonight."

Tyrone thought about Nathan and their time together. Only he and Nathan really knew what happened that night and he had no intentions on telling Shannon. In fact he lied so much to himself that he started to believe his lies. But there was one person other than Tyrone who remembered exactly how the incident went down.

Years ago, Nathan was in town from Atlanta to visit his sister Shannon after not seeing her for five years. Their relationship was always strained since she could remember, her oldest brother always abused some sort of drug. First he started off small with weed and since it's often considered a gateway drug, before long he upgraded to heroin.

The day he visited Shannon, she hadn't gotten home from work as a makeup artist. So she asked her husband to make sure her brother got settled in. Although they fought a lot, she was actually looking forward to seeing him again.

But the moment Tyrone laid eyes on Nathan, he knew he wanted to fuck him, even if Nathan didn't know. As the day went on, neither of them could have imagined how much they had in common. Nathan really could not have imagined their connection because he knew how much his sister despised him because of all of the lies he told while on drugs. And since everyone in Shannon's family hated Tyrone, after hearing rumors that he was gay, he didn't think he had an in-law alive who would like him. He was wrong.

After a few cups of hard liquor were drank between the two of them, the conversation moved to drugs. And although Tyrone was no stranger to getting high or snorting cocaine, he never dealt with anything else. But when

Nathan offered him heroin, he gladly accepted. What Nathan didn't know was that after he took his first hit, and handed the needle to Tyrone, he only pretended to put it in his arm. The expensive drug dripped to the floor. Tyrone chose to be as conscious as possible, for what he was about to do.

Sharing a couch with Nathan, Tyrone said, "I ain't feelin' shit." He tapped his arm in the place the needle should have entered and said, "Let's do anotha one, man."

"Damn, here I was thinkin' I was puttin' you on to somethin' new, and you handle this shit betta than me." He said nodding a little. "Okay…okay…I was gonna save this for later, but let's cook this one too."

So again he shot up and again Tyrone pretended to get high. He even allowed his eyes to roll toward the back of his head and lean to the side. And when he saw Nathan falling in and out of consciousness, he put the deadbolt lock on the door, threw Nathan over the edge of the sofa and raped him over and over again. When Nathan who had never been with a man before, while in and out of consciousness saw what was happening, his spirit weakened. His sister's husband had taken advantage of his body and violated him in the worst way.

When Tyrone was done, he cleaned him up and put him in the guestroom as if nothing happened. The next morning when Shannon arose to greet her brother, she saw he was gone. He never even told her why. Her sadness turned into anger and she eventually counted her brother's actions as another way to prove he didn't care about her or her feelings.

A year afterwards, Nathan dove deeper into drugs doing whatever he could to take his life. And when he was finally sentenced to rehabilitation after going on top of a department store roof naked, claiming snake people were trying to kill him, his life changed for the better. The first thing he did when he was sober was attempt to right the wrongs in his life. He started with telling their mother about the rape, so that she could warn his sister about her husband. His mother believed him and pled with Shannon to file for a divorce. But she stood by her husband and swore he could never do something so heinous. She never spoke to her brother again.

"Okay baby. I'll try to put somethin' together, based on what I got with me anyway. But you know I don't live my life like that anymore. I'm openly gay now, Shannon."

"Who fault is that? Yours or mine?"

"Shannon, it's nobody's fault. I just don't want to give you the wrong impression when I come over. Although I want to spend time with my family, we can't be like we were anymore."

Silence.

"Tyrone, I said my piece. I'll see you when you get here."

◆ • • • • • • • • • • • • • • • • • • • • • • • • • • • • • • • • • • ◆

# *Indecent Proposal*

"What the fuck is he doin' here, Shannon?" Grace screams at her daughter when she opens the door to see Tyrone standing there. "This monster violated my son...your brother...and you allow him into your home?"

"Mother this is my house and I do what I want! Plus I'm not trying to hear my brother and all them lies he be tellin' you! He been on drugs so long he don't know what's goin' on no more."

Tears streamed down Grace's face and she yells, "Baby, this man is sick! Look at him…he comes in here with no shoes, wearing smeared makeup all over his face and jeans so tight I doubt if he has balls anymore! When are you gonna open your eyes?"

"I don't care, mama! He's my husband!" She yells louder. "And so what…what if he is gay? You can hate a person because of that?"

"Gay I don't have a problem with, Shannon! But a rapist and a cheater is another story! 'Especially when my daughter is involved with one."

"Mrs. Holbrook-"

"Don't you Mrs. Holbrook me, mothafucka! Don't you ever speak to me again!" She says pointing at Tyrone. "Shannon," she continues in a much softer and caring tone than before, "you can't have him around you. You have to let him go. Look at your son…"

"Go in the room, Tyrone. I have to talk to my mother alone." When he's gone she says, "That's right, mother. Look at my son! And then take another look at the man you just disrespected back there because believe it or not, he *is* his father."

Silence.

Grace lowers her head, stands up straight and says, "I'm done. Have it your way. I just hope you live long enough to remember the day your mother warned you." She grabs her purse and walks out the front door.

◆ • • • • • • • • • • • • • • • • • • • • • • • • • • • • • • • ◆

# *Over an Hour Later*

After arguing with her mother for over an hour, all Shannon wanted was sexual relief. She tried to fuck him but he wouldn't get hard. She wasn't going to let that stop her though.

"Oooohhh, kiss it for me like that," Shannon moans as Tyrone spreads her legs and licks her wetness. "I love when you do it like that."

As a woman, Shannon was very attractive. Her thick legs and small waist turned heads every time she walked down the street. But that was just his problem, her body reminded him constantly what he really wanted was a man. His disgust for her grew so bad that toward the end of their marriage, he demanded that she allow him to penetrate her from behind, so he wouldn't have to see her angelic face. She accepted because it was the only way to keep him in her life.

Shannon was so entrapped in his touch, that she pulled his head toward her wet mound and pushed her wetness against his face.

"Shannon," he says clutching her wrists, "don't grab the back of my head. You know I don't like that."

"I'm sorry," she says looking down at him, "it just feels so good and it's been so long. I'll try to be careful. Just don't stop. Keep flickin' that tongue."

As her head drops back to the pillow, she moves her hips wildly to get back the feeling she lost when he stopped. But this time something was wrong. Tyrone felt his stomach rumble and a bitter taste fill his mouth.

"Are you okay?" she asks noticing he wasn't performing the same.

"I...I..." his sentence was cut short as he spewed vomit all over her vagina.

Aggravated, she leaps off the bed and he runs to the bathroom to finish releasing the cheese steak sub he ate at a rundown carryout a few hours earlier. With both hands on the rim of the cold toilet bowl, he feels his stomach buckle with pain.

"Are you okay?" she says entering the bathroom to clean herself off in the sink. "Don't worry about it. I'm fine and I know you had a long day." Placing her foot on the edge of the tub, she wet a washcloth to wipe herself. "I'll give you a few minutes so you can start again. I was almost there, silly," she continues rubbing his back.

"You gon' need to give me a longer than a few minutes," he manages to say looking up at her.

"Oh...well...I'll be out there waiting."

When she's done she leaves him in the bathroom alone. Ten minutes later he walks into the bedroom.

"Shannon, I can't do this anymore." He says sitting on the bed next to her. "I can't live this lie no more. It's gotta stop here."

"But why?"

"As much as I want to please you, I just can't fuck you no more."

"I know you feel that way right now, but if we can just get counseling, I know we can make things work."

"You not listenin' to me, sweetie. I'm gay!"

"But you're married to me!" she says touching his arms. "Look, honey, I'm willin' to understand that part of your life. Just don't remove the part from your world that includes me." She says rubbing his back again. "Remember when use to fuck at my house and you liked it?"

"The key word is *use* to. Look at me! And then look at your house! My pictures are everywhere around here!" he says grabbing one which sits next to the bed. It was taken on the day of their wedding. "Can't you see we aren't the same? I'm not the same man in this picture, Shannon!"

"I still love you anyway, and I don't think of you like that." She says placing the picture down. Tears roll down her face. "Maybe if you stopped hanging around your friends as much, we could work on our marriage. I know I can please you if you just give me a chance."

Tyrone grows frustrated but he doesn't know what to do. Part of him, the selfish part, loves that she is so committed that no matter what, she'd still be by his side. And the other part, the part that is disgusted by their lives together wishes she just move on.

"You believe what you wanna believe."

When Tyrone gets up to walk out of the room to sleep in the guestroom she says, "If you want to sleep here...you will fuck me. And you will fuck me like you love me. You owe me that!"

Tyrone turns around and looks at her in disbelief. Her love for him was so strong it left her obsessed.

"What?" he says.

"I think you know what the fuck I'm saying. Look at you...you're in your late thirties, you can't read or write and you're homeless. Who the fuck will want you more than me?" she says cutting her eyes at him. "I'm there for you whenever you need me...give you money when you ask...take care of your son. But what about me? You mean to tell me that you can't even lick my pussy like you love me? With all the dirty dicks you done sucked? My pussy is worse than theirs?"

"Shannon..."

"Shut the fuck up, Tyrone! No more excuses. You don't get to call the shots right now, I do. Now if you wanna stay in my house, you will get in this bed and fuck me like I know you can," she says wiping the tears from her eyes.

Tyrone considers his options briefly.

He has none.

So against his will, he walks slowly toward the bed.

"You still got the kit?" he asks in a low voice.

Having gotten her way, she hops off the bed and removes a brown plastic bag from underneath the mattress. Like it was second nature, she removes an old worn out poster of LL Cool J with his ripped up abs exposed and places it on the wall. Then she goes in her closet, grabs a red varsity jacket and baseball cap and places them on. Not a strand of her shoulder length hair shows.

With her ass pointed in his direction, she gets on her hands and knees and spreads her legs. At first glance, she looks like a young boy waiting to be fucked and it works for him.

Focusing on the poster he did what he had to do. But if he were smart he'd realize that anyone that dedicated to one person was mentally off balanced, and he needed to run and fun fast.

# A Month Later

## ❀MISS WAYNE❀

I hadn't been to the Bachelor's Mill, a gay club in Washington DC, in years. Sweaty queens who ain't got shit on me, covered the floor as they danced and sashayed to the latest house music. But I'm so busted I couldn't even tell you what's playin'.

Today the nursing home called me again about my mother. They said they're worried about her but for some reason, they think she's trying to hold on. But I know why. She's waiting on me to tell her it's okay to die...and that I'm strong enough to take care of myself now. But I just can't do it. I'm not ready.

I was on my fifth drink when Miss Adrian and Miss Dayshawn wiggled inside the doors more than fashionably late. They had something to tell me and although I already thought I knew what it was, I agreed to meet with them out for drinks anyway. When all I really wanted to do was go home and stretch out, after my recent flight from LA to D.C.

"We missed you so much, mama!" Miss Adrian says hugging me. "How was LA?"

He looks cute in his black tight slacks and black button down shirt, which exposes his small-sculpted chest. He's so gorgeous that even in butch he's slaying the queens.

"It was fine, but you know it wasn't a pleasure trip. I had to get Miss Daffany squared away. She should be fine for now."

"So how is she?" Miss Dayshawn asks, sporting a cute black blazer by Lyle Scott with a white t-shirt underneath and his DSquared blue jeans.

"Girls...Let's stop the fakeness and get to the fuckin' point."

I wasn't about to tell them that Daffany was doing bad and that the doctor put her on bed rest. I knew that the stress of possibly losing our business was too much for her to take. I spent hours telling her I had her back and that everything including her health care expenses would be paid for...I just wish she relaxed and believed in me.

"I wasn't trying to upset you. I just wanted to make sure she was okay," Says Dayshawn.

"Look, what's up? 'Cause I ain't got time for all this shit you bringin' me. Our first party is tomorrow and I wanna go home and rest up so it can be a success."

Miss Dayshawn takes a deep breath and says, "He wants back in the house."

"Does he want back in the physical house or the house of dreams?" I ask referring to our crew.

"Both. His wife is over there giving him the blues, Miss Wayne. Making him fuck and suck her every five minutes. He can't handle it and he feels like we've all turned our backs on him. I miss him, Wayne. Don't you?"

"I can't say that I do. Tyrone ain't the same, Day. Doesn't it bother you that every time we turn around, some crazy ass drama is surroundin' her ass? I remember lookin' at this special Oprah had on one day talking about how you are what you think. If that's really true, what does that say about him? The longer we hang around him the more our lives are in danger. I don't know, Day, I think we betta off leavin' him the fuck alone."

"But he's sorry."

"Yes he is, darling! But I no longer care. He's also ungrateful. I mean…if I didn't agree to stay in DC, what were ya'll gonna do? Where were ya'll going to live? Yet you get mad at me because I tax that ass? It makes no sense."

"That's true," Miss Adrian adds. "Wayne has carried us so far. And just so you know, mama, I'm with you the entire way. I just don't want you to throw me out."

"Why do you keep sayin' that shit? I'm nowhere interested in gettin' rid of you, twinkie. Who told you that?"

She hangs her head low and says, "Nobody."

"Are you sure?"

"Yes." I sigh and turn to Miss Day and say, "The cunt can't want back in the system and buck it too. She has to make her fuckin' mind up."

"You right, but she understands now that if she's not helping out the house, she's against it. Just give her another chance, Wayne…please."

I think about their campaign for Tyrone and everything in my soul tells me to walk away from her. The feeling is so strong it makes my temples throb. But I also know that when it comes to whoring, Miss Tyrone is the best girl for the job. And, with Miss Daffany being sick, I realize any money we can raise will help my cause.

"Look, if he wants back in, he has to come up with five hundred dollars, and then I'll see."

"Yayyy," Miss Dayshawn smiles, jumping up and down.

His dedication to Miss Tyrone confuses me. Miss Tyrone is selfish in every sense of the word so why would he and Adrian be so loyal to him? I sure hope Tyrone realizes he's lucky to have friends who care about him, no matter what, by his side.

I know I do.

◆ •••••••••••••••••••••••••••••••••••••• ◆

## *Reflecting On The Younger Years*
## *Miss Wayne*

*Miss Wayne walked quietly into the school cafeteria. That's the part he hated most...being new and not fitting in anywhere. Spotting an empty lunch table, with his beige meal trey in hand, he moved slowly toward it until he heard, "Wayne! Over here!"*

*Turning around to see where the voice would lead him, he smiled when he saw the girl he helped protect a few days back waving at him. In a fabulous swagger only he possessed, he strutted toward her and sat down at the table.*

*"Hi!" Sky smiled. "I never got a chance to thank you for helping me. Them jealous ass bitches always worried 'bout what I'm doin'. By the way, the name's Sky, and this is Daffany," she said pointing to a scraggly looking girl sitting next to her. Wayne knew automatically that Sky liked to be around girls she ran rings around physically, to make her look better. "This is her first day."*

*Wayne smiled at Daffany and focused back on Sky. "Sky huh?" he said opening his milk carton with soft and feminine mannerisms.*

*"Yep, 'cause my mother and father told me that with my beauty, the sky's the limit!"*

*He laughed and said, "So, Sky, why were you gettin' your ass kicked? I mean...what you do to piss them off?"*

*"I ain't do shit but be me," she said with a sassy attitude. "I guess they couldn't handle it."*

*Wayne giggled and said, "It looked to me like you were the one who couldn't handle shit and me and that girl had to mix in."*

*As they were chatting like little girls, the voice meter in the cafeteria rose and Wayne turned around to see why.*

*"Look at that black bitch! I bet you she won't do to me what she did to Diamond! I don't even know why she jumped in," said one girl. "Nobody was even talking to her."*

*"Ain't been here a month and already starting shit," said another.*

*"Look at that dusty bitch's shoes," added someone else.*

*When Wayne saw whom they were referring to, for some reason, he was consumed with rage. Nothing ruffled his feathers more than people picking on weaker people. So when he saw it was Parade, the girl he also met in the yard, he couldn't be still.*

*Parade was doing her best to ignore the girls' harsh words but her tightly pierced lips were a dead giveaway that she was mad. Still, she took the treatment like a trooper until someone threw a carton full of milk at the back of her head. It bursts at her feet and drenched her legs.*

*Seeing the culprits laughing, anger overcame her and it took her five seconds to lunge on top of the table and wrap her hands around the girl's neck. All of the loud-mouthed girls' friends, who had so much to say moments earlier, were as quiet as church mice hiding in a corner.*

*Wayne dashed to the scene seconds before a few teachers reached Parade. He pulled her off of the girl and the teachers missed the actual events. They did see one girl rubbing her neck and Parade standing nervously in front of her.*

"*Miss Knight, I know you aren't starting trouble again!*" *Yelled a young black male teacher.* "*Because you were warned that the next time we had an incident with you, you could be expelled from this school! Even your mother said she'd snatch you out by your hair if she had to come up here again.*"

The children standing by giggled at the comment. Wayne was enraged.

"*Parade what is going on?*" *asked the white teacher with kind eyes.* "*Why are you always in trouble?*"

Parade was breathing heavily, tears streamed down her face and her fists were still balled up. She was embarrassed by the teacher's comment regarding her mother.

"*Do you hear her? Were you causing a disruption in my school for the tenth time or what?*" *The black teacher yelled.*

"*No she wasn't. It was me.*"

Both teachers transferred their glare from Parade to Wayne.

Parade whipped her head toward him to be sure she'd heard him correctly.

"*What is your name young man?*" *the female teacher asked.*

"*Wayne. Wayne Peterson.*"

"*Well Wayne Peterson, how come I don't believe you?*"

"*I don't know,*" *he shrugged.* "*But why don't you ask her?*" *He said pointing to the girl who Parade had choked out just moments earlier.*

"*Young lady, is this true?*" *the male teacher asked.* "*Was he the one who hit you?*"

The girl looked at the teacher and then at Wayne. She was hesitant with her answer and it was obvious that something or someone had her shook.

*"Yes...it's true. It was him."*

*"Well then," the male teacher said irritated he wouldn't have the chance to make good on his promise to expel Parade. "Wayne, if it was really you, then you have to come with me."*

*Before he left with the teacher, he tucked the pocketknife fully in his pocket he slyly used to threaten the girl with earlier. It was positioned so that only she could see it. Then he gave Parade a smile.*

*"Thank you," she said softly.*

*He smiled back, and walked out the cafeteria's doors.*

*Miss Wayne* & THE QUEENS OF DC

## *Shake Your Money Makers*
# ✤MISS WAYNE✤

I can't believe he raised five hundred dollars. And then I remember, his wife would do anything to keep him including give him money. To tell you the truth, I was kinda hoping he didn't raise the money. So much for wishful thinking.

Anyway, the setup for the party was hot if I do say so myself. First I turned on Comcast music channel and let the slow jams play. Then the girls and me placed scented candles and fresh linen in every bedroom. Then there was the food. We had fried chicken, collard greens, French fries and liquor on the dinner table. And the girls were stunning...each one of my queens' faces were beat to death compliments of me. I made sure their makeup was perfect. I even chose the outfits they wore...trust...we were definitely ready for business.

"All queens, to the living room please," I say. "We only have an hour before the party."

Tyrone, Dayshawn, Adrian and the four queens I hired from Quincy Manor come rushing into the living room. They're dressed in different colored beautiful dresses but all were in full drag. I wore a long royal blue silk dress with a cut so high on the side, you can almost see my black silk panties.

"Now, tonight is our first party and I wanted to thank each of you in advance. We will be workin', but I want each of you to have a good time too. Because the more relaxed you are, the more money our guests will spend to be entertained. We're in the money makin' business ladies and we *are* queens. Remember that shit tonight. Don't let anyone take you to the playroom, without discussin' a fair price. What you charge is up to you, as long as I get my ten percent cut. Don't drink too much or give up the pussy too quickly either."

"I'm ready, Miss Wayne." Says Alicia, one of the manor queens. "And we love you in your blue chi-chi-ka-ka dress!"

"And I love you back," I say blowing a kiss.

"How many guests are we expectin' tonight?" Tyrone asks out of nowhere.

"Fifteen. And these gentlemen were handpicked by Sincere, my daughter from the House of Dreams in LA. So they understand what we offer and more importantly know what has to be paid. But don't be fooled, children. Boys will be boys and we must protect ourselves. So I left condoms in every room…use 'em. Any questions?"

Silence.

"Well let the games begin!" I say clapping my hands, my short black curly wig brushing my shoulders.

Five minutes after the meeting, we opened our doors wide!

"Welcome to the House of Dreams fellas," I say to the men coming in one by one, "let your inhibitions run wild and all of your dreams will come true."

When they walk in, they see Queen Tyrone, Dayshawn, Adrian and the manor Queens all sitting on the couch looking like sex kittens. When the guests pile inside, they pay my fee and pick their flavor. My plan could not have worked any better.

I'm counting my door fee money when my phone rings and I wonder who it is.

"What's the T?"

"May I speak to Wayne?"

I recognize the voice instantly as the nigga who called me when I was at Popeye's. "It depends on what you want to speak to Wayne about."

"Wayne…this is Chris."

"Twinkie's Chris?"

"Yes."

Now I'm all confused. "Did you call me awhile back?"

"Yes…and I really need to talk to you…about what's goin' on with me and Chris."

"Honey, I don't jump in folks personal lives…and even if I could you wouldn't want me to if you knew how I feel about you." I say scanning the room for Adrian. The last thing I needed was for him to be upset.

"But you don't understand. Things are not as they seem."

The fact that he is calling me means he's ready for me to put it to his ass like it needs to be put. "Let me tell you somethin' fuck boy, the way you beat that chile was terrible! And it don't make no sense to me. Now if you were near me, I'd show you how I feel about you, instead I'ma just say you betta not ever call me again."

"Wayne please…you have to listen. This is serious."

"Chris, fuck off! And lose my number!" I say ending the call.

What kind of shit is that? After everything he did to that boy, why would he think I'd listen to him about shit? I'm over these dudes who fuck us at night and beat us by day. Make up your mind what you wanna be. Gay…straight or whatever!

After I swallow a glass full of vodka, I focus my attention back on business. Things were going better but as the night grew older, some of the guests had a little too much Jesus juice and started acting simple. I guess they forgot we were still men and as strong as they were if not stronger. They found out soon enough.

"No...no, you paid one hundred dollars to get in these doors, but anything else," Adrian says rubbing her ass cheek over one of the guests face, "is gonna cost you."

Some of them tried to buck the system but one by one they'd dig into their pockets and pay me a little somethin' extra for the queens' time. I held the cash for the ladies until they were done. Over the course of the night, fifteen men trickled into the house and I was already up three thousand dollars until I saw Tyrone on his phone. And since we had two more guests waiting, I was wondering what was up.

"Do what the fuck you want! I'm not doin' this shit no more." He yells into his cell phone.

He's silent for a minute with the phone against his head until he says, "If you wanna kill yourself then that's on you, maybe then you'll leave me the fuck alone."

I gave him a few seconds to handle the call but I remember that he's been acting really strange lately. Sometimes he gets up in the middle of the night to make calls and he always seems to be sneaking around. Be that as it may, there's money to be made right now.

"Queen, you do realize we still have guests waitin' right?"

Tyrone leans up against the wall and says, "Yeah...but I don't think I can do nothin' else today. That last guy wanted me to stand on my head, against the wall, while I let him lick my ass. Now my neck hurtin'."

"I feel for you but not finishin' up is not an option. Now...after tonight, I'll set you up an appointment with a friend of mine who does massages. Okay, darling?"

She looks at me, walks to the guests and introduces herself. That ugly fish is workin' my nerves already! She's the laziest bitch in captivity.

Twenty minutes later, the queens had worked the hell out of the men, refilling their cups with cheap drinks every time an empty one hit the floor. In the end, we finished the night with no real problems and I was hopeful that our good luck would continue for weeks to come. The money I pulled out of my pockets were overflowing and that's wasn't including the money that belonged to the girls.

But when I open the door, to let the last trade leave, I see someone standing outside who looks out of place. The thirty-somethin' cunt I believe I recognize walks up my stairs. She's Tyrone's wife. She's wearing a black raincoat and the handles are tied tightly around her waist. Black massacre is smeared down her face.

"Is Tyrone here?" she asks in a delirious glare.

I look behind me, close the door and step fully outside. "Honey, I can't let you in my house. But is everything okay with you? Is there somethin' I can help you with?" I ask, placing my hands on her shoulders.

"You don't understand," she says shaking me off. "I need to see Tyrone now and it can't wait 'til later."

"Shannon, I don't know what's goin' on, but you look upset and because of it, I'm worried. I mean, did you call Tyrone before you came over here?"

She looks up at me with sadness in her eyes, and then her glare is replaced with rage. For some reason, when my eyes focus on the ground, I see a red streak leading from her white Cadillac at the curb, to my house. It's obvious that the trail is following her, but where is it coming from? Then I see a red thick liquid escaping her arms. This bitch slit her wrists.

OMG!

"You will let me in, Wayne!" she says pulling a gun out of her coat pocket. "Now open that fuckin' door or I'm gonna blow your shit off!" When I didn't move fast enough due to shock she says, "Please, Wayne, don't make me kill you. I didn't come here for you, but that can all change."

When I back inside the house, my stare remains on the weapon. I'm also careful about how I deal with her. A woman scorn is one thing, but a cunt with a gun and slit wrists spells murder.

Seeing his wife, Tyrone walks up to her and says, "Shannon, I told you not to come over here! What the fuck are you doin'?!"

"Tyrone, be careful with her," I whisper.

"I came to see you. We have to talk now," she demands. "You owe me at least that, since you drained my bank account of over twelve thousand dollars, which was all I had left." She laughs hysterically. "It was my fault though, I should've taken your name off of my account when I had the chance. Just never thought you'd be so grimey to me."

"I said I'd pay you back later," he says as I wonder where in the hell all of the money went. "I'm in over my head and I really needed it. But I ain't got no money to give you now."

"And like I said on the phone," she says raising the gun. "I'm sick of waitin' on you to make right by me. That shift ends today."

"Shannon, please…don't do this. You're goin' to regret it if someone gets hurt. Look at you." I say. "Why are you doin' this?"

"Why?" she laughs crazily. "Ask your friend Tyrone! Since he told me earlier that he didn't care if I died today or tomorrow. I decided I don't care anymore either. So I told my mother to get my son, quit my job, and came over here to take Tyrone with me. Why die alone right?" Tears roll down her face and she wipes them away leaving blood smears all over her skin.

Walking into the living room for the first time, when Adrian sees the gun, he screams.

"Shut the fuck up!" Shannon yells, banging the handle of the gun against her temple. "I can't stand the noise! Be quiet!" she continues shaking the gun wildly at all of us. "Everybody sit the fuck down!"

Afraid the gun might go off, we all sit on the couch and out the corner of my eyes, I see Miss Dayshawn run toward the back of the house. Sneaky Day always knew how to get away.

"Wait...was that Dayshawn? The one you told me died in the fire?"

"No...I mean yes. I mean...not really."

"I asked one question...and as far as I'm concerned, there ain't but one answer to it." Shannon demands.

"Okay...baby I need you to listen," Tyrone says in a masculine voice although she's wearing a dress, "Dayshawn died...but then he came back to life."

She burst into laughter and Adrian and me whip our heads in his direction.

"So what...he's Jesus now?" Shannon giggles.

"No...he got burnt really badly and was unconscious. Then they reccessated him and gave him some medicine. After that he was cool."

I couldn't believe my ears. I knew Tyrone was illiterate, but I never thought he was that ignorant too. The lie he gave her was so obscene, in good faith I couldn't hear him say it again.

"Oh my God! You *are* sick!" she laughs. Then she falls into the seat across from us...the blood leaving her body was probably making her weak. "My mother told me there was no way on earth I could trust a person like you…but I kept telling myself that you were my husband. You know, after all these years, I never saw the man you were until now."

"Please, Shannon. Let's talk."

"There's no more talking!" she screams, letting off a bullet into the ceiling. "I'm done talkin' to you! You are my husband and we made a vow through sickness and health, 'til death do us part, that we'd be together forever. It's time to die."

"Shannon, please…please calm down."

She fires another bullet into the floor next to my foot and I understand then that she can't be reasoned with. When I look at Adrian and Tyrone, I see that they feel the same. If we want to live, which we all do, something has to give now.

With nothing else to lose, we all look at one another and charge her ass. She's immediately knocked out of the chair and onto the floor, but the gun is still in her hand. Then Tyrone proceeds to punch her in the face multiple times until the gun falls to the ground.

"Tyrone, I think that's enough!" Adrian says.

"Yeah, Tyrone! She's not movin'." I add.

When he finally stops, she's laying lifelessly on the floor. I don't know what killed her. Blood escaping her body by the pounds or Tyrone pounding her face to a pulp. And then I hear sirens in the background. Betty Badge could not have come at a better time, thanks to Dayshawn calling them when he ducked to the back of the house.

The police were there for two hours taking our testimony. And although we all confirmed Tyrone's self-defense story, I wonder what else was behind his blows. It was like he hated her or something.

At the end of the night, I know the cops will always remember three gay men dressed in drag, and the murder on 28<sup>th</sup> place. But what can I do? Like most incidents in my life, I have to move on. So that's exactly what I'm gonna do.

With the house clean and Adrian and Dayshawn sleep, Tyrone walks up to the couch and sits next to me.

"Can I talk to you, girl?" he asks.

"What' up?"

"I'm sorry about Shannon. I wasn't expectin' none of that shit tonight to happen up in here."

"Tyrone, why did you hit her like that? And what money is she talkin' about? And why would you tell her Day was dead? I'm confused."

"The money was ours and I took it. But as far as me hittin' her, you saw how crazy she was. She was tryin' to kill us. That shit with Day was just to get her to let me stay at her house. I ain't have no place else to go."

"I think you could've been talked Shannon down off that ledge. But it's like you didn't care that she was your wife and the mother of your child."

"But she had a gun! What the fuck was I gonna do? Let her kill me?" he pauses staring at me with wild eyes. "It was her or me and it wasn't gonna be this girl, honey."

I can't believe how selfish he sounds. Shannon must have really been insane to choose Tyrone to be a part of her life.

"All I know is that the situation could've gone a lot worse. Somebody else could've gotten killed. Really, Tyrone…you're gonna have to start carin' about somebody other than yourself. Too much shit follows you wherever you go."

"Care about people?" he says with sass. "You mean like you care about your mother?"

Have you ever had an experience…where you've been in someone's presence and felt like punching them in the mouth, snatching out their tongue and strangling them with it? Well when he said my mother's name, that's exactly what I felt like doing.

"Tyrone, let me tell you somethin'," I say pointing my finger in his face. "What went on around here ain't got shit to do with my mother. And I'm gonna leave it at that. But if you ever mention her again, there will be problems for me and you. Are we clear?"

He smiles and says, "Crystal."

Silence.

"Good…now remove yourself the fuck outta my face…I wanna sit down alone and sort some shit out."

"So I guess you don't want to hear anything else I have to say."

"Tyrone, if I hear your voice again I'ma throw up. So you tell me?"

He gets up and says, "I guess you don't want to know who burned the house down and almost killed us." He walks away.

"What did you say?"

He turns around and says, "I know who burned the house down."

"What are you talkin' about? I thought it was an electrical issue."

"It wasn't. The fire department did a full investigation and found out that shit was done on purpose." He continues. "I heard it was Queen Paul."

To be honest, I hadn't given the burned house any more thought once we made our move to 28th place. Besides, had it not been for the fire, I would not have come up with the scheme to hold the parties. But now that I know a person was actually responsible for that shit, I wanted blood.

"How do you know for sure it was him?"

"W…what you mean?" he stutters.

"Why would anybody tell you anything? Somethin' don't sound right to me."

"They didn't tell me. They told Garisha. They told him Paul was tryin' to get some money from his house insurance."

I think he's lying but can't prove it.

"Go head, Tyrone."

"The 'T' is that Paul was mad that you beat him into another state and he wanted to pay you back and come up on some cash. So instead of facin' you queen to queen, he burned the house down his mother raised him in." he continues. "But I know where he lives, Wayne. All we gotta do is pay these people five hundred bucks to beat the brakes off of Queen Paul and it's done."

I consider my options. Do I hurt somebody off the strength of what she says, or do I let shit go and take it as a loss? Then I remember, I hadn't heard anything from that fish name Paul since I taught him a lesson. And since queens believe in revenge and would sell their mothers to get it, why didn't he come for me?

"Do it." I say pulling the money from my stuffed bra. "And let me know when it's done."

"No problem," he says accepting the money.

"Let whoever does it know that I'll give them an extra fifty if they show me a picture of his fractured face. But...and hear me good, you betta not fuck this up. I don't want you nowhere near the scene. Understood?"

"I got you."

"Good, 'cause if he burnt down his own house, there's nothin' to stop him from tryin' to do it here and I don't want to have to kill his ass."

"It's as good as done, Wayne." She smiles.

I hope I didn't just make a GRAVE mistake.

## Reflecting On The Younger Years
## Miss Wayne

Wayne, Parade, Sky and Daffany built an unbreaka-ble bond. No longer did Wayne feel like an outcast or any of them for that matter. They finally belonged...together.

One afternoon over Wayne's house, they were all en-joying some turkey sandwiches and cool homemade le-monade in the kitchen when Wayne noticed Parade's dingy clothing.

"Parade," he said after sipping his juice, "how come your clothes never look clean?"

Parade looked at him and then the rest of her friends. "What you mean?" she asked swallowing hard.

"I love you, honey but you just never look fresh," he said softly. He truly wasn't trying to embarrass her. Their friendship had grown so much that he knew he could ask her such a personal question around the rest of their crew with no hard feelings because they all loved her.

"I try to wash my own clothes but if my mother don't give me no money, then what can I do?"

"Well," Wayne said dipping into his pocket, "I have ten dollars and you can have it." He pushed the money across the table to her.

Sky and Daffany looked at Wayne and followed suit.

"I have two dollars," Daffany said. "I tongue kissed this boy at school the other day and he gave it to me. You can have it though."

"Here's ten from me. I can get you some more any-time you need it. All you gotta do is ask," Sky bragged. "You know my peoples' pockets stay fat."

Parade took the money into her small hands, looked at her friends and cried. Stuffing the money inside her pocket, she stood up and said, "Thank you...but ya'll don't know what kinda life I got, and you wouldn't understand it even if you did. Nobody would."

"Help us understand." Wayne said standing up from the table.

"It's too hard. I have to go!" She said before bolting out the front door. She could be violent if followed and her friends knew this so they left her alone.

Parade ran to her house, which was in the same apartment complex that Wayne and the rest of her friends lived. The moment she opened her front door, she saw her father sitting on a leather recliner, rocking and watching Family Feud on TV.

"What's wrong, baby?" he asked seeing her upset.

"Nothin'," she said wiping her tears. "I'm okay."

"You sure?"

"Yes."

"I can't tell. I could swear I see tears in my daughter's eyes," he said kindly.

Parade walked up to her father amazed at how different he was from her mother. He talked to her when they were alone whereas her mother acted as if she didn't exist.

Parade walked slowly over to her father, and sat on his lap. "Now...tell me what's wrong, baby?"

"My friends are so much better than me. They have new clothes and money to do stuff with and I never got nothin'. I'm embarrassed to go to school sometimes, daddy. I hate my life."

"I know money's been tight around here," he said holding her lovingly in his arms, "but things will get better. You're in middle school now and you have four *friends who care about you. Be happy for the small things."*

*Parade listened to her father attentively and her stomach fluttered. She loved him so much. He always knew what to say to her when she was upset and she was grateful.*

*When he finished with his words of wisdom, she turned to him and kissed him softly on the lips. He rarely showed emotion, or even hugged her, unless they were alone.*

*When their lips separated, he looked into her eyes, smiled and their lips met again. The kiss was passionate and Parade loved the secret relationship she had with her father. He picked her up and carried her to her bedroom.*

*He was the one who taught her how to move her hips and perform oral sex. She enjoyed the tingling sensations that overcame her body when he kissed her softly on her special place and out of appreciation, she returned the favor. During these times, she felt wanted and loved. To her what they were doing wasn't wrong. It was love. They spent the next thirty minutes indulging in everything but a healthy father and daughter relationship.*

*What they didn't know was that Parade's mother had come home early and caught their indiscretions. She couldn't believe what she was seeing and their betrayal ripped her apart. Sure she had her suspicions all along...but she hoped it wasn't true. Sadly she turned around and walked away from her daughter's bedroom door, never saying a word to either of them. But what she witnessed made her hate her only child even more.*

*A few years later the secret relationship Parade shared with her father ceased and vanished from her memory. Remembering only bits and pieces of it in her dreams. But soon, that all would change.*

# *Smash*

## ❧BIG BOODY BRANDY❧

Big Boody Brandy waited impatiently at the Anacostia Park train station for Tyrone. Ever since she found out she tried to set her up by having Garisha's brother rob her, she'd been extorting money from him. This was the main reason she didn't want to kill him like Paul wanted. She figured she'd wait until Tyrone couldn't pay anymore, and then take care of him. She'd already gotten ten thousand dollars out of him with plans to take more.

Walking out of her brand new white Saab, she left her dog Maxie inside because it was raining. She left the windows down so her puppy wouldn't suffocate but was still worried about him. Tyrone called her a few minutes earlier and said he was around the corner with her five hundred dollars.

When she saw the car pull up, she stood up straight and gripped her Fendi purse closely. Although she knew Tyrone knew better than to fuck with her, she always carried heat just in case.

"Hey, Brandy," Tyrone says once out of the blue Nissan Sentra Garisha was driving.

"Don't hey me." She says eyeing Garisha who was so scared of her, she didn't look in Brandy's direction. "You got all my money right?"

Tyrone dug in his ugly black pocketbook and handed her the cash. "It's all there."

After Brandy counted all of the money she says, "Good. And what took you so long?"

"Garisha took forever to pick me up," he pauses. "But can I ask you somethin'?"

"What?"

"How long is this gonna go on? I mean, I think I paid my debt to you by now, Brandy. Don't you?"

"Oh...you think so?" she asks sarcastically. "So tell me, how much do you think my life is worth? 'Cause I can tell you now it's worth more than ten thousand dollars."

"I'm not sayin' it like that, Brandy. I'm just sayin', it was only a fifty-dollar bag of weed bag. And since my wife killed herself, I don't know how I'm gonna get you no more money."

"I heard! But damn, you really did have that bitch wrapped around your little finger."

"Seriously, Brandy. You call my house all hours of the night, show up when you need money for the club and I just want it to stop."

"Then what you waitin' on, Tyrone? Do somethin' 'bout it?" he smirks. "I'm standin' right here. Make a move."

Tyrone's lips tighten and he says, "I'm not tryin' to start no shit wit' you, bitch."

"You already did."

"I know...but this is fucked up. It's not even fair."

"And I don't give a fuck what you think. When I'm done with you, you'll know. Just make sure that you have five thousand a month for me until I say so. Or I'm goin' go to the cops about that football player I know you and Garisha's manly lookin' ass murdered. Don't fuck with me, Tyrone."

"I won't."

To kill two birds with one stone Brandy says, "Oh yeah...what you gonna do about Paul? I told you he wanted me to kill you."

"I'm goin' over there now. You sure he havin' the party?"

"What you think? I ain't got not reason to lie. I'm out. I'll holla at you later."

After Brandy walked away leaving Tyrone to himself, she smiled realizing her good luck. She knew Tyrone was a punk but this was ridiculous. Once Brandy made it to her car, her heart dropped when she saw her dog Maxie lying lifelessly on the floor of the drivers seat.

"Maxie!" she screams in horror.

Her purse fell to the ground as she wrestled to open the door. And when she did, her guard went down and she was grabbed from behind. Placing his forearm around Brandy's neck, he used his other free hand to place a napkin containing Chloroform over her mouth and nose. And when she passed out, he pushed her in the car, and drove to an undisclosed location. Brandy would never be seen alive again.

# A Who Ride

## QUEEN TYRONE

"I shouldn't even be talkin' to your ass right now." Garisha says to me as she's driving down the road. "I can't believe you still dealing wit' Big Boody's bitch ass."

"Look, stop whinning over dried shit."

"Stop whinnin' over dried shit?!" He repeats. "Did you forget that *that* bitch stabbed me?"

"Don't put that shit on me, Garisha. How I know he was gonna catch you in your car lookin' stupid? If anything I should be mad at you."

"How you figure?" he asks whipping his head toward me.

"Because had your brother been smart enough to wear a long sleeve shirt, I wouldn't have gotten into a beef with Big Boody to begin with. Now that hag extortin' money out of me and shit. Where Detroit at anyway?"

"Girl, locked up! Again!"

"Has he ever considered the fact that crime may not be his thang?"

"I don't know, girl" he says waving me off. "But why you payin' this bitch anyway?"

"You playin' right?" I ask staring at her.

"Heaven's no...why?"

"Because she was with us the day we were with Andy. All she gotta do is tell the cops we were the last who saw him and Betty Badge would be all over our ass. There's no statute of limitations on murder, ugly."

"Fuck all that...are you sure Queen Paul gonna be over there? Shit, I got some place else to be and I'm not waitin' around all day fuckin' wit' you."

"Yeah...just drive, Garisha, damn!"

"Well let me know when you see Parker Street." She says. "I'm texting my new boo right now."

"He must haven't seen you yet," I laugh.

"No. But when he does it's gonna be all good," she says with a scowl. "Pleeeaaase believe! You just look for the street."

Although me and Garisha were cool, she still didn't know I couldn't read and I wasn't gonna tell her either. She talk too much and I didn't feel like everybody being in my business.

"Do you see the street yet, bitch?" Garisha asks me again. "'Cause you lookin' like you don't know what the fuck is goin' on now."

"Ummm...you know I can't really see these street signs, girl. I wear glasses. You gonna have to help."

"Damn bitch, you worthless!" She says putting her phone away. Like she should be texting and driving anyway. "Ain't that the street right there?"

"I don't know...I think so." I squint looking at the sign.

"Yeah that's it! Fuckin' wit' you, I almost missed it." She complains whipping onto the street, almost knocking over a mailbox.

When we finally reach Queen Paul's house, just like Big Boody said, Queen Paul and his crew were in the backyard having a bar-b-que. Music was booming from the speakers and everyone was dancing and talking shit.

"Pass the house a little," I say. When we were a few houses away from Paul's house, she parked. "This cool right here… you got the camera?"

"No but I got my camera phone."

"Okay, let's go."

Garisha and me grab our bats and creep out of the car and up to Queen Paul's house. Queens were all over the backyard in dro's, laughing, drinking and having a good time.

"How we gonna get his ass out here? I'm not fuckin' wit' all of them at one time," Says Garisha. "I hope you know that."

When he says that, Paul walks around to the front of his house to talk on his phone and we could not believe our luck.

Quickly we run up behind her with bats in hand ready to handle our biz. But Queen Paul turns around and sees us right before we can land a blow. In fight or flight mode, Paul squares up and steals Garisha square in her extra large nose. Blood splashes everywhere. When she falls back, Paul continues to kick her with his pink pump repeatedly in the stomach. When she's sure Garisha is dealt with, she smiles at me.

"Bitch, you must be a glutton for punishment," says Paul.

"Miss Paul, it's not even like that," I say dropping the bat. "I was just comin' over here with Garisha. I hadn't a clue he meant to do you harm. You know we were cool after the last incident right? We even spoke at the Mill that night and everything. Remember?"

"Stop lying you wretched troll," Garisha yells from the ground. "This was your project not mine! You got me all the way fucked up!"

"No I don't either! I ain't got no beef with Queen Paul."

"Bitch, tell this lady Miss Wayne sent this mission!" Garisha continues, holding his face. "And miss me with all them lies! Tell him how Wayne wanted us to bring back the picture once we beat him down."

Garisha didn't know that although Wayne paid me to have Paul dealt with, Brandy was the one who wanted the work done for her own personal reasons. Since I needed the five hundred dollars anyway to give to Big Boody, I thought of a smart way to get it by telling Wayne them lies.

"Stop lyin'!" I yell at him. "This all you, guuurl!"

"I don't know who's lyin'! I do know you didn't run me my rent and out of the blue show up at my house. Then my house burns down. What the fuck is up with that?"

"That wasn't me. I know you know that, Paul. We were in that fire too and could have gotten killed."

"Well what you talkin' 'bout, Miss Wayne sent this mission?" Queen Paul asks Garisha.

"It's true!" Garisha confirms. "He got it in for you and sent us. I wish Miss Ty stop lyin'! I don't know why I even fuck wit' her sometimes."

"What Miss Wayne want with me?" Paul asks confused. "I ain't got no more business with her."

"He said you had something to do with the house burnin' down." I say.

"You mean my house?" he asks touching his chest with one hand, placing the other hand on his hip. "Oh Miss girl how you sound? "What I look like burning my mother's house down?"

"I said the same thing." I say. "I knew you wouldn't do somethin' like that but Wayne wouldn't hear it. Can you just let me go? I don't want no problems."

"Well bitch which one is it? At first you said I sanctioned this shit and now you said Wayne! See Queen Paul, this bitch is fabricating scenes!" Garisha yells.

Paul looks at me and in a high pitch voice yells, "Bitches on deck!"

When thirty drag queens came running from around the back of the house, my ass sweats.

"Stomp attack!" Paul says. "I want them mud!" he continues snapping his fingers.

For two long minutes, Paul's crew beat and stomped us so badly, some of the queens got squeamish from all the blood and ran to the back of the house. They just couldn't beat us anymore.

"Don't let up! I want them dead!" Paul orders.

I have never been more scared, than I was right then. I had a feeling he really wanted me dead. And then one of the queens whispered to him.

"Not on your property," he says. "You don't want it done like this."

When he was done Paul says, "Garisha, stand the fuck up and grab your phone too!" He does. But barely.

"Now…you did say Wayne wanted a picture right?"

He nods yes.

"Good, let me see your phone," he says snatching it from his hand. "I wanna take a picture of you and this hog. So he can see our handywork. Ya'll stand together."

"What?" Garisha ask as if he wasn't just speaking English.

"Bitch, I said get your ass over there next to Tyrone!" Garisha, who was in so much pain and could barely move, scoots next to me. Then Queen Pauls says, "Smile."

We manage a weak ass smile. I just imagined how it would look with my broken teeth and black eyes.

Queen Paul laughs and says, "You got Wayne number in here don't you?"

"Yes," Garisha says, holding her stomach.

"Good." He scrolls through the numbers and finds Wayne's. Then he sends him the picture message he just took handing the phone back to Garisha. "And when you speak to him tonight, you two bitches betta tell him that the next time he wants it with me, to come see me personally."

# Bold Face Lies

## MISS WAYNE

I was sitting on the sofa with Dayshawn on my right and Adrian on my left. We all were looking at Tyrone who was standing in the living room floor looking like a washed up ass drag queen. He had so many bruises on his face it was ridiculous. Not to mention his teeth were cracked.

"Give me what happened again, girl, 'cause this shit don't add up. And don't pause a play eitha."

"Okay…I just gotta stretch out." She says lying on the floor. "Ya'll don't understand what I just been through. Even my nuts hurt!"

Adrian gasps and says. "Miss Ty, a real queen never talks about her balls."

Now I don't doubt she feels some kind of way after getting the black beat off of her, but she's doin' stunts and shows with all the gripping of her stomach and head. I have no room in my body for sympathy for her so I don't even pretend to care. All I know is that I gave her some money to handle a job that ain't done. And what does she do? Take her country ass over there, get beat for points and spends my money.

"When you finish your performance, I need to know what the fuck happened."

"Wayne, please don't look so mad. I know you probably pissed at me for doin' the job myself, it's just that I felt I could do it better. And I needed the money."

"How is it that you felt like you could do it better? Didn't she beat your ass back to the future before?"

"Yeah...but I wasn't thinkin'." He pauses. "I use to be able to hold my own back in my day. Adrian, tell him about the time I put work in on that queen who hit you last year."

Adrian uncomfortably says, "I wanna stay out of it."

Tyrone shoots him an evil glare.

"I don't give a fuck what she remembers. I'm interested in finding out why I'm out of five hundred dollars and why I was sent a picture of you and Garisha's monkey lookin' ass on my cell phone. So please...save yesterday's storylines and get to today's paper!"

"Okay...so I go over there and tell her that you came to collect from her ass for the burning she put down on the house."

"Why would you say my name?"

"Because she caught us."

Damn this bitch stupid! "Go 'head, Tyrone."

"She was all like, 'I burned down the house so the fuck what. It was my house and ya'll were in it!' She said she told us to leave but we wouldn't listen. The next thing I know, thirty big ass girls come from around the corner and stomped me and Garisha into next week. Then he sent the picture."

"But why would you go over there? I know you can't read but are you retarded too?"

He frowns and looks as if he wants to strike me but trust me babies, she knows better. "It's done, Wayne. Alls I can say is sorry now."

I had it with her.

I'm over.

I can take no more disobedience from her fat ass.

"Give me one reason why I shouldn't write you out of my life *and* this house?"

"Well...for starters, I can tell you how to really get at him."

"I'm not listenin' to you."

"Please...I know what he really wants and takin' it from him would hurt more than anything else you do."

"And what's that?"

"He wants to win the House of Star's Drag ball next month. You know it's the biggest ball yet and everybody sayin' how he's goin' for the Legendary category. If you beat her, and take her crown, she will be fucked up."

As I think about the new information I'm given, for some reason, I'm more than interested. It's been a while since I participated in a ball but I'm sure I could dust myself off and still shine. Still, Tyrone has to go.

"I know you ain't got no place to stay so I'ma make it simple. You got three weeks to find you another situation because the one right here ain't workin'."

"Wayne!" he wails. "I ain't got nowhere to go. You know Shannon died."

This bitch hasn't said a mumbling word about his wife since he halfway killed her. He's not even going to the funeral. But he fixes his lips to say that shit? He's the worst.

"Cunt, that's nowhere near my problem! And you wouldn't know the word sorry if it sat in front of you on paper...literally. What I'm gonna do is let you keep that five hundred dollars you spent and give you a chance to save up to find another place. Consider yourself lucky."

Tyrone stands up, looks at me and says, "I'm not about to beg you again, Wayne. But thank you for the extra time."

As she walks to her bedroom, I think about the first time I met her and Dayshawn. I should've known then that she was nothin' but trouble.

# Miss Wayne & THE Queens of DC

◆ • • • • • • • • • • • • • • • • • • • • • • ◆

## Reflecting On The Younger Years
## Miss Wayne

"Did ya'll hear about Old Man Dennis?" Parade said, sucking on a lollipop. They were sitting on the steps of Wayne's apartment building.

"Naw...what happened?"

"He was murdered for no reason yesterday."

"How?"

"They didn't say much, just that it's not pretty. I think he was shot and burned up or somethin'. That's sad 'cause he was always so nice."

"You always know the neighborhood gossip," Sky said.

"That's 'cause my mama always runnin' her mouth on the phone."

"Well I got gossip too," Wayne said.

"What?" they all asked with widened eyes.

"Did ya'll hear that I'm mad at ya'll 'cause ya'll wanna do the same stuff everyday instead of going to the block party today?" Wayne said.

"Wayne, please stop talking about that dumb party. We can't go today." Daffany said.

"Come on ya'll! It's gonna be off the hook! I just know it."

"But we going to the movies," Sky reminded him. "I told you my mama was taking all of us. She was taking you too until you changed your mind."

"We can go to the movies anytime."

"Yeah but she's paying for us too," Parade added. "I don't pass up no chance to get out of my house."

151

*"I wish you didn't pass up a chance to brush your hair before leavin' the house," Sky laughed. "It's all knotty and shit."*

*"Shut up, Sky!" Said Daffany.*

*"Forget it," Wayne said ignoring one of their usual fights. "I'ma go by myself."*

*"Don't be that way, Wayne." Daffany said. "It's not like we don't want to go. We just made other plans."*

*As Wayne begged and begged harder, Dayshawn and Tyrone, the neighborhood gay boys walked down the street.*

*"Hey...why don't you ask them," Parade offered, pointing in their direction.*

*Wayne looked at the two of them. Although Dayshawn was cute and walked with a slight switch, Tyrone was trying too hard by tying the back of his white t-shirt up in a knot and carrying a big ass red purse. His jeans were real tight and he was wearing a red pair of converse, no socks.*

*"Yeah...it ain't like they not like you." Sky laughed. Although she wasn't a bitch all the time, when she was, everyone noticed.*

*"And how is that, Sky?"*

*"Fruity." She laughed.*

*"Bitch, I'm not fruity, I'm fabulous! There's a difference." Miss Wayne corrected her.*

*"Well you betta go ask them," Parade said picking at a scab on her knee. "They about to walk away."*

*Putting his pride to the side, he ran up to them and said, "Excuse me, what ya'll 'bout to do?"*

*Dayshawn said, "We headed to the block party. Why? What's up?"*

*"Yeah...what you want with us? You neva got no time for nobody but your little crew over there. So what gives*

*now?" Tyrone said. Wayne wasn't sure, but he had a feeling that Tyrone was drunk.*

*Wayne looked back at his friends who were staring at him with hopeful eyes wondering if he should just leave things alone.*

*"They are my friends, but I do get up with other people when I want to. And I want to now. I see ya'll around high school all the time." He continued, slight silence filled their space. "Anyway, the name's Miss Wayne. What's yours?"*

*"I'm Tyrone and this is Dayshawn."*

*"So what's up? Ya'll mind if I roll with you or not?"*

*"Don't make me no neva mind." Tyrone said.*

*When they got to the block party, it was packed. People were everywhere and it was hard to move around. But what surprised Wayne was that he was having so much fun with them that he didn't mind the crowd and people stepping on his toes. It felt good being with people who looked slightly like himself.*

*"So Wayne, have you tried it with boys yet?" Tyrone asked sucking a strawberry sno-cone ball.*

*"What you mean?"*

*"You know...let them put it in your mouth and stuff?"*

*"Naw...I ain't gay-gay. I just like dressin' the way I do."*

*They laughed so hard Wayne looked behind him to see if someone was there.*

*"Hold up, did you say that you aren't gay-gay?" Tyrone asked.*

*"Yeah...well, you know what I mean."*

*"Honey, there ain't but one type of gay and you're it!" Tyrone said. "Trust me I know."*

*"Well if I never been with a boy I must not be gay at all then."*

*"How is it that you don't know who you are yet?"
Dayshawn asked seriously. "It must be rough bein' in
denial. I can't believe you ain't been with no boys either."*

*"Well I haven't and for real...I ain't trippin'."*

*"Well...the reason I'm asking is because my boy-
friend Cramer and his friends are having a get together
in a few minutes. Other boys gonna be there too. You
sure you don't wanna hook up?"*

*"First of all Cramer is not your boyfriend," Day-
shawn said. "He has a girlfriend and as far as I
know...you do too. Don't you be with Shannon all the
time?"*

*"That's a long story. But forget all that...Wayne you
wanna roll or not?"*

*Wayne thought about saying no, after all, just be-
cause he was gay didn't mean he wanted to have sex with
boys. Just thinking about being with someone he didn't
know made him uncomfortable. Sure he'd look at the
football team at school and feel small flutters within the
pit of his stomach, but that was the extent of it. And now
that the offer had presented itself, he wondered what to
do.*

*"Okay."*

*"Okay?" Dayshawn repeated as they stood in front
of a hot dog stand.*

*"I'll go." Wayne confirmed.*

*"Let's hit it!" Tyrone cheered. "I don't' want to miss
them."*

*Fifteen minutes later, they were in a crampy house a
few blocks away from Wayne's apartment complex. Six
teenagers were present, including Dayshawn, Tyrone and
Wayne. And Wayne's guess about Tyrone being drunk
was confirmed when he saw him drinking vodka.*

"So what ya'll wanna do?" Cramer asked Tyrone and his crew, as he played with a video game system. He sat on a chair in front of the TV.

"I don't know...what you wanna do?" Tyrone asked.

"Nothin' for real, I was gonna show you my new sneakers if you want to see 'em." He said. That was his way of getting Tyrone alone without admitting that he wanted to fuck him like he normally did.

Tyrone smiled and said, "I'll go look at them with you." Before Tyrone left he said, "Wayne...don't be all stuck up either if you wanna hang with us from now on. Have fun now and ask questions later."

Minutes later, Dayshawn and James also excused themselves to another small bedroom within the basement, leaving Wayne and Michael alone.

Michael was a cute teenager with hazel eyes and light brown skin. Wayne had been looking at him all-night and hoped he was for him. He liked that he seemed shy and quiet like himself.

"You live around here?" Michael asked.

"Yeah. Up the street."

"Oh...me too."

Michael mindlessly changed channels on the television and it was obvious that he was trying to find something to keep him busy.

"So...you like boys or something?" Michael asked.

"No! Do you?!" Wayne asked defensively.

"No...I mean...I don't think so."

For some reason, when the words exited his lips, Wayne's heart fluttered. It wasn't what he said but how he said it. He could tell in that one instance, that Michael was as conflicted as he was about his sexuality.

"Well...I don't think so either," Wayne smiled, crossing his legs.

*"Come over here. Sit next to me."* Michael directed. *Wayne sat next to him and Michael asked, "Can I have a kiss?"*

*"I thought you said you don't like boys."*

*"I don't, but I like you. So you gonna kiss me or what?"*

*Suddenly it was as if the shy kid had left and his confident twin brother had remained in his place.*

*Wayne kissed him quickly and removed his lips to look into his eyes making Michael smile.*

*"Don't be nervous. Kiss me again." Michael chuckled. "I ain't gonna hurt you or nothin'."*

*"Before I do all of that, do you have a girlfriend?" Wayne inquired. "'Cause I'm not kissin' you if you have a girl."*

*"Naw. I ain't got no shawty."*

*Having heard enough, Wayne moved back in toward him and kissed his lips again. This time it lasted longer and was more passionate. Their tongues ran in and out of each other's mouth and Wayne felt himself growing inside of his pants.*

*"Can you kiss it for me?" Asked Michael. "Look what you made me do."*

*"That wasn't me?"*

*"It was. Stop bein' a tease."*

*"I'm not."*

*"I like you, but if you not willin' to try new stuff, I'm not messin' with you no more. I want you to kiss it for me and tell me if you like it."*

*"But I never done it before." Wayne advised.*

*"I'll teach you," Michael said unfastening his jeans. When his pants and boxers hung over his brand new sneaks, he stroked himself and said, "Come over here and get on your knees."*

Wayne slowly complied and waited for his next command. He liked the boy a lot and was hoping he liked him too. Although he never had a boyfriend before if Michael acted right, he wanted him to be his first.

"Now, open your mouth and suck it softly."

Wayne put his mouth over his thickness and inhaled the smell of soapy smelling skin. He made a mental note to find the soap he used so he could buy some for himself.

Doing the best he could, he opened his mouth wide and mindlessly licked the shaft of his penis. And when his mouth grew tired, he closed it a little too much biting down on him.

"Ouch! You put your teeth on my joint!" Michael screamed in an angry tone. "Be fuckin' careful and you betta not do it again either!"

Just like that, Michael had changed. He wasn't the same nice boy he met moments earlier.

Grabbing Wayne's cheeks to together he said, "Now...do it slowly and open your mouth WIDER. You hear me? If you scrape my joint again I'ma fuck you up!"

He released his face and Wayne doing what was asked of him, opened his mouth and continued sucking his dick, carefully, keeping his hands on the shaft to control how much was being thrust into his mouth at one time. That was until Micheal smacked his hands away and palmed the back of his head. He could barely breathe as he pumped in and out of his throat.

"That's good! Keep that shit right there you faggy bitch! You like to suck dicks and shit do you? That's what you like? Then that's what I'ma give you."

Wayne wanted to cry and he never imagined being with a boy would hurt so badly. All he wanted was for it all to be over. And then he heard a loud noise upstairs, followed by heavy footsteps leading toward the basement.

Michael trying to bust a nut, appeared to be unphased by the commotion upstairs.

Seconds later, he filled Wayne's mouth with cum.

"Where is my son?!" a woman's voice screamed from above them.

Wayne thinking he was going crazy, jumped up and did a poor job of wiping the semen off of his face.

*It can't be mama! He thought. It can't be!*

His thoughts were incorrect when he saw his mother shoot down the stairs as fast as her body would carry her. When she finally reached the bottom, her angry face turned to sadness when she saw her son. Following her stares, Wayne was scared when he saw Michael hadn't pulled up his pants yet.

"Wayne, let's go!" she said to him although looking at Michael. "And young man, you better never let me see your mother...or I'ma tell her about this incident. And you better never tell anyone, not even your friends, what happened between you and my son. You get me?"

"Yess mam."

When they were in the car, Marbel drove in silence for two minutes before speaking. "Wayne...why would you disrespect yourself that way? I'm so disappointed in you. I can't believe you'd do this to yourself or me."

In all the years he'd known his mother, she never said the word disappointment and his name in the same sentence. Tears flooded Wayne's eyes and as quickly as he wiped them away, more appeared.

"I don't know...I just wanted to...fit in with my new friends."

"What do you mean? How is what you were doin' back there fittin' in?"

Wayne hung his head low and said, "I think I'm gay, mama. And the boys I were with today are too. I just wanted to be with people that are like me. I didn't know none of this was gonna happen."

Marbel parked the car in front of their apartment building. When she saw Parade, Daffany and Sky walk toward the car like they normally did whenever Wayne got home, she fanned them away. She needed to spend some more time with him alone.

When they were gone she said, "Son, I've known you were gay all your life. Even if you didn't."

"How? I mean, whenever someone called me gay, you'd get upset."

"I was upset because they were trying to use the way God made you against you. Havin' sex with boys or degradin' your body is not a part of being gay and I hated that they wanted you to feel bad for it.

"They were stupid and I wasn't going to allow it...not while I had breath in my body anyway," She paused. When she saw his tears still streaming she said, "Son...those two boys you were with today at the block party are damaged. I know both of their parents from the hospital I worked at some years back. They'd tossed in their cards a long time ago when it came to their sons, but not me. I care about mine. And I'm gonna live as long as I can, until I'm sure that you can understand that."

"I feel so bad. I'm sorry you had to see that, ma." Wayne's head hung low.

"I don't want you to beat yourself up anymore, son." She said as she held his sweaty hand. "And I'm sorry for shoutin' at you too. My screamin' and hollerin' doesn't mean I don't love you though. It means the exact opposite."

"I'm sorry too, mama. I didn't mean to make you upset."

"I know you are son." Spotting a small white-crusted spot in the corner of his lips, she grabbed a tissue from *her glove compartment, put a little spit on it, and wiped it away. She knew what it was and it broke her heart.*

*"Mama...how did you know where I was?"*

*"Daffany's mother saw you going inside the house. Apparently she was on her way over there to earn some cash doin' what she does best," she started, speaking of the blow jobs everyone knew she dished to the neighborhood boys, "when she saw you and your friends walk in. She said she was concerned for my child but I know what it really was. She was afraid you kids would get in her way and take money out of her pocket."*

*Wayne was saddened at someone else knowing about his shame, especially one of his friend's mothers. What if she forbade Daffany from seeing him? That would crush him.*

*"But son, you can't tell Daffany about what her mother did. That little girl has too much to deal with as it is."*

*"I won't say anything, mom. I promise."*

*"Good, son." She said gripping his hand.*

*Suddenly, Marbel looked out ahead of her and then back at Wayne in a confused state. It appeared as if something serious was on her mind.*

*"You okay, mom?"*

*"Huh?" she responded.*

*"Is everything okay?"*

*"Uh...yeah...everything's fine."*

*"You sure. You look like something else is wrong."*

*"Son...where are we going?" she asked seriously. "Why are we in the car?"*

*"What you mean, mama?"*

*"Were we getting ready to go somewhere?" she asked in a low voice.*

*"No...we...were getting ready to go in the house. You just came and got me. Don't you remember?"*

*Silence.*

*"Oh...I see. Come on, son. Let's go inside." She said opening her car door.*

*Wayne was confused by his mother's sudden memory lapse...but it wouldn't be the last time he'd have to deal with it either. It would be the beginning of their relationship changing forever.*

# *Shit Is Never As It Seems*

## ❦MISS WAYNE❦

I had just left Miss Rick's house and was happy I was home. He can be fun at times, but since he got a new boo, who apparently cared about him a lot, he changed. He couldn't talk openly about *the life* anymore and seemed to be more concerned with being a housewife. To the outside looking in it was a match made in heaven, but her boyfriend didn't know that she was HIV positive, and she had no intentions on telling him either. Still, when I left, I found myself wanting to share my life with someone again, but who?

I told the girls I would be home late but came back earlier than I thought. The moment I reached the door, I heard a lot of commotion inside my house. So I quickly took my key out and opened the door. When I did, I saw Miss Tyrone rush in the living room with Adrian following behind him. Adrian was holding his stomach and seemed to be doubled over in pain.

"Fuck is going on in here?" I ask looking back and forth between them.

"Uh…me…uh…me and Adrian got into it because he went to see Chris again. You know he's not good for him so I told him how I felt. He had the nerve to come in here with a bloody nose," Tyrone continues, looking back at Adrian. "I'm not hatin', I'm just statin'."

"So you hit him? In the stomach?"

"Naw! Chris did that in the car. That's why I was yelling at him."

My heart was beating fast and I was about to kill Tyrone. Somethin' didn't feel right, I just didn't know what.

"Adrian…what happened to you?" I ask pushing past Tyrone, not without giving him an evil stare.

"Nothin'…really."

"Adrian, tell me what the fuck is goin' on 'round here. I got the instincts of a woman and somethin' don't feel right. Don't you lie to me."

"Chris…Chris had just dropped me off and Tyrone saw me get out of his car. We had another fight about nothing really. I was sneaking in the house because I knew ya'll would be upset if you found out I was seeing him again, and Tyrone saw me anyway. That's all."

"See!" Tyrone says raising his hands in the air. "I told you."

"You sure?" I ask, looking deeply into his eyes. I wanted to feel the truth not necessarily hear it. "Because you don't have to lie to me. I ain't got no problem fixin' what's wrong right here and now. But I can't help you if I don't know what's up."

Silence.

"Adrian…are you sure?!" I yell.

"Yeah…I'm sure."

He was lying and I decided that it was time that I hear what Chris had to say after all. But this time it would be face to face.

◆ • • • • • • • • • • • • • • • • • • • • • • • • • • • • • ◆

## *Later That Day*

"Thanks for coming over," Chris says as he sits on his burgundy sofa. We were at the home he owned in

Bowie, Maryland. Everything seemed cozy and warm and it was definitely not how I expected a drag queen beater to live. "Can I get you some coffee or something?"

"Look, I didn't come over here for all that, I want to know what the fuck is up with you and Adrian?!" I ask standing over him. "Did you come over my house today?"

"Yes I did."

"And did you hit him?"

"That's what you wanna believe isn't it?"

"I'm sick of him looking beat down and your name always comin' up. So what I want to believe is the mothafuckin' truth."

"I know...and that's what I wanna talk to you about. The truth." He says. As I stare into Chris's eyes I can't help but realize how fine he was. His light skin, green eyes and muscles make him extra sexy. "But in order to hear the truth, you have to have an open mind."

"How 'bout you *open* your mouth and start talkin', suga!"

"Can you please sit down, Wayne." I don't move. "Please...you're making me nervous."

I finally sit down and say, "Tell me what's going on."

"Adrian has been lying to you about me and him. I would never hurt him and I need you to know that. I wanted to tell you the moment I found out you were in town, but Adrian threatened to leave me. So when he came over one night, I took your number out his cell."

"Stop the bullshit."

"Wayne, hear me out. I've never hit Adrian in the entire time we've known each other. As a matter of fact, I love him and wanted to be with him. And I'm not talkin' about no side dick either. I'm talkin' about for life.

"I've even asked him to move in with me after he gave up the apartment I had for him. But for some reason he's protecting the person who's really hurting him. And for the life of me, I just can't understand why."

"Nothin' you're sayin' right now is makin' sense. If you're not hittin' him than who in Samual Adams hell is?"

"Tyrone, and I'm tellin' you now, you got to watch him. He's dangerous and I often wondered if he wasn't the drag queen slayer I've been reading about in the news lately. He's mean…cold and selfish. And when I refused his advances awhile back, he became dead set on breaking me and Aid up.

"I took two days to tell Aid about him coming on to me, because I was trying to find the right words to say so I wouldn't hurt his feelings, but it ended up being too late. Tyrone beat me to him and claimed that it was me who came on to him instead. I would never choose Ty over someone as beautiful as Aid. Look at him."

"Honey, that was about the realest shit you said all night."

"It's true. I believe Tyrone is very calculating and would not stop short of murder. You know him better than me…what do you think?"

"Now you're going too far."

"For real, he was the reason for most of our problems. And a while back, I found out some shit that happened to Tyrone when he was younger. He came up fucked up and now he's deadly."

"What things happened to him?" Although Tyrone and me were cool at one point, I didn't know much about him outside of the fact that he lived with his father and his mother killed herself when he was ten.

"I don't know if you know, he lived with his father but his uncle Base, stayed with them most of the time. Base was a gay man who had parties in the apartment all the time. I was told that both his father and uncle use to rape him at those parties and pass him around like some toy.

"They fed him alcohol and all kind of shit to make him forget what they'd done. I don't know if you know it, but he was addicted to alcohol since middle school."

*I do remember him drinking a lot.* I thought.

"I can't deny that life was hell for him, but now he don't care 'bout nobody or nothing but himself."

"How you know all this shit?"

"Adrian told me some stuff, but I also met his aunt who still lives around Quincy Manor a couple of weeks ago. She was mean at first, but was willing to tell me about all of the stuff she seen her nephew go through as a child. She said she couldn't afford to take him in herself permanently when he was younger, but would go get him every other weekend. That was until he started stealing from her and taking her liquor. She put his ass out after that and never saw him again."

I was listening but my mind was working overtime. Could Tyrone actually be that crazy?

"Look...I have to sort some things out." I say standing up. "I gotta go."

"I know...but please, watch after Adrian. For whatever reason he feels loyal to Tyrone. But if he keeps hurting him like he does when he gets angry, I'm afraid he'll kill him. It's like whenever Tyrone has some shit going on in his life, he takes it out on a weaker person and for him Adrian's it. He may even be jealous that I love Adrian the way that I do considering he has nobody. I don't know."

"I...really must go," I say not being able to take much more of the bomb he just dropped on me. But when I see the love in his eyes for Adrian I say, "Don't worry about shit, if what you telling me is true, I'm never gonna let him hurt Adrian again. He'll be safe. I promise."

When I left I knew I had to confirm the facts with Adrian. But I can tell you this, if it's true what Chris said, I don't know what I might do to Tyrone either. I'm gonna need a wing and a prayer to get me out of this shit.

# Ugly Gary and the Money Scheme

## QUEEN TYRONE

"Oh my Gawd! What happened to your lips?! And what the hell are those lopsided lumps in your chest?" I ask Garisha after she lifted her shirt when I got in her car. Apparently all the silicone in her body has shifted and she's starting to look like a real life monster.

"Bitch, you were there!" He says pulling his shirt down. "Them queens stomped me out and fucked up my boob and face job. Now I got to pay Miss Tracey to put in my silicone injections again." He continues driving down the road. "But before we do all that, I got to stop up the street and meet my new boo. He 'spose to be given me some money."

"Now?"

"Yeah…it'll only take a second."

When we pulled in front of an old apartment building in DC, I ask, "How you gonna know it's him when you see him?"

"I told him what car I'm driving. And he said he's driving a black Capri."

Garisha stands outside of the car to wait on her blind date and I think about my living situation. I need to get some cash to get a place to live quick. Too much is happening to me lately and I don't' even know why. I'm a good person, I mean, what the fuck!

"Here he comes." She says excitedly.

The black Capri slows down by her car and soon as the dude rolls down the window and sees her face, he presses the gas and speeds off. The back of the car swerves a little. He got away so fast smoke was blown in her face. Garisha runs behind him and says, "Wait! Wait! I want to talk to you!"

"Garisha get your ugly ass into this car and come on! That boy is gone!"

She sadly walks back to the car and I do all I can to not laugh in her face. Miss Wayne once said the only person uglier than me is Garisha, and he was right. That's why I hang with her all the time. She makes me look like Beyonce in comparison.

"Damn, he must didn't know it was me." She says getting into the car.

"Garisha you can't be that stupid! That boy knew it was you and was not tryin' to be bothered."

"Man! I need to get my face fixed back!" She says driving down the road. "And I don't have enough money."

"Wait, someone implanted them lopsided lips you had in your face and chest on purpose?"

"Girl, yes! You didn't think I was born looking that beautiful did you? Had my face been fixed he woulda stayed." She say hitting the steering wheel. "Anyway I wanted you to go with me so you can drive me home when we leave. Seeing as though it's your fault I'm all fucked up."

Damn! I hate driving, not to mention the fact that I didn't have a license and couldn't read the signs on the road. Hopefully the place we were going wouldn't be too far and I could find my way back.

"My fault...how you figure?"

"Had you not seduced me into your bullshit, I wouldn'tve had to get fixed back up. I mean really, Miss Tyrone, take some responsibility for your shit. You stood up there and lied like shit in front of Queen Paul! What kind of shenanigans is that? I'm 'spose to be your friend."

"Miss me with all that shit. It was every man for him self and you would've done the same shit to me. Hell, you have done the same shit me!"

"What you talkin' 'bout?"

"What about that time them stick boys came into the store we was in to rob it? You saw them comin' and ain't so much as tap me on my shoulders to let me know. Matta fact, you rolled out and I got robbed *and* had to find a way home. So please! Are we Thelma and Louise? No! It just is what it is."

"Miss you wit' nothing…and where's my half of the money anyway?"

"What? Miss Wayne took that shit back the moment I got home…you know that."

"Girl I'm so over you," Garisha whines. "You as worthless as two left shoes."

"And you as ugly as my mother's wrinkled black pussy!"

Garisha parks his car in front of an office building in Lanham Maryland. Good, I know where we are and how to get back to her place from here.

"You tried it, but I still want my half of the money because even though we didn't finish the job on Queen Paul, I still got my ass kicked like I put in work."

We entered the building and then an elevator and he says, "Hit the button for the basement."

I stare at the words confused on which one to touch and the doors remain open. I can't read any of this shit.

"Bitch hit the floor!"

"You know what, do it yourself!" I tell him. "I'm sick of your attitude."

"Sometimes you act like you can't read or somethin'!" he tells me.

When Garisha hits the button to the basement floor I say, "Fuck all that! Like I was sayin', we both were victims the other day and I don't owe you shit."

"Hag I'm not tryin' to hear all that! How I'm supposed to land a husband with a face like this?"

"You gotta ask your mama all that?"

"Bitch, don't talk about my mother! You know Miss Charlene been gone for ages."

As we continue with bullshit talk, I observe where we were. The basement looks dirty and dark, like an ugly secret went on down here. When we walked into the doctor's office, twenty transvestites were present waiting on their procedure. Garisha signed her name on the list and waited beside the rest of them.

"How long you been doin' this?" I ask looking around.

"For a couple of years, why?"

"Is it expensive?"

"It depends…he charges $800 dollars for a cup of silicone and I usually get about a half of cup to a cup in my cheeks and lips alone. I'm only gonna work on my face today though 'cause thanks to you, I can't afford to get my breasts fixed."

"Bitch, thanks to Batman who got the fuck outta dodge when he saw your face! Anyway, them mangy couple dollars Wayne gave me wouldn'tve been nothin' but piss in a cup."

"Every little bit helps," Garisha continues. "Anyway, why you wanna know about how long I've been comin' here? You thinkin' 'bout gettin' work done or soemthin'?"

"Fuck no! But look…this shit is illegal right? Ain't no real doctor injectin' this shit in ya'll faces."

"What you think? Look where we are."

"Have you ever watched him do it?" I ask.

"Uh…yeah! I'm here all the time."

"Where can you buy the silicone from?"

"Walmart or Home Depot. Why, what you thinking?"

"I'm thinkin' for that kind of money, we can change our lives."

"How?"

"Garisha don't be stupid *and* ugly! I'm thinkin' we should do this shit ourselves. It ain't like the person doin' you got a license or nothin'. We can stack up on the money we bring in if we start our own operation."

"Bitch is you smokin'?"

"I'm serious!"

"Me too. And have you forgotten that we don't have the money for start up or to buy supplies? Not to mention we need a place to do the shit at. I live on the floor of Mr. Howard's convenience store at night and he barely wants me there." He pauses. "And what about this, I may have seen them do me, but it don't mean I know how to do nobody else."

"If I come up with the place for us to do the work and get the cash, can you buy what we need?"

"Yeah…I guess so."

"Well I'll get the money."

"Aw, shit! I guess we 'bout to make a little change!" Garisha cheered.

"Don't fuck me over with this. I'm not the one. When I get the money it's for supplies only."

"Girl ain't nobody trying to fuck you over. If anything you don't fuck me over. Come up with the cash and I'm in there. And now that I think about it, Miss P who be workin' the stroll over off New York avenue will show us exactly how to do the shit. We just got to pay her a hundred dollars."

"Set it up! And I'll get the money."

"If we do this right, we gonna be rich boots!"

# *An Unreasonable Request*

## ❦MISS WAYNE❦

"Why are you pullin' this shit on me right now? We got a house full of people out there and you askin' for favors?" I ask Tyrone, as I replace the empty liquor bottles on the table with new ones. The mere sight of him disgusts me.

I still hadn't gotten a chance to talk to Adrian because he left for a couple of days to visit his cousin in Baltimore. But now that he was back home, I couldn't wait for the party to be over so we could talk about what Chris told me when we were alone.

"Because you said I have to go. So I gotta earn some money to take care of myself otherwise I'ma be out on the streets, Wayne. You know you still love me even if you mad. I mean, we were friends. So I'm askin' for help."

As he's talking to me, I get a flash of him being on top of me again. That vision comes to my mind every now and again but I never know why. What is this vision that is obviously trying to make itself known?

"I don't see how that's my problem. I gave you three weeks so as far as I'm concerned, I've done enough."

"It's not your problem. But can you please let me earn a couple of extra dollars on the night we have our parties by bringin' in my own clients. I'll even make sure that they pay you something at the door. And it's only for three weeks and after that, I'm gone anyway."

I know this fish is up to something…but what?

"You can bring in no more than two clients on party night. Mind you, this ain't got shit to do with our regularly scheduled guests. And they still have to pay $100.00 at the door but you can keep the rest to yourself. Cool?"

"Yes! Thank you so much, Wayne." He says hugging me.

"Girl move! With them underarms as strong as a backed up toilet bowel."

"You won't regret this I promise!" he says hopping away.

Just what is this bitch up to? I was still conducting a mental investigation when my phone rang. It's Parade and she's probably calling to give me an update on Miss Daffany's condition, which had worsened since last we spoke. And although I was sending the money I earned from the parties to pay all of her health and living expenses, she was still depressed.

"Hey, Parade. How's Daffany?"

"Miss Wayne, I need you to sit down," as she's talking to me, the fireman who saved Adrian from the fire walks inside my house. And since you had to RSVP to even attend our party, I was surprised to see his face. I had a feeling he was gay and this may prove it.

"Miss Wayne, look who I ran into at the store," Adrian says. "He says he had been trying to find you."

I smile and say, "Give me a second. I'm on a call." My heart flutters wildly and I can't wait to talk to him.

"Miss Wayne...I really need you to sit down," Parade repeats.

"I can't sit down, girl. I have a lot of stuff going on over here. We're entertaining and I gotta make this money for me and Daffany."

"Miss Wayne...please...for me." Parade continues.

I stop what I'm doing and my eyes focus on the fireman again. "What is it, Parade? Just say it."

"Daffany's dead."
I can't feel my legs.
I can't feel my feet.
Total blackness

◆ • • • • • • • • • • • • • • • • • • • • • • • • • • • • • • • • ◆

## Reflecting On The Younger Years
## Miss Wayne

"Can ya'll believe we're in high school?" Wayne asked Daffany, Parade and Sky, as they sit on his floor by the Christmas tree. "It seems like yesterday I just met you all in elementary."

"I know...and I don't know what I would do without you guys." Parade said looking at all of them. "Truthfully, you're all the family I got."

The friends hug each other.

"So...let's get down to exchanging Christmas gifts," Sky said. "Me first since I had Wayne's name."

"I knew you pulled my name out of that bag. You tried to lie to me when I asked you."

"Yes and I was surprised you bought my bullshit too. Usually you do a good job of reading me." She giggled.

Wayne grabbed the gift and said, "Well thank you, dahling!"

When he opened the green and red Christmas paper and saw his first Gucci wallet, he almost shit himself.

"Oh my gawd! You got me the wallet I wanted to match my red leather purse! Thank you, Sky!" he said embracing her.

"Open the wallet up!"

Wayne opened the wallet and revealed two hundred dollar bills, "Miss Sky, you betta work it bitch! This Christmas is off the chain already!"

"No problem, sweetie," she said blowing him a kiss. "You don't 'spose to give nobody a wallet or purse without money in it."

"And it got a nerve to be Gucci!"

"Come on...you know my peoples got it like that so it ain't a thing." She said bragging a little.

"Wayne! Who in there with you?!" Marbel yelled from the bedroom, interrupting their moment.

Without waiting on his answer, she walked into the living room butt ass naked. Wayne hopped off the floor and covered her up with his body, trying to push her back into the room.

"Mama, you ain't got no clothes on. You got to go in the room."

Parade and them looked at the scene.

"Don't worry, 'bout all that! Who the fuck is in my house?"

"It's Parade and them. Remember I told you earlier they were comin' over, ma?"

"Hi, Miss Marbel," they said.

"Ya'll betta announce ya'll selves next time!" she said walking around Wayne, her titties hanging like two saddle bags.

"Ma it's just my friends...please."

"Oh...well I don't care who they are, if I ask you a question mothafucka answer it!"

"Yes, ma."

Now that her memory had gotten worse, she became defensive when she couldn't remember things. Every day was a struggle and Wayne was starting to despise her.

When he finally got her into her bedroom an eerie silence filled their space.

*"What's wrong with Miss Marbel? She ain't the same no more."* Asked Sky.

*"Ain't nothin'wrong with her...she just gettin' old."*

*"You okay?"* Sky asked.

*"Yeah...I'm cool."* He said forging a smile. *"Let's get on with the gift givin'."* He said. *"Now...it's my turn to give a gift, and I pulled Daffany's name."* He held the gift in his hands, handing it to her.

Daffany looked hesitantly at Parade and then at the purple and gold wrapped package.

*"Wait guys,"* Parade said softly, *"Me and Daffany want to tell you something first. We couldn't come up with the money for your gifts. Things are still bad at our houses and we're sorry. We tried to get the money to get somethin' for ya'll all the way up 'til today. It just didn't work. So it's not fair that we take gifts from you."*

*"Yeah...I wouldn't feel right,"* Daffany added, her head hung low.

Miss Wayne and Sky looked at each other and smiled.

*"We know ya'll couldn't make it happen and it's not your fault. But we still got you somethin' anyway."* Miss Wayne said. *"We don't care nothin' about all that."*

*"But you were just hype because Sky got you a Gucci wallet,"* Said Parade.

*"Right! That bitch got it like that so I expect nothin' but the best from the cunt. But it don't take nothin' from what we already know is goin' on at your crib. It's cool...and we still want you to have the gifts."*

*"But why?"* asked Daffany.

*"We're friends, Daffany! Enough with the questions. So...this is from me,"* Sky said handing a gift to Parade.

*"And this is from me,"* Miss Wayne said handing the gift to Daffany again.

*"Open them up,"* Sky said when she saw sadness still covered their faces.

"Listen, stop being pitiful," Miss Wayne told them. "It's cool. Don't let your peoples take away the day that belongs to us. My mother just walked in here bare ass naked and I'm fine."

They laugh. "So no worries right now," he continued. "That shit will be waiting for you when you go back home, for now, be happy."

Daffany looked at Parade and they both hugged Wayne and Sky. When Parade opened her gift, she couldn't believe she was staring at a brand new pair of diamond stud earrings.

"Are these...are these....real?"

"Come on now, don't play me," Sky laughed. "What you think? I would buy you some fake shit?"

"I never owned anything like this before."

"Now you do."

"I love you so much, Sky! Thank you."

"Okay, Miss Daffany," Miss Wayne said, "Open yours."

Daffany carefully tore the paper off of a small box, when she opened it, she saw a heart shaped gold locket and chain inside. When she opened the locket, she saw a beautiful picture of the four of them smiling in the hallway at school. Their favorite teacher snapped it on the day of a field trip to Baltimore.

Tears streamed down Daffany's face and she continued to wipe them away.

"This...is beautiful." Daffany said. "Thank you so much. I'm gonna cherish this for as long as I live."

"I'm glad...and the picture means something to."

"Aw, here comes the sentimental bullshit." Sky said.

"I'm serious. This is not just a locket suga, I put a lot of love into this gift idea."

"What does it mean, Wayne?" Daffany asked.

*"It means that I don't know where our lives will lead us. Hell, I don't even know if we'll all be alive in ten years at all." They all laughed. "But, I want you to know that even in spirit, we can't be torn apart. Always remember that no matter what happens."*

# *Off Balance*

## ✤MISS WAYNE✤

I buried one of my best friends today.
Something I prayed I'd never have to do again.
I guess I was wrong.

When I heard a few raps on the bedroom door, I pulled myself out of bed, opened it, and hopped back under the covers. All I wanted to do was be alone with Raheem Davaughn's melodic voice on the stereo system.

"Wow, you're playing that pretty loud aren't you?"

"I guess," I say, the covers over my head so only my face shows.

"Are you coming downstairs? Your friends are waiting for you." Ryan says walking fully into Miss Parade's guestroom where I was staying.

"I'm really not in the mood. Just wanna stay in bed...you know?"

Ryan the firefighter couldn't be more amazing. Had he not been there after hearing the news that Daffany was gone, I wonder if I would have made it. And I wonder more why he's here, in LA with me. Once again Ryan comes to the rescue but this time he never left my side.

When he showed up at the house that night, I thought he was there to score some boy-butt like the rest of them. Turns out Adrian spotted him at the grocery store when she made a run earlier in day and invited him over. I'm so glad she did.

"I can't say that I know what you're going through personally," he says after sitting on the edge of the bed touching my leg softly, "and I'm sorry you have to go through this at all. I really am."

"I really just want to be alone right now, Ryan" I say, trying to hear him over the loud music.

"And I'm gonna give you that, but you need to listen to me right now," he demands. He's forceful and I like it. "I'm sick of you turnin' me away. I'm not goin' nowhere right now."

"Go 'head."

"Wayne, I can tell you're a good person but you have to pick yourself up right now. That girl downstairs needs you. She's an emotional wreck, too. Not to mention that you have a Goddaughter to take care of now. You have to find that place inside to do what you gotta do."

I want to hear him better, but the music is still loud. And I'm too lazy to turn it down and too comfortable with him touching me to suggest that he do it for me.

As I look into his eyes, I wonder how God could have brought a nicer person my way. With everything going on, the thing I miss the most is companionship. I hadn't had a man since my ex-boyfriend raped Daffany, contracted HIV and died. But now…now…well, I wonder.

"Why aren't you taken?" I ask sitting up straight, "Or are you?"

"Well…I was in love. Me and my partner Eddy were together for ten years and I loved him most of my life."

"What happened?" I asked.

"He contracted AIDS and died. All I wanted to do was protect him and be there for him. Sometimes I even put my life on the line trying to make sure he'd be okay. Changing his IV's and risking the chance of contractin' that shit myself," he says a little angrier. "I blamed him for a long time. He just had to be a slut and put himself out there, putting both of our lives on the line. To tell you the truth, after awhile, I was glad he got that shit."

"That's mean."

"It's also true. He was a heavy heroin user but it wasn't always that way. He got into that shit after we were together. By the time I found out…it was too late. I was in love."

"Are you…I mean…positive?" I asked.

"No although I can't understand why. We were together sexually and even during his unfaithfulness, he never really left my bed. I guess God saw it fit for me to share his testimony but not his fate. Now I just take care of myself and go to work. I don't like the gay club scene so I haven't met anybody new. Until now."

I smile and say, "You would make somebody a good husband."

He grins and I can't get over his pearly white teeth. "I don't know about all that. I just want to spend my life with the right one…when he comes along."

"Listen, how was you able to get away so long from work? I mean…you've been with me for about a week now?"

"You didn't hear me going at it with my boss the day that we left?"

I laugh and say, "I can't remember shit about that day."

"Let's just say it wasn't easy. But, I have some vacation time I never used. It just kept accumulating. After Eddy died I threw myself into work with no break. What better time to use my vacation then now?"

Thank you God for doing me this huge favor.

"You ready to go downstairs now? It's time to pick yourself up and face life." He says. "I'm not gonna allow you to mope around anymore."

He turns the music down and opens the door for me to walk ahead. While we walk down the hall, I wait for him to put his hand on the small of my back. I always know when the right man comes along when he does that one small gesture. He doesn't do it.

Oh well.

◆ •••••••••••••••••••••••••••••••••••••••••• ◆

## *The Earlier Years*

## *Miss Wayne*

*"Wayne! Wayne!!!!! Get in here!"*

*Wayne runs into his mother's bedroom and when he opens the door, she's naked from the waist down. Feces fill her bed and urine drenches her sheets.*

*"Why did you shit in my bed?" She asks him.*

*"Ma, what are you talkin' about?"*

*"You shit in my bed and put me in it! What the fuck is wrong with you?! If you not gonna act right, I want you out of my house!"*

*"Mama, I don't live here anymore remember? I just came to visit you because you're getting sicker. Where is the nurse? I thought she was supposed to stay here."*

*"I put that bitch out! She was tryin' to rape me!"*

*He knew that was a lie. He loved his mother dearly and even he couldn't stand the way her vagina hummed if it wasn't clean. Times like this made him regret not going to college like his mother begged him to. Marbel knew she was getting worst and before she forgot everything, she begged him to use the money she saved all her life for what it was intended for...his college education. Instead he spent every penny on nurses to take care of her twenty four seven, and now most of it was gone.*

*"Mama, that can't be true."*

*"Don't tell me what the fuck is true! And don't call me your mama neither! I ain't your damn mama!"*

*"Mama, please. Calm down."*

*Mentally Wayne was finding it hard to deal...Sky was murdered a month earlier and now his mother's condition was failing terribly. It was discovered some years back that she suffered from progressive Alzheimer's disease and each year she got worse.*

*"I don't wanna hear that shit, nigga! You ain't nothin' but a lazy bastard who wants to kill me! I shoulda neva married you!"*

*It hurt Wayne that his mother referred to him as his father on a regular basis. It didn't help that with age, he was starting to look more and more like a man who cheated on her consistently when they were together. He left her many years earlier.*

*"Mama, let me help you up. I gotta clean your bed linings." Wayne said walking to her bedside trying to ignore her harsh words.*

*"I don't want you to clean shit!" she said striking him on the arm with a closed fist.*

*"Mama! Stop this! Stop doing this!"*

*"I want you to leave me the hell alone you black bastard! I shoulda let my sister have you since you liked to fuck her more than me anyways. Just don't try to take my son! You hear me! Don't try to take my baby from me!"*

*Unfortunately Wayne found out more about his father's infidelities since his mother had been sick than he had when they lived together.*

*"Okay Marbel," he said pulling the covers back from her legs, the smell of her own bodily fluids filling the air. "I won't take your son from you." It was no use in arguing with her about who he was. He had to face the*

facts. His mother was going to get worse before she got better.

"Get your hands off me! What are you tryin' to do?!"

"I'm helpin' you up so I can clean you." He said as calmly as possible.

"Well I don't want you helpin' me!"

"I'm gonna help you anyway, mama. Because I love you."

Although he had to manhandle his own mother, he was eventually able to get her into a tub of water, wash her body and replace the bed linens. But it was time to make some decisions regarding her health too. And to do that, he would have to call the one person he didn't want to ever hear from again. His father.

# Can I Call You
# Mama Wayne
## ❧MISS WAYNE❧

"Shantay, I need you to sit down for a minute, baby. I have to fix your hair and put your shoes on so you can go to school."

"But I don't wanna go back to school." She says dancing around. "I wanna stay here with you."

"I understand that but you can't stay with me today." I say looking down into her pretty eyes. "You've been out of school long enough."

"Awe, man!"

I laugh and say, "Come sit over here with me on the sofa so I can tie your shoes and do your hair."

She does and I take the jar of green grease and brush her hair into a pretty ponytail. Then I place a yellow ribbon on her hair to keep it together.

"Are you gonna be gone when I get back?" She asks me.

"Yes…but don't worry, I'll be coming back to get you in a few weeks. Okay?"

"I don't want you to leave." She says as I put on her shoes. "If you go I won't have nobody to talk to."

"Nonsense. You still have Parade, Landon, Logan and the new baby Ella."

"Ella can't play with me yet and Landon and Logan are mean to me sometimes."

I laugh and say, "I'm sure that's not true because Parade and Jay not havin' all that carryin' on."

"It is true...they don't like me. They think I'm a baby."

"How is that when you're four and they're three?"

"It's true."

"Listen I know you don't believe me, but when you all get older, trust me, you'll be friends for the rest of your lives."

Shantay smiles when I say that and I feel warm inside. She looks so much like Daffany that I can't love her any more if I tried.

"Okay." She says doing plane motions with her arms. "Miss Wayne?"

"Yes, baby."

"Why did mama die? Why did she go to heaven and leave me all alone? Didn't she know that I need her?"

"You're not alone. We talked about that just now remember?"

"Well why did she leave me without a mommy? She didn't love me?"

"Yes, baby. Of course she did. It's just that God needed her help in heaven. But listen," I say pulling her to me the way my mama use to do me when we shared a couch, "I don't want you to worry about stuff like that. I want you to focus on bein' a kid and enjoyin' life. Okay?"

"Okay."

"Well, let me take you to school," I say staring down at her.

"Miss Wayne," Shantay pauses, "can I call you Mama Wayne instead?"

"Sure you can, honey. But understand that you only have one real mommy. And even if she's not here, she's still shinin' down on you from heaven."

Shantay looks up to the ceiling and waves. "Hi, mommy. I love you."

◆ •••••••••••••••••••••••••••••••••••••••••••••••• ◆

## Reflecting On The Earlier Years
## Miss Wayne

*Wayne was uneasy as he waited for his father to come over the apartment he shared with his lover of the moment. He couldn't believe he was inviting him into his home, after all the things he put him through.*

*Because he didn't want to be subjected to his father's ridicule about his clothes, earlier in the day he purchased a pair of blue slacks along with a white men's dress shirt. Had he not, he would've worn one of the many too tight outfits he kept in the closet.*

*"What are you wearing?" his lover asked examining his apparel. He was on his way to work.*

*"What you mean?"*

*"You look like a...well...man."*

*"Newsflash, I know I may tuck myself pretty good to the back honey, but at the end of the day, I'm all man."*

*"You know what I mean."*

*"I do...and I decided to change it up a bit. My father's comin' over and I'm not tryin' to upset him."*

*"Well I don't like it."*

*"And why not?" He asked putting his hands on his hips.*

*"Because it's not you, Wayne. Why would you allow him come into our home and make you feel indifferent? He doesn't deserve that kind of power, sweetheart."*

*"I know." He said with his head hung low. "But what else can I do?"*

*"You can remember who you are and let him worry about the rest."*

*"I do know who I am! Trust me honey, nobody knows who they are more than me."*

*"Good...because I'll fuck him up if he makes you feel bad for it," he said, grabbing his black Louis Vuitton briefcase, which Wayne bought for him during one of his credit card schemes. "When I get home tonight, I expect my baby to be here and not whoever stands before me now."*

*When he left, Wayne walked into his bedroom and looked at himself in the full-length mirror. He looked bad pretending but more importantly he felt uncomfortable. Taking off the new clothes and throwing them into the trashcan, he chose to wear a pair of tight stretch jeans and a fitted white t-shirt which read, 'Cuter than a new-born baby', instead. Then he waited for his father to arrive.*

*Five minutes later, Bells knocked on the door and Wayne allowed him inside. Bells looked thin and frail and walked slower than Wayne remembered. But what Wayne couldn't get over was the fact that they looked so much alike. It was like looking into a mirror.*

*"Why are you dressed like that?" Bells asked sitting on the sofa. "You look like a fucking sissy."*

*"I'm dressed like this because this is me and it's none of your fuckin' business."*

*"I don't believe it...after all this time Marbel still didn't do a good job of raising you. A grown ass man dressed like a ten year old chick. You're a disgrace."*

*"Look, your slights won't hurt me anymore. Gone are the days in which I need your acceptance. I know what I am and afraid of you is not one of them."*

*"You know what," he said getting up to leave before the meeting even began, "I'm out of here. I don't have to*

listen to this shit from a child I disowned a long time ago."

Wayne felt awful because he'd hoped their meeting wouldn't end that way. Right before Bells reached the door he said, "Dad, I need your help."

Bells stopped but his back remained toward Wayne and his hand rested on the doorknob.

"You need help alright, but I don't know how I can help you."

"Well you can. Mom is sick...really sick and I don't know what to do anymore. On paper, you both are still married and I need permission to put her in a hospital that can help her. She has Alzheimer's."

"Alzheimer's?" He laughed. "Well I don't believe any of that shit She's probably just faking to get some attention as usual. I wouldn't be surprised if that was her way to sit on her fat ass all day and not work."

"Maybe that's true," Wayne said biting his tongue, "but she also thinks I'm you whenever she sees my face. And considering I'm wearing a pair of stretch jeans and tight t-shirt, I think she's far off. If that doesn't prove she's sick I don't know what does."

Silence.

"Marbel ain't hardly my problem nomore. I gots me a young girlfriend to take care of now. What I care about an old dried up ass bitch for?"

Wayne swallowed hard. It took everything in his power not to tackle him and kick his ass. Because unlike when he was a kid, he was positive he could take him now.

"If you ever loved her, if you ever loved me, you'd help us. I don't know what to do dad...and I need you. I'm not what you hoped for, but I'm still your son." He continued tears rolling down his face. "She's at the same place she was when you two last seen each other. Please *go to her. Just see her and you'll know what I'm saying is true."*

*Silence.*

*"I'm gone. Bye, Wayne."*

*Wayne didn't know what his father would do but he certainly hoped it would be the right thing. He was his last hope.*

# *Murder*

## ❦QUEEN PAUL❧

Kevin walked into the living room to see two police officers just leaving and his heart dropped.

"Oh my gawd! What did Betty Badge want with you? I mean, why are they interrogating us?" She asks staring out at the window watching them get into their unmarked squad car.

"You need to calm down, Kevin!" Paul says walking to his office. Then he takes a seat in his chair. "You bein' real paranoid when you don't need to be. Everything is under control."

"But you say they wouldn't think it was us. And that they'd think it was the drag queen slayer instead if we killed her in the same way. If that's the case, why were they here?"

"Since you wanna be all loud and stupid, bitch, let's talk about why they were here. He does think I had something to do with Big Boody Brandy's death but not you. They don't even suspect that you were there. And if they question you, act like you don't know nothin'. All you gotta do is stay calm because it's not even that deep. We just have to remain cool."

"But...I don't know...I mean...how did they know it was you?"

"They don't *know* anything for sure," Paul corrects him. "If they did I wouldn't be talking to you right now."

"Well what happened? We covered our tracks. We did everything like we planned including puttin' on gloves. We even cut her penis off and put it in her mouth like the slayer does."

Queen Paul starts to bore with Kevin's anxiousness. So he ignores him and as if a light goes off in Kevin's head he says, "Unless...unless you're really behind all the shit that's been happening in the news to begin with." He says staring down at him. "Queen Paul, I asked you before, but I'ma just ask you again, are you behind all those other murders too?"

"And like you asked me before, I told you it wasn't me. And if you don't believe me, then that's on you." Paul rises from her chair and struts toward her bedroom.

"I got your number, bitch!" He says to himself. "And I'm not goin' down with you either."

◆ • • • • • • • • • • • • • • • • • • • • • • • • • • • • • • • • ◆

## *Two Hours Later*

Kevin waltz's into a Washington DC police department wearing a cute black dress and ugly orange shoes. Sure her massive neck and head on top of her body made her look like Wesley Snipes in drag...but as far as she was concerned, she was beautiful.

At first she considered turning around and going home, after all, she also participated in the murder of Brandon Bar. Instead of incriminating herself, she had plans to remix things in her favor.

Walking up to the counter she says, "I'd like to speak to a detective please."

"And what is this in reference to?" An officer asks looking Kevin up and down.

"I'd like to report a murder."

# *Lunch with Parade*

## MISS WAYNE

The fried fish was done and I just finished making a fresh salad with leafy greens, tomatoes, onions and shredded cheddar cheese. I walk the bowl over to the table, dish out two plates and sit next to Parade. She's staring at her food but isn't eating a bite.

"It looks good," she says moving the meal around in her plate. "And the fish smells great."

"Baby...You 'sposed to eat it you know." I joke.

The kids were at school and baby Ella was at the daycare center because Parade and me really needed this time alone.

"What time does your flight leave?"

"At 6:00 PM...I wanna show Ryan LA and then we headed back home."

Parade is quiet for about two minutes and she forces some food down and says, "So...when are you coming back? To LA?"

"I'll be back in a few weeks to get Shantay after this ball I'm walkin' in is over. Hopefully I'll win and can earn some money. Then I'm gonna settle down and raise Shantay and I was thinkin' about buying a house."

"Really," she asks with hopefulness in her eyes, "Where you want to buy your house?"

"In Accokeek, Maryland or somethin'. I want to be closer to trees and serenity. And I still haven't seen my mother. I'm thinkin' it's time."

She smiles and says, "You know it's been years since you said her name?"

"That's because it hurts too much to be around her right now. You know her memory is fucked up, but for some reason, she remembers to think that I'm my father. A man she hates."

"Oh...I'm sorry, Wayne." She says touching my hand. "I didn't know it was that bad because you never talk about her."

"Don't be sorry, honey. After all the death and despair around me recently, I'm startin' to realize I can handle anything."

She sighs.

"But when your mother passes...or if she passes, are you gonna come back to LA then?"

"No, Parade. I don't think I will. There isn't anything here for me anymore, girl."

She slams her fork down on her plate and yells, "Why do you wanna hurt me?! You know I want you and Shantay to be here with me! Daffany is gone and you're taking yourself and her away from me too? Those faggies mean more to you than I do? I thought I was your family?"

"Parade, this is why I asked Ryan to do some shoppin' without me today. I wanted to talk to you alone." I say in a low voice. "Look, I know things have been crazy around here and trust me when I say it's been hard on me too. I'm so use to cryin' when I lay down that I haven't slept in days."

"I know...I mean...I do understand you lost her too and that you have a life. It's just that this whole thing is bothering me more. You're stronger than me, Miss Wayne. You've always been."

"You haven't been yourself for awhile, Miss Parade. Before Miss Daffany passed you were actin' like somethin' heavy was on your mind. You're angry all the time and you lash out for no reason! Not to mention the fact that you're so concerned with holdin' on to me, that you're destroyin' your marriage! What the fuck is really goin' on with you? Talk to me!"

"I don't know what I'm feeling! I'm confused," she sobs. "I have a man who couldn't love me more yet every time I look at him, he reminds me of Sky and I feel like I'm betraying her since she was with him first. And then...and then..." She hesitates.

"What is it, baby? Don't hold back. Get it out, tell me what's up!"

"I've done something I'm not proud of." She sobs heavier. "I never shared this with anyone because I forgot all about it until recently. When I found out I was pregnant with Ella...I started having nightmares about my past again. It was like I was remembering things I suppressed deep in my mind that I never wanted to know."

She pauses and I say, "Go ahead, Parade. Please."

"I...I...use to sleep with my father, Wayne. When I was younger." She pauses and wipes her tears. "It stopped when I got into high school but it went on for a long time before that. I think that's one of the reasons my mother hates me...I wonder...I wonder if she knows. I wonder if she ever walked in on us having sex before."

"I don't understand. What do you mean you use to sleep with your father? Do you mean Mr. Knight, raped you?"

"No. I mean...I don't think so."

"I'm confused. Did he have a sexual relationship with you or not, Parade?"

"Yes!" she cries. "And I liked it. I liked how he made me tingle and I liked the attention he gave me. I heard of molestation but my father wasn't the monster I thought molesters were. He was good to me when we were good. But now I'm afraid that the same thing will happen be-

tween Ella and Jay. And I'm realizing what we shared
was not right."

Wow.

This explains everything.

Now I understand why she is so clingy and has been
rejecting her husband...she's been a victim of molestation. I put my arms around her and we're both crying so
hard it's difficult to understand one another.

Somehow I manage to pull away from her grasp and
say, "Parade, I don't care how good it felt, your father
took advantage of you. He raped you! He is a fuckin'
bum bitch who took advantage of your sadness. He knew
you didn't have anybody and he used you for your body.
And just because it felt good, doesn't mean you weren't
raped. Some rapes do feel good which is why you're so
fucked up afterwards."

"No...no," she said shaking her head. "I said he
wasn't like that."

"Yes it was like that, baby! You were failed by a man
who was supposed to protect you, just like my father
failed me. Do you understand that?"

"I...I don't want that to happen to Ella. I don't want
Jay to hurt my baby girl like my father did me."

"I've looked into Jay's eyes, Parade. I've seen how
he looks at you and how he gloats over those kids. That
man would never do no shit like that. Give him a chance
and let him be there for you and his family."

She wraps her arms around me tighter. "I thank God
for you every time I close my eyes...and this is why."

"I finally understand why you're so hurt but I have to
tell you somethin'. Parade, you have to realize that real
friends don't grow a part, they just take different paths in
life. We aren't kids anymore on the stoops of our apartment building. You have a beautiful family and I'm tryin'

to get one started of my own one day. But it doesn't mean I don't love you."

"I understand."

We hug again.

"I can't believe Miss Daffany is gone," I say remembering what was more important. "I can't believe I won't see her face anymore."

"Me too. She drove herself to sickness because of worrying about that IRS shit! And a day after she dies, we get the information from your lawyer that we can be put on a payment plan to save our businesses. Had she just held on, things would have been okay."

"I know but you have to remember, Daffany went from havin' nothin' to havin' everything…and then the IRS came and threatened all that shit. Let's not forget that just before Shantay was born, she was sellin' her body for drugs, food and shelter. She was scared of goin' back to that again. "

"You're right," she says softly. "I guess I never thought about it like that."

"I understood her reasoning, just wish she understood I had her back, and that it was okay to be loved."

"What are you going to do with the boutique?"

I sigh and say, "Well, right now the staff is running it pretty well, but when someone makes me an offer I can't refuse, I'm gonna take it. It reminds me too much of Daffany and I don't think I can keep it."

"Let me have it!" Parade suggests.

"You can't run the apartment building, your houses, the make-up store and my boutique."

"Sure I can! I can buy it from you by the end of next week. I'll have my attorney put the paperwork together and everything. Our funds are free now so it's not a problem anymore."

"Oh Mercy…Listen at you. You'll have your attorney put the paperwork together." I laugh.

"I'm serious."

"Why do you want to keep the shop?"

"For the opposite reason you want to sell it. Because it reminds me of Daffany and I kinda want to hold on to it."

When I think of her reasoning, without question, I take the offer.

And then, a totally irrelevant flash of Tyrone being behind me enters my mind again. And then I remember.

Everything.

◆ •••••••••••••••••••••••••••••••••••••••••••••••••• ◆

## *Reflecting on The Earlier Years*

## *Miss Wayne*

*Bells came through for Wayne after all, even though he complained the entire. Wayne decided then to contact a lawyer about having power of attorney over Marbel's finances and body.*

*The day he put her in the nursing home, he was devastated. He felt like he let her down. But he didn't…even the doctors told him that there was nothing else he could do.*

*He was on his way home to grab a few drinks when he got a call from someone he hadn't heard from in a few years.*

*"What's up, bitch? What's the 'T'?" Yelled Tyrone into the phone.*

*"Ain't shit. Just dealin'."*

*"I hear that...what you doin' right now? Dayshawn and me are havin' some friends over for our weekly Spades game. You comin'?"*

*"You live with Day now?"*

*"Girl, yes! I been livin' with him for a few months now. What's up?"*

*Wayne thought about the offer. The one thing that stayed in his mind was that every time he got with Tyrone and Dayshawn, some crazy shit happened. So he considered his options but realized quickly that he had none. He caught his lover cheating earlier in the week and he threw his ass out on the street. So unless he wanted to be alone, hanging out with them was his only choice.*

*"I'm on my way."*

*"Cool...See you when you get here."*

*Wayne wore a cute pair of stretched black tights, a free flowing pink blouse that exposed his chest and a big pair of gold hoop earrings. Since he had just gotten some tracks sewn in, he let his hair hang over his shoulders.*

*When he walked through the door the house was packed and everyone was in attendance.*

*"Bitch, you look so good! What's up with it?" Tyrone said opening the door examining Wayne's muscular but sexy body.*

*"It depends on who's asking," Wayne told him as he struck a pose in the doorway.*

*"I heard that, sashay your skinny ass in here."*

*Wayne walked inside and jumped right into the Spades game, and five minutes later, the animation began. All of the lights were dimmed with the exception of the ones that were in kitchen and in an ardent way, it acted as the spotlight for their loud and rambunctious performances. It was always about who talked the loudest and who had the best comeback. If you were weak at heart, the Friday night Spades game was not the place for you.*

*"OOOhhh, Bitch, they cuttin' early, I shoooow hope I don't see no hearts fly out them monkey paws for the rest of this hand!" Dayshawn yelled at Wayne who had partnered up with Tyrone.*

*"Monkey paws? Okay, Bitch, you must be referrin' to the gorilla toes attached to those petite size 18 feet of yours! I don't even know how you find sandals for 'em." Miss. Wayne snapped back.*

*"Miss Wayne, baby, don't worry. I'm watchin' her ass. You know Dayshawn is famous for being a re-nigga-a!" Tyrone said.*

*"LIES...I ain't neva reneged in a game of spades in my life...unless you count last week," he recollected. "But Bitch, you can't count that game 'cause I was rollin' and I thought we was playin' go fish. Ha...ha...honey, the X and the Dro had the ole girl done, baby...yeousss!!!" Dayshawn laughed as his breath meshed with the alcoholic frenzy within the room.*

*Spades was just one of the ways Wayne, Dayshawn and Tyrone passed time with other people in the life. Being amongst people who did the same things and talked the same way they did brought a sense of normalcy to their lives. And with his mother's condition, which he rarely talked about, being worst, he really needed the getaway. Food was cooking, drinking glasses were clinking and shit talking was at an all time high.*

*There were so many people in the house that some of them found a seat on the lap of another. And no one cared because when you're Family, everything was all good.*

*As the night went on, liquor poured like it came out of a faucet and suddenly, Miss Wayne felt woozy.*

*"You okay?" Tyrone asked noticing him swaying. He placed his hand on his shoulder. "Cause you don't look too good."*

*"Uh...yeah...I think so. I had a long day though with my mother. I guess I'm more tired than I thought."*

*"You wanna rest up?" Dayshawn asked him.*

*"Ya'll mind? All I need is an hour am I'm ready to keep the party goin'."*

*"Yeah it's not a problem," Dayshawn said. "You know my home is your home."*

*"Let me give you some pain medicine and some water and you can stay in my room." Said Tyrone.*

*Wayne took the pills, walked past the people who were socializing and laid down in Tyrone's bed. Once his head hit the cushion, he felt even more off balance. Tyrone helped him get situated in the bed and said, "Damn, it looks like you had way too much to drink this time, Wayne. You sure you gonna be okay?"*

*"Yeah. I'll be fine. I don't even remember drinkin' that much."*

*"I'm gonna go back out there. But let me know if you need anything...okay?"*

*"Yeah...just leave the door..."*

*Wayne felt light headed and could not complete his sentence. Through a mental haze he saw Tyrone smile at him slyly, close and lock the door and flip the light switch off. Two minutes later, Tyrone had turned him over on his stomach and was entering him anally. Wayne could hear him panting heavily in his ear as he gripped his shoulders and thrust into him over and over again.*

*"You feel so good, Wayne," Tyrone said. "This ass all soft and wet. Just like I knew it would be."*

*Tyrone talked to him as if Wayne was a willing participant when in actuality, he was a victim of a drug-induced rape. He tried to fight him off, but his body wouldn't do what his mind requested. He had no idea that Tyrone had been planting drugs in his drink all night.*

*Ever since Tyrone met Wayne, he wanted him sexually. He loved the lightness of his skin and the way he walked around like he owned the world. But part of him was jealous that Wayne garnered so much attention. Tyrone wished he could be as smooth as Wayne but felt he could never measure up. So since he couldn't be him, he decided to take the next best thing, his body. And that's exactly what he did.*

*The next morning, Wayne would not remember the event.*

*But that would all change many years later.*

# *Top Flight*

## ❦MISS WAYNE❧

We had thirty minutes before we boarded the plane and there were three things that were blowing the hell out of me. First, my best friend was gone and I missed her already. Second, Ryan's cell phone kept ringing off the hook and he wouldn't answer. Third, the memory of Tyrone being anywhere near my body made me want to cut everything back there off.

Was the vision real? Or was it bullshit? I couldn't call it! And then I remember how Big Boody Brandy claimed that everyone knew Miss Tyrone raped people. Could he have done the same thing to me too?

I had an idea on how I was going to deal with Tyrone and I call it 'Operation Hole Dig' but I wasn't sure how I was going to deal with Ryan and his ringin' ass phone because after all...he wasn't my man. And to tell you the truth, he hadn't even asked me out let alone elude that he wanted more. Even though he stayed with me for two weeks in LA and we shared the same bed together, at no time did he try to touch me. So I guess I'm being petty right? Fuck that shit! I still wants to know.

When he wasn't looking I concocted a plan to find out what kind of nigga he really was. So the moment he turned away, I removed the SIM card from my AT&T phone.

Then I place the phone to my ear and yell, "Oh my goodness!" I scare the hell out of a child sitting next to me.

"What's wrong, babe?" Ryan asks turning toward me.

"I can't get a signal! Gosh darn it!"

Now that those words left my lips, I realize 'gosh darn it' was a bit too much but there was no taking it back now.

"Were you in a middle of a call?"

"Yes and I need to finish it up before I board the plane, not to mention I'm thirsty."

When he pulls his phone out of his pocket, I know my plan is working.

"Look...use mine and I'll go grab you something to drink. What you want?"

"You sure?"

"Of course. I wouldn't offer if I didn't feel like going," he says handing me his phone. For a man who has something to hide, he seems carefree. "What you want to drink?"

Thinking of something that may take some time I say, "A double espresso...and add milk but only *after* it's seeped for two minutes."

"Ooookay," he laughs. "I'll be right back."

When he's gone, I focus my attention to his phone. There are seven missed calls from Eddy and two unread texts.

Eddy?

WTF!

I thought he said Eddy was dead! Already I'm not feeling Mr. Fireman. I should've known that a gay man and a fireman being together was just too much of a cliché.

Curiosity was killing me. Now if I read the texts, how was I going to hide it? He has an actual cell phone unlike everybody else on earf who uses a PDA. Which means that once I read the messages, it will no longer show as UNREAD.

Before I invade his privacy, I look up to be sure he isn't coming. He's not so I click the button to read his messages. One reads, *'Ryan, I need to talk to you. You said you'd be here for me and I can't find you. What gives?'* The other reads, *'Can you at least return my texts?'*

I knew it! He's a bum and a fraud and I wanted nothing more to do with him. I'm so mad that as I close the lid of his phone, I miss calculate my timing. Because Ryan is walking up to me and yes, he saw everything.

"It doesn't look like you're making phone calls to me." He says with an attitude. "Fuck are you doin' going through my phone?"

"I'm sorry...I was just..."

"Disrespecting me. You know what, Wayne, when I first met you, I couldn't help but think about you after we met. I wondered what kind of person you were and if you were for me. But after this, *Madam Wayne*," he says sarcastically, "I realize I should've turned around the moment your ass dropped on your living room floor."

He takes his phone from me.

"You know what, it was wrong for me to look at your messages. But what about you? You said you were single and even went as far as to feed me some bullshit about Eddy bein' dead! When for real, unless you run into Eddy's all the time, he's alive and well and textin' you now!"

"First of all my lover's name was Teddy...not Eddy! Had you turned the music down when I was talking to you in the room you would've heard me clearer. And Eddy is a co-worker of mine who wanted me to cover his shift but I'm not there am I? Instead I'm in LA with a lunatic who doesn't understand the meaning of privacy!

Here's your fuckin' espresso," he says pushing it in my hands before walking away. "I ain't got time for this shit! I'm out."

I'm so embarrassed I can barely move.

"Is that man mad at you?" asks a child next to me.

"Yeah." I say slightly irritated at his ear hustling.

"Oh...he seems nice. I saw him help the lady in the wheel chair over there when you were looking through his phone."

Pissed this snotty-nosed-bastard is making matters worse I say, "And I saw you diggin' for gold in your nose five minutes ago and eatin' your boogers. But did I say anything to you?" I pause. "So mind your ugly business!"

When the child cries I stomp away in my heels and place the SIM card back in my phone. Then I lean on a wall and call home.

"Miss Wayne...we miss you!" Adrian yells after he picks up. "How are you doing?"

"I'm fine."

"That's good...but there's so much going on out here."

"Like what?"

"They arrested Queen Paul for murder. It's all over the news. They say they've finally solved the case of the Drag Queen Slayer."

"What?!" I scream a little louder than I realized. "How?"

"He killed Big Boody Brandy too. That's how he got caught."

"I haven't been watching anything out here with Daffany's funeral and all."

"Oh...well shit is crazy in DC."

I'm blown away. "So that means he killed Marlene too?"

"That means he's responsible for *all* of the Drag Queen Slayer murders."

I'm happy the case is solved but for some reason, I don't believe it. I always thought in the back of my mind after speaking to Chris that Tyrone was responsible even though I never said it out loud.

"Wow…well, how is everything else goin' there?" I say looking for Ryan in my peripheral vision. He's no-where to be found.

"It's cool," he says hesitantly, the tone of his voice changed.

"What's wrong, Adrian? I can tell in your voice something ain't right so just tell me what's up."

"I really don't want to start stuff, Miss Wayne. I just want to stay out of it."

"You won't be in it if you tell me, if you don't…well that's another story. Is it the parties? Are they running smoothly?"

"Are you sure you won't be mad at me for telling you?"

"Adrian…tell me what the fuck is goin' on! I hate playin' promise me more, or promise me not, with you!"

"Okay…well…did you tell Tyrone he could have clients over…outside of the ones you set up for Party Night?"

"Yeah…why?"

"I knew I should not have said anything. Please don't tell Tyrone."

Although I hear his words, I'm more interested in what's behind them. I immediately recall how every time Tyrone name comes up, that he goes overboard to protect him. I also remember the day I came home, and heard him and Tyrone fighting supposedly over Chris. I never got a chance to ask him if what Chris said about Tyrone was true. Was he an abuser?

"Adrian...I'm gonna ask you somethin' and I want you to be real with me."

"Okay."

"Has Tyrone ever hurt you?"

Silence.

"Adrian...answer the fuckin' question! Now I need to know this shit and my plane is comin' so you got to tell me now!"

"Yes. He has."

I swallow hard and say, "Did he hurt you the night I came home early and heard him yelling at you?"

"Yes. He does that all the time. It's like he's jealous of me and whenever he finds out I'm spending time with Chris, he'll pick a fight. And then it will turn physical."

"So all those times you had bruises, Tyrone did them?"

"Yes."

"What about the scars? On your body?"

"All him."

I slide to the floor and sit down because the room feels like it's spinning.

"So Chris has never hurt you?"

"He couldn't. He loves me too much."

"Then why lie to me? And why lie on him?"

"I was scared, Wayne."

"Ain't that much scared in the world, Aid! Has he raped you too?"

"A lot."

"Adrian, why wouldn't you tell me this shit?" I ask in horror. "Why wouldn't you let somebody know somethin' like that was goin' on? I don't understand."

"You were in LA. And I wanted to tell you...really badly. I even tried that day you caught Tyrone in the bed with a man, when the other guy was on the couch. But you said he told you already and I left it like that."

"Damn I remember that shit too."

"The abuse started after I caught him raping me one night. He put something in my drink and when I remembered the next day, he said he wasn't trying to hurt me. But that he was all alone and needed somebody. I just wanted it to stop. So I told Chris and he approached him the next day. Tyrone got mad and told me he'd kill him if I didn't leave him alone. There was something in his eyes that made me believe him. So I left the apartment Chris rented for me and tried to cut him off. I lied to Tyrone and told him Chris stopped paying for the apartment so he would really think I was through with him. I didn't want him to get hurt."

I know what he meant when he said something in Tyrone's eyes made him believe he was capable of murder. I thought the same thing when I saw the way he beat his wife.

"When was the last time he raped you?"

"The night of the fire."

"What?!"

"The night Marlene died, he put something in my drink, the way he normally does. Usually I pass out and can't remember much but this time I woke up and felt him on top of me again. I couldn't pretend anymore so I told him I'd tell you and he got mad. He hit me in my face and I think he was going to kill me, but you came over.

"Ya'll started cooking and you came downstairs to check on me. He was nervous the entire time and told me that if I said anything to you, he'd kill you too. He threatened to kill anybody in my life that got too close."

I gasp.

"Are you serious?"

"Yes. Later that night, he locked my door from the outside and set fire to the house. With all of us in it."

It felt like I was taking off without the plane. What kind of maniac was I living with all this time?

"Are you telling me that Tyrone burned that house down?"

I thought about how I paid somebody to hurt Queen Paul. What if my hit was successful? I could've gotten tied up in all kinds of shit. Although with Paul's recent arrest, I may have done the world a favor.

"Yes. And I tried to bang on the walls when I smelled the smoke because he wedged a pole under the doorknob so I couldn't get out."

"I remember that too! Tyrone told me it was his next door neighbor making all that noise."

"Is that why you told me on the night of the fire that you wanted to die?"

"Yes… I couldn't take it anymore."

"You don't have to worry about Tyrone…not as long as I'm alive. And the parties will be over soon too because I want you to make a life with Chris and be happy. We just have to play it out for a few more weeks so I can get back at Tyrone."

"Okay."

"Don't tell Day either. I don't want anybody else involved."

"I won't."

"How many clients has Tyrone invited over my house anyway? For party night?"

"Well that's what I wanted to tell you when you first called. When I got up in the middle of the night one time, I heard extra voices in his room. So I started paying attention and found out he has two people over a night. I don't think he's trickin' either. I think he is doing some kind of procedure and Garisha be with him too. They have all kind of surgical stuff in their room and I even saw gauze."

"Surgery? With Ugly Gary in my house?"

"Yeah."

"Okay, honey. Just be easy and don't alert anybody that I know." I say taking the entire bullshit in. "Is there any good news?"

The attendant says the flight is boarding so I know I must hurry.

"Yes...your ball gown came! It's so beautiful, Wayne. You're going to love this I promise."

"For real? How does it look?"

"It's a pink sequin bra top with long pink beads dangling from it. And the bottom is a sequin bikini bottom with the same design. I never saw anything like it. Trust me...you're going to look beautiful in it." She exclaims. "Oh!! They sent a soft pink feather boa with it too. It's hot!"

"Good! 'Cause I have plans to bring home the money from that ball. Did you and Day's gowns come?"

"Yep! I'm rocking a pink sequin one-piece mini dress and Day has a cute pink sequin one-piece pants suit. We are going to kill it!"

"Okay...I gotta go," I say when I see Ryan stand in line to board. "I'll call you later.

When I rush over to him I ask, "Can I stand in line with you? So we can talk?"

He turns to me and say, "You just don't get it do you? You fucked up with me. Be gone."

As I walk sadly to the back of the line I realize that he got *me* all the way fucked up. Don't nobody carry me without my getting in at least one word edgewise. So I hustle back toward him.

"You know what...I was wrong for lookin' at your little weak ass texts. In fact it was bitch like behavior and unfortunately I am not immune even though I'm a man. But have you ever stopped to think that maybe I did it because I was feelin' you? And that maybe I wanted to make sure you were who you claimed to be before I gave you my heart? And had you around Shantay?" I pause not long enough for him to answer. "Well think about that when you wake up in the morning and realize you lost the best thing that never happened to you narrow ass. Fuck you! I'm out." I say as I switch my little ass to the back of the line.

I decide then that he's done!

I got ninety problems and he ain't one.

# *Work The Runway*

## ⚛MISS WAYNE⚛

It's party night and home for only two days, I already regained control of my house. I acted as if everything was good between Tyrone and me because I wanted my plan to work just right. If he weren't such a selfish ass fish, one look in my eyes would tell him something was up. But he had one thing on his mind, HIMSELF.

Even though I learned that Tyrone burned the house down instead of Paul, who was my biggest competition, I still wanted to win the ball that was going down in two days. My reasons are personal. So, to win, I consulted the lovely B Scott, a transgender woman, to help prepare us for the night. She's the best of the best and since we are judged on our walk, costume, and attitude, I knew she'd be great. She worked with us on proper hairstyles, offered makeup suggestions and even gave tips on our performance. I truly felt after talking with her that I was ready.

When the meeting with her was over, I placed an important call to LA that would prove beneficial for me later. It would be the most hateful thing I did in my life and I didn't even care.

"Miss Wayne, I have a client comin' over today. Are we still cool with our agreement?"

"Sure," I say. "I told you, you can have two clients over the night of the party. Remember?"

"I know. I just want to make sure everything still stands," he smiles.

"Why wouldn't it?" I imply. "You been real with me, I'm bein' real with you."

"Oh...thanks, girl."

"No problem," I say slightly touching him on his shoulder. "Nice watch," I continue spotting a black Toy Watch on his arm that runs in the upper one hundreds. "When did you get it?"

"Oh...this?" he says pointing at it. "I've had it for a while now."

"Well I hope you're savin' your money, Tyrone. Remember that was part of the agreement too. You were to save up so you'd have enough money to get a place of your own."

"I am, Wayne. Don't worry about me...I'm set up real good."

I laugh, "Glad to hear that."

"And Wayne, Garisha is helpin' me out with my clients tonight. Is that okay?"

"Now wait one fuckin' minute! What human in their right mind would pay ugly Gary's ass for anything?"

"Our clients. We found a niche market."

"A niche market huh?" I laugh. "And what is the market? Men who want to fuck men who look like shit? Literally?"

"You know what they say, there's somebody out here for everybody," he says dismissively, "well...let me get ready for work. Thanks again, girl!"

He dipped off into his room and I was really curious about the scheme he was running now. But I also knew everything would be revealed in time and I had to be patient.

Twenty minutes into the party, my phone rang. The number is blocked.

"Hello?"

"Wayne, can we talk about what happened at the airport the other day? I mean, I been by the house and you don't answer the door, despite your car being out front. I call all the time and you send me to voicemail, what's up?" Says, Ryan.

"Nothin's up," I say, happy he's been calling me everyday since we split. "I told you I'm done with you and don't appreciate how you tried to come for a bitch in public. You don't grandstand on me in front of people. I don't play that shit."

"I know, and I'm sorry. But if we can just go out, and grab something to eat, maybe you'll change your mind about me. I want a chance to show you I can be the one. Just like you made a mistake by going through my phone, I made a mistake by talking to you the way that I did."

"I doubt going out with you will change my mind. Take care, sweetheart."

After I hang up the phone with him, a thin young boy knocks on the door. And since he looks to be about seventeen, I figure he was in the wrong place and definitely at the wrong time. He was cute and dainty but looked scared.

"Honey...I believe you wandered on the wrong side of town."

"No, I think I have the right place." He says pulling a piece paper from his pocket. "Is Tyrone here?"

"What do you want with Tyrone?"

"I'm not supposed to say."

"Well I can't let you in." I say preparing to close the door.

"Please don't turn me away," he says holding it open. "I really need to see him."

"What is an ugly ass man like that going to offer a cute little thing like you?"

"Like I said, mam, I really can't say," he says digging into his pocket again, pulling out cash. "But I have one hundred dollars for you like he said to bring."

I take the money and look at him again.

"Listen, I don't proclaim to run a legal operation in here, but I'm still gonna need to see some ID from you. Just for my own personal sake."

He looks behind me at everyone having a good time and pulls out his wallet. Then he shows me his ID. He wasn't 21, but he was 18. I guess that'll have to do.

"Right this way," I say pointing to Tyrone's room.

When he disappears inside, I make mental notes to clock him when he comes out. I need to know what the fuck is up now more than ever. I tried to do regular shit but the Capatain Save-a-ho mentality in me wouldn't allow me to mind my own business. Two hours into the party, the young man did not leave Tyrone's room. What was going on in there? I was five seconds from knocking on the door when I see Adrian.

"Adrian, did you ever find out what Tyrone's doin' for money? 'Cause the moment he told me ugly Garisha was helping him, I knew sex was not a part of the equation. Ain't nobody in their right mind fuckin' him!"

"I'm not *really* sure but somebody did tell me he might be doing silicone injections." He laughs. "But I don't hardly believe that shit. Do you?"

"No!"

"I said the same thing, but you remember Miss P from New York Avenue right?"

"Funky bussy, P? The queen who does any freaky thing a trick wants no matter what?"

"Yeah! I saw her come through here for him when you were gone one day. And you know she use to do the silicone injections all the time until a trick stabbed her in the left eye and she couldn't see straight no more." He says. "Well maybe the rumors are true. I can't believe you can learn that quick."

"That bitch can't even read!" I say.

"I guess you don't need to read to stick and push shit into people."

That was it! There was no way I was allowing this kind of shiftlessness to go on in my home. I couldn't risk the chance of something ELSE bad happening here.

So I run toward the bedroom and fling open his door. Time felt like it stopped because there on the floor was the young man I let into my home hours earlier. 'Cept for now, he was out cold. Ugly Gary and Miss Tyrone were standing over him sweating.

"Tyrone...what the fuck is going on?" I say looking at the boy.

"Wayne, we got trouble." He says walking up to me.

"Bitch *we* had trouble the moment I started dealin' with your crispy black ass."

"Wayne, I'm sorry. But I need your help again. I don't know what else to do."

"What is wrong with him, Ty?" I say, seeing two small shiny objects peeking from under his bed. When I see what they are, I remain quiet and direct my attention elsewhere.

"He's dead." Tyrone says nonchalantly. "The mothafucka up and died on me!"

I know he didn't just say what I think he did. Still, I walk deeper into the room despite wanting to go the other way. Then I slyly kick the objects I saw earlier further under the bed. In my mind I know I have a house full of guests slash witnesses and here Nurse Betty is, botching up cosmetic procedures.

"What happened?"

"We were doing the silicone injections to increase his breast size, because God knows he only had two bee stings, when he started spazzin' out." Garisha offers. "We did this all last week and never had a problem until now."

"All last week?!" I scream. "Doctors go to school for years to be able to do this kind of shit and you think you can sum it up in a week? There's a reason this shit is illegal in America! Have you two mothafuckas ever thought of that?"

"But I get it all the time." Garisha continues.

"Bitch and look at your face! I would not have even told nobody that shit."

Silence.

"You know what...you two bitches make this shit disappear. I'm not in it and I ain't see shit." I say closing the door.

Then I direct my attention to my guests who are going on about their business as if nothing is wrong. They're having a lot of fun and I hate to be the bearer of bad news but I don't have a choice.

"Listen up, babies. Unfortunately the party has to be cut short tonight. However I will be sure to refund all of your money for having to leave right now."

When they don't move I yell, "Get the fuck out of my house you limp dick bastards!"

That works and when the house is clear, I make a quick back-up phone call before I do anything else. When the call was over, I hope the person I reached out to will do what needs to be done. Truly I was counting on it. Then I grab Adrian and Dayshawn and we head to the Hilton Hotel because I don't want us anywhere around this shit.

While sitting in the hotel room, Dayshawn asks, "Can you please tell me what happened back there? I kinda liked the trade I was keeping time wit' tonight."

"I don't think you want to know because then you'll be involved."

"But can you tell us if we're going to be in trouble? 'Cause it looks like somethin' happened to that boy who came in but didn't leave out." Asks Adrian.

"As of now no, we aren't in trouble, but I can't make any promises." I say as we all lie face up on the king size bed in the room.

As I'm thinking about the way the young man looked on the floor, I look over at Adrian and then Dayshawn. Why am I always in life or death situations? I remember dealing with this guy who was big on law of attraction awhile back. He told me that the Law of attraction says, 'that which is likened to itself is drawn'. In other words, if all I see and talk about is drama, then by law the universe has to bring me more drama to see. It makes sense. I can't be happy if everything I do is to the contrary.

I look at Dayshawn again and think about Tyrone. I always thought he was a saint for dealing with him for so long. The two of them just don't seem like they'd be that close.

"I need to know something from you, Day. And I need you to keep it real with me."

"I always do."

"Good…'cause I need to know how is it that you befriended Tyrone as long as you have? He's sneaky, untrustworthy and trouble. I mean, we were also cool but we maintained our friendship from a far. I could never deal with him on a regular like you do. He certainly doesn't match your fly so what does he have on you, baby?"

"He told you didn't he?" he asks sitting up straight in the bed. "He told you my business?"

I'm even more curious because it's obvious that whatever secret he's about to let out of the bag, will more than answer my questions.

"Yes," I lie. "But I'd rather hear it from you instead."

Dayshawn gets up, stands at the foot of the bed and looks down at Adrian and me.

Taking a deep breath he says, "When I was younger, just finding out who I was, I felt alone. My mother pretty much told me that any gay son of hers was not her son at all. So I didn't have anybody I could identify myself with and then I met Tyrone who had a rack of friends and knew a lot of people. He was living with his father and was going through some family shit too. Just like me.

"Even though Tyrone was popular, for some reason, he gravitated towards me more than his other friends and we became closer. I think he saw a weakness in me and wanted to capitalize on that shit. Anyway, we were pretty much all we had. My mother worked at least 14 hours a day and his father stayed in the streets. The more different we were from everybody, the tighter our bond became.

"Well one day, my mother was entertaining friends at her mother's house up the block from the Manor. So she sent me to get some charcoal lighter fluid and some matches. Tyrone went with me, but on our way back from the store, we saw a man lying on an old mattress in between two apartment buildings. We thought he was a bum and that was the night everything changed...

*"Oooh look, we should stick that pole over there up his ass or somethin','" laughed Tyrone as they crept slowly up to him.*

*"That's some gross ass shit! His hot wet ass probably stank and everything." Dayshawn laughed. "You know he ain't washin' shit livin' out here."*

# Miss Wayne & THE Queens OF DC

"Come on man...why you always act so scary? That's why I don't like hangin' out with you sometimes. The rest of my friends are fun and do wild shit...but you act older than my father."

"I'm not scary."

"I can't tell."

Dayshawn, worried about losing a friend said, "Okay...what you want me to do? 'Cause you got me fucked up if you think I don't have heart."

Tyrone's sinister mind went into overdrive. Removing the lighter fluid from Dayshawn's brown paper bag, he said, "Let's burn him."

"What is wrong with you? I ain't burnin' nobody! You trippin' now!"

"Please!" Tyrone whined as if they were talking about burning anything other than a human. "Nobody will know we did it. Hardly anybody ever come down this alley anyway." He smiled. "Let's have some fun!"

"What's the purpose, Tyrone?"

The smile was removed from his face and he said, "I'm not fuckin' wit' you no more, and I'ma tell all my friends not to fuck with you either." He shoved the fluid into Dayshawn's chest. "You're probably the snitchin' type anyway and I'm glad I found out before we did this shit." He said, as he began to walk away.

When he took a few steps Dayshawn said, "Do we have to burn him?"

"Bye, young!"

Dayshawn remained quiet for a moment and yelled, "Okay. I'll do it!"

"For real?" he said turning around.

"Yeah."

Dayshawn opened the spout and doused the man with the liquid. Then he struck the match, considered the consequences and paused.

223

*"Go head...throw it." Tyrone cohearsed. "I promise I'll never tell anybody you did this. But I'll also know that you got my back just like I got yours. Go 'head, his life is over anyway, look at him."*

*Dayshawn's heart beat out of his chest. Taking one last look at the fire on the stick, which was very close to burning his fingers, he tossed it in the air and it landed on the stranger's dingy grey coat. His entire body erupted in flames and they ran from the scene, Tyrone laughing the entire way and Dayshawn crying inside.*

*Little did he know, Tyrone would forever hold the murder over his head to keep him in line. It was Dayshawn's single most costly mistake and one he always regretted.*

What Dayshawn just said blows me away and I wonder...who are these people I have around me? Just when you think you know somebody you don't.

"You didn't know....did you?" Day asks me.

"Naw...I ain't know shit, girl. But I did know ya'll relationship was unnatural."

"Damn, Wayne! You tricked me," he says flopping down on the edge of the bed.

"Wow, Dayshawn. You told me so freely...it was almost like you been wanting me to know."

"Maybe I just wanted to tell somebody else that shit. When I heard that man had a family but because he lost his job got put out by his wife for only one night, I never forgave myself. I wanted to take my own life."

"Why didn't you?"

"The next day, we became friends. You remember? The day of the block party. Just bein' around you made me feel better...so I never got around to doin' it."

I smile and say, "Well I'm glad you ain't do no shit like that. If anybody should've killed themselves, it needed to be Tyrone's fat ass."

"Hey, Day...what happened on that case?" Asks Adrian.

"Nothin'. His wife stayed on the news trying to find justice, but it never came. Pretty soon the press stopped caring and stopped talking about it."

"I remember that case too." I say.

"I'm sure a lot of people from around the way remembered that shit."

"Let me ask you somethin', is this the real reason you let Tyrone talk you into letting Dell leave?"

"Yeah. He never wanted me to have anybody. It was like he felt threatened or something."

"That's the same thing with me. He wanted us to be as miserable and as alone as he was."

I exhale and say seriously, "Well every hog has its day...and Miss Ty's is right around the corner. But Day, never repeat the story about the murder ever again."

"I didn't want to this time."

"I'm serious, Dayshawn. I'm not sure but I have a feelin' everything is goin' to be okay from here on out. But you gotta trust me and remember that quiet is kept."

"I hope so."

"Hoping is over, it's time for revenge."

# Fight Night

## ❧MISS WAYNE❧

Dayshawn, Adrian and I get out of the car and walk toward my house when Ocean, who was in the House of Diamonds with Big Boody Brandy walks toward me. Her red Mercedes Benz sits on the curb in front of my house.

I knew it was Ocean the moment I saw her long lace front weave, tight jeans and double D size breasts. Ocean's honey colored face was covered expertly with a nice makeup job. I must admit, the girl's face was beat and the white Louis Vuitton purse she carries swings on her arm.

"Watch out, Miss Wayne!" Adrian screams. "Mad QUEEN walking!"

Dayshawn stands beside me as I look at Ocean stomp in our direction.

"Everything is cool, I just want to talk to Miss Wayne for a minute." Ocean says looking at them. "Alone. This kinda private."

Dayshawn and Adrian look at me for confirmation and I because I'm never scared I say, "It's cool, Diva's...I'll talk to her alone."

Adrian and Day walk into the house taking one last look at me before going inside. Although the door is closed, they look out the window. Now I don't have a problem with Ocean, but I did have a problem with Big Boody Brandy and how she shot up the house with all of us inside. Just 'cause she wanted Tyrone.

"What's up, Ocean?"

"Everything, Wayne. For starters my house mother is gone and I'm left to keep the House of Diamonds legacy alive by myself."

"Yeah…I'm sorry to hear about Big Boody. I can't believe Paul did some shit like that."

"It's cool," she says adjusting her Fendi shades, which rests on the bridge of her nose job. "In the end she got what she deserved."

"With that said, Ocean, me and Big Boody weren't cool, so what does all of this have to do with me?"

"Nothing…except Brandy did tell me if anything were to happen to her, to give you this letter. And I may be a queen, but I keep all my promises."

When she reaches into her purse to grab something, Adrian and Dayshawn run back outside.

"What is goin' on out here?" Dayshawn yells.

"Uh…nothing," Ocean frowns. "I just want to give Wayne this letter from Brandy that's all."

She hands me a sealed envelope with my name handwritten on it. I take it from her hands and examine it briefly before opening it.

"I don't know what it says…but I hope it clears up whatever for you. I'm out."

"I'm coming ya'll. Go inside."

Adrian and Dayshawn look at me before walking away.

After Ocean switches away and jumps into her car, I take a few seconds to read the two-page letter outside. It revealed some incriminating information. What shocked me the most is that she took the time to write it.

When I open the front door, the letter is still on my mind and I see Tyrone sitting on the couch with his face in his hands. Make-up is streaked up and down his face. Adrian and Dayshawn come behind me and close the door.

"Hi, Wayne," Tyrone says pitifully. "Everything cool outside?"

I tuck the letter in my pocket, look at Adrian and Dayshawn and say, "Yeah."

"I'm sorry about last night. I ain't know none of that shit was gonna happen!"

"Before you say anything, Dayshawn and Adrian don't know the facts of last night's events," then I turn to them and say, "Do ya'll wanna know what happened?"

Both nod yes.

"Okay, proceed."

"We handled the situation."

"How?"

"We hid the body."

I sigh and wipe my hands down my face. "Tyrone, I knew it was too much for me to expect that you would do the right thing, and maybe take him to the hospital or somethin'."

"I know you didn't want the cops around here askin' questions again. So I did what I thought was best."

"The key word is...Again!" I yell. "But why is that the second time somebody died in my house? And both times you're the main culprit!"

"Wait...what body?" Dayshawn asks looking at Tyrone and then me.

"Let me start from the beginning, Wayne, because you probably don't understand everything I do either. I learned how to do silicone jobs from Miss P. because I was tryin' to make enough money to get my own place. I was doin' 'em with no problems but my client yesterday had an allergic reaction or somethin' and started spazzin' out, holdin' his chest and shit! Had I known he was allergic, I would never have done that shit!"

"Had you been a doctor you would've known to ask. You can't even fuckin' read, Tyrone! So please tell me how you're up in here doin' surgeries?"

"Hindsight is twenty/twenty, Wayne and for real it ain't shit I can do about it now. All I can tell you is that I never meant for anybody to get hurt."

"I find that funny…because everybody who comes around you gets hurt or killed. Nothing in between."

"What does that mean?" he asks.

"It doesn't even matter anymore. I have a question though, how much were you chargin' people for that silicone shit?" I ask.

"Six hundred for face procedures and 800 for breasts corrections if you already have them."

I was floored. Didn't even realize how much money could be made in that shit.

"Knowing you, you probably don't have any of that money left do you? Because we all know you can't save shit."

"Well I guess ya'll don't know as much as you think you do about me. Because I saved up ten thousand dollars already."

"Really?" I laugh.

"Really," she smiles and then my cell phone rings.

The number is blocked out and I put the handset to my head and say, "It's me…who are you?"

"It's me, Parade…I just wanted to say thank you for being there for me and that I can't wait to see you again. I also want you to know that no matter what happens, you have real family here."

"I know, darling. I'll call you later."

"Okay," she says, nicer than she has in a long time.

"You know what," I say turning around to them, "all of this shit is too much for me. I should have stayed in LA and never came back. And I'm finally realizin' after gettin' off the phone with Parade, someone who actually gives a fuck about me, that this shit is not even worth my time. So...I propose *you all* find another place to live. I just buried my friend and as far as I'm concerned all the shit that's been happenin' up in here, don't even matter anymore."

"What are you saying, Wayne?" Dayshawn asks in a surprised tone.

"I'm sayin' you all have to go by the end of the week...together if you want to, apart if it's better. Either way I don't care."

"Wayne...me too?" Asks Adrian.

"You too. I got a little girl I have to think about now and I'm not takin' care of three faggies no more."

"After all that...in the hotel?" Asks Dayshawn. "After everything we talked about in private?"

"Like I said, I'm sorry." I say walking away from them. "But my life and the life of my family matters more to me than all of you! And since my name is the only one on the lease, I have the luxury of cleaning house, and that's exactly what I'm going to do."

# *New Management*

## ⚜QUEEN DAYSHAWN⚜

Adrian sat on the sofa along with Tyrone and Dayshawn after Miss Wayne gave them a piece of his mind.

"I'm confused," says Adrian. "I mean...I thought everything was okay between the three of us at least. I know he was beefin' with you, Tyrone, but how we get tied up in this shit?"

"It's like he snapped," Dayshawn adds.

"I don't know what to think, but what are we going to do now?" Adrian asks.

"I don't know. What are you goin' to do, Tyrone?" Asks Dayshawn.

"Well I have enough money to get a place of my own, I just need some roommates I can trust."

"You sure you don't really need someone to fill out the rental applications for you? Since you can't read?" Asks Dayshawn.

"That too," he laughs. "But think about it...after this shit blows over, we can make enough money to take care of ourselves because I'm still doin' the injections. It's a lot of money in that shit and I could use the help. We don't even need Wayne no more."

"I feel like I should talk to Wayne first," Says Adrian. "Maybe he's just mad right now but will be better later."

When Tyrone sees he wasn't getting through to them he says, "We can even split the profits three ways."

Now he had their full attention.

"We still need a legal job to qualify to rent an apartment. You know wherever we go they're going to ask us for pay stubs." Dayshawn replies. "I really wish that house didn't burn down. That was a good look for us."

"Wait a minute…isn't Miss Rick renting out another place?" Adrian asks.

"You're right! She do got a spot." Says Dayshawn.

"We can see if she'll rent it out to us. You know she'll be lenient on the paperwork and shit too, just as long as we pay on time."

"I don't know, it's all the way in Laurel, Maryland. You know we don't go that far up the pike on a regular."

"Come on, Day! We don't have a choice." Adrian persists.

"What do you think, Tyrone? You think we can move that far?"

"I just need a place to live." He says although they detect slight hesitation in his voice.

"Let me call Miss Rick now and see if the place is still available."

Grabbing his phone from his pocket, Dayshawn calls. The phone rings four times before he finally answers. He puts the call on speaker.

"What's up, bitch?!" Miss Rick screams. "Where the fuck you been?"

"Nowhere important but everyplace else. You know how it is."

"I hear you."

"I'm calling to see if that place is still available. The one you were renting out in Maryland."

"For now…but if you want it you better move quick. I had five people come look at it today alone. You know I'll keep it for you because you're my peoples but you got to move now."

"Cool...can we make a deposit at the end of the week?"

"I don't think I'll be holding it that long. I need to rent that place sooner than later."

"What happened to us being your peoples?"

"You know how it is. I'm a greedy bitch first. But to be honest, if you really want the place you should come down here today with a five thousand dollar deposit."

Dayshawn laughs and says, "Okay...let me see if the deposit is possible on my end." Dayshawn takes the phone off speaker and says, "You heard him. If we want the house, we got to go down there today to sign the papers and bring the money."

"Good!" Tyrone pauses looking at the slight frown on Dayshawn's face. "What's the problem now?"

"Well, we don't have the money for the deposit...unless you can front us, Tyrone."

"Wait a minute...is this a set up? Are ya'll consipirin' with that bitch back there to take my fuckin' money? It is awfully funny that Ms. Rick doesn't mind renting her house to me when she doesn't bump with me for real."

"Ty, I don't have time for this shit. We 'bout to be homeless! You heard Wayne. Now if you don't want to move with us then that's up to you. I'll just find another place to get the cash. As a matter of fact, let me go back there and ask Wayne now. He wants us out so bad, he's liable to pay us to leave."

Dayshawn walks to the back and Tyrone yells, "Wait! I'll put up the money. But how do I know I can trust ya'll?"

Dayshawn walks back and says, "Tyrone, just because the bitch doesn't want to live with you don't mean she don't wanna get money! Ms. Rick will rent to you as long as the money right and she ain't gotta stay with your ass." Deshawn pauses when he still senses hesitation. "Look…if you think we bullshittin' you let's do this… we'll let you sign the lease alone. That way if we act up, you can put us out. It'll be your world, and we'll just be livin' in it."

"Why would you do that? After all the stuff I've done to ya'll?"

"Did you hear, Miss Wayne? He wants us the fuck out of here, Ty." He pauses. "Now come on! What the fuck are we gonna do? Nair one of us has good credit or a job! This is it."

"Let me go grab my purse." The smirk on his face shows that he loves having full control.

When they get to the house, they were overwhelmed at how beautiful it was. Although the rental was only in Prince Georges County Maryland, it had a large back yard filled with trees and a below level pool. It also had five bedrooms and that meant they would each have a space of their own. After Miss Rick showed them the place, he sat them down in his office and went over the details of the agreement.

"So, do you like it?" He asks.

"It's beautiful!" Says Adrian. "I'm going to hook this place up!"

"You mean *I'm* going to hook this place up. This is my place not ya'lls," Tyrone reminds them like he had all the way to the house. "Ain't shit goin' on in this house unless I approve it."

Adrian lowers his head and looks at Miss Rick and Dayshawn.

"Well since you're the renter, where is my money?" Asks Miss Rick.

"Here you go."

Miss Rick tucks the money into his bra and slides the contract across the table.

"Here is the first contract," Miss Rick says, sneezing several times. "Let me know if you don't like something in the verbiage because we can change it right now."

Tyrone looks at Dayshawn and Adrian for their help. Adrian scans over the paperwork and with an attitude says, "It looks fine to me."

With that, Tyrone places an illegible signature on the only place on the agreement he could comprehend. The blank line.

"Here's another document too. I need you to sign this also." Miss Rick says.

Again he signs. Once he finishes, Miss Rick quickly snatches the documents before Tyrone has a chance to change his mind and his sneezing becomes worse.

"Are you okay?" Asks Adrian.

"Allergies…that's why I'm renting this house. I can't take the trees no more in the spring."

"I'm not tryin' to be rude, but can you hand me my keys *without* touchin' them. I don't want none of that snot on my hands," says Tyrone.

"Uggh! It's just allergies, girl but okay," he says grabbing a napkin and placing the keys in them. "Congratulations home renters!"

Miss Tyrone, Dayshawn and Adrian embrace each other in a hug and leave. They go on and on about how they lucked up on such a good deal.

But when they're gone, Miss Rick picks up the phone to make a call, "I got what you need. So hurry up and come get your half of the money. I got to go pick up my husband at the airport."

"I'm on my way."

# Red Light Special

## ❦MISS WAYNE❧

All of the ladies are in attendance including the ladies who usually help us out at the parties. We're in the living room going over the details of our last event, and this would be one some of us would never forget.

"Okay babies! We have a busy night. The party list is jammed pack and we are sure to make a lot of cash. So…make sure we keep the liquor flowin' and turn up the swag. Any questions?"

"No!" Adrian says. "But too be honest I didn't know you were still going to throw the party this weekend. Considering that you want us gone."

"Well we already had people on the way so the last show must go on. Plus I know you wanna make a little cash before you leave."

"I guess we're ready to go then!" Dayshawn adds.

"What about you, Tyrone? Are you ready to work?" I ask.

He's quiet and the look in his eyes shows he *thinks* he knows something I don't.

"I'm ready as I'm goin' to be but I work at my own pace now. You need to know that tonight, Wayne. You're not the boss of me anymore."

I laugh and say, "Thank the queens on high for small favors." With that I clap my hands together and say, "We have five minutes 'til show time. Chop, chop!"

Twenty minutes after my little speech the house is jammed pack and I am excited. I had a heavy weekend ahead of me because tomorrow is the ball and I'm confident that we're going to kill it. My house members from LA are already in town and were ready to walk the hell out of that ball girl. But instead of staying with me, I put them up in a hotel. A lot of shit popping off tonight so I wanted them as far away from here as possible.

While in the kitchen, someone knocks at the door and I wonder who it is. I look at my watch and walk to the door. Through the peephole, I see Ryan and on impulse, I look behind me to be sure Tyrone isn't near, he isn't. So I open the door.

"Here is what you needed." Ryan says handing me an envelope. "I did everything you asked me to."

"Thanks, Ryan. I appreciate you doing this for me." I say tucking the envelope in my bra like I do everything else.

"It's not a problem." He smiles. "Can I talk to you for a minute?"

"What's up?"

"I kinda want to sit down, and talk. Mind if I come in?"

He's wearing a fresh pair of jeans, a dark blue button down and smells so fuckin' good I want to bite him. The sleeves on his shirt are rolled up exposing his diamond Rolex watch.

"Ryan, I have a house full of people in here. So now is not a good time. But here is the money I owe you. It's all there."

If he takes it, I won't fuck with him at all. And if I do give him the time of the day, it will only be on my terms.

He takes the money and frowns.

*Bitch ass nigga!* I thought.

Then he looks into the house and sees Adrian, Tyrone and Miss Day walking around.

"Every time I come here they're here."

"Why?"

"'Cause you never have no time for me, but you always got time for them."

Not wanting him in my business I say, "They don't live here but they're my friends. I'll leave it at that. But Ryan, I really have to go now."

"Damn! Fuck is wrong with you? I said I was sorry!"

Okay, this bitch is tripping for real. "Look, I forgive you...I really do. But like I said, I'm not interested in you like that. I'm a diva... and divas demand love and respect and you just showed me once again that you don't get it."

As I'm talking to him in the doorway, a man walks up behind him and says, "Is Tyrone here?"

"Yeah...go inside. It's the third door on the right."

When he walks deeper into the house I say, "Alright, Ryan. I'll talk to you later. I need to keep an eye on what's goin' on."

"You know what...I had no idea you could be so fuckin' cold. So what...you don't believe in second chances?"

"Well you won't be hanging around long enough to find out," I say tapping the envelope. Then I slam the door in his fuckin' face.

He can kiss my ass. When I close the door, I swagger my sexiness back inside. By the way he went off, I can tell he's feeling me way more than I could ever feel him. But I'm gonna make him sweat. And then maybe...just maybe, I'll give him another chance to taste this fruit. But he could never make me do shit I don't want to do. Believe that.

# *I Know What You Did Last Night*

## ❦SPECIAL STRANGER❦

"Excuse me…you can't come in here." Says Tyrone to the man entering his room. He was getting ready to entertain the guests Wayne scheduled for him in the living room.

"Oh you can make time for me." The tall handsome man says. Wearing black slacks and a red shirt, he looks more reserved than the men he usually entertained.

"Sir…maybe you not hearin' me. I said you can't be in here right now. I'm waitin' on someone else."

"Who could you be waiting on, Tyrone? Tell me what else could possibly be more important than the man who wants to know what happened to his nephew?"

Silence.

"I…I don't know what you're talkin' about."

"I think you do," he says in an angry voice. "Now take a seat." When he doesn't he says, "I won't ask you nicely again."

Tyrone stops what he's doing looks into the stranger's eyes and sits on the edge of the bed.

"Tyrone, let me not cut corners with you." He starts sitting next to him. "I know everything about you and I also know you have something to do with the reason my sister is going crazy right now. She can't seem to understand why her only child never came home last night. But

I know what happened." When Tyrone appears nervous he says, "But have no fear, I'm not going to tell her anything about you. That is, if you pay me."

"I don't know who you are, but I really think you have the wrong person."

"Okay," he says standing up. "Maybe the police will be more interested in what I have to say."

"Please don't go. I...I want to talk to you."

"I'm glad you finally understand what's going on," he says sitting again. "Now this is what I want...I need five thousand dollars today and five thousand by the end of the week to be quiet. Once I collect the last five, you'll have my complete silence and promise to never bother you again." He smiles slyly. "Deal?"

"I don't have that kind of money."

"Tyrone, stop fuckin' around with me! I know you got the money. I know what you do in here. Don't make me take back my promise and settle for the two thousand dollar reward my family is raising instead. Either way it goes, I'm going to get something out of this."

"O...Okay. Calm down."

"Don't tell me to calm down!"

"Please...I understand now. But can I ask you somethin'?"

"What?"

"How did you find out he was here?" he asks in a low voice.

"He told me he was coming. We were close. *Very* close."

"What you mean?"

"I was the one who sent him to you. He wasn't as feminine as I like my men to be, so I suggested he have the procedure. You know...get larger breasts." He laughs. "At first we went to Miss P but she told me she wasn't doing them no more and gave us your info. It was pretty much as easy as that. I also know that when I ain't hear from him anymore, he must've died here."

"Why would your nephew do something like that for you?"

"To keep me from leaving him. Let's just say he didn't want to be alone. So he did whatever I wanted him too. That boy sure did know how to suck a mean dick."

"You were fuckin' your own nephew?" he says with an evil glare. "You're just like my uncle! A fuckin' user!"

"Think what you want. But give me my money now."

Tyrone frowns at him stands up and says, "Can you get the fuck off my bed please?"

"Sure."

When he does, Tyrone raises the mattress and removes a purple velvet satchel. Then he takes out five thousand dollars and hands it to him. With the money he gave Miss Rick, he was dead broke.

"Thanks." The stranger smiles tucking the money inside his jeans. "Now let me let you get back to work. You have a lot of money to make up before the end of next week. And I don't want any slacking on the job either." He says pointing at him, "Because do or die, you will give me what's owed to me."

# *Long Shanks*

## ❧ANOTHER SPECIAL VISITOR❧

"Tyrone, help me restock the liquor table." Miss Wayne says to Tyrone who is in a slump. Ever since she'd been blackmailed out of her money earlier that night, she wasn't in the mood to do anything else.

Reluctantly, she walks slowly over to the table and assists, Wayne anyway. While there, Adrian rushes toward him with a question.

"Tyrone…can I borrow your whip? I got a kinky trick over there and he's my last one for tonight."

"Yeah…whatever." He says throwing an empty Vodka bottle in the trash, and putting a new one on the table in its place. "It's in my room."

"Is the door locked?"

"No."

"Thanks, Ty!" she says bopping away.

"So what's up with you? You been actin' funny ever since that guy left." Wayne inquires. "Who was he anyway?"

"Nobody you have to worry about."

"I hope not. Because after last night, I don't want no more drama in here when it comes to you." Wayne says throwing another empty bottle in the trash next to the table.

Tyrone rolls his eyes when Wayne isn't looking and asks, "Wayne…I need a favor. I'm in a bind."

"And what is this favor you're askin' me for?" Wayne asks in a suspicious tone. "'Cause you ain't got no more favors comin' your way from me no time soon."

"I know I shouldn't be askin' you, but this is serious. I really need your help or we all may be in trouble."

Wayne turns to look at her and says, "*We* all will be in trouble? Why do I get the impression that whenever you say *we*, you really mean *you*?"

"Wayne, I don't got time for all this shit...all I know is that I need to borrow five thousand dollars. You got me or what?"

Wayne laughs so hard his stomach aches. Placing his hand on her back he says, "I can tell you right now that that's not even happenin', and I know you know that."

Pissed, and not sure what to do next, He storms away.

"Tyrone...come back." Wayne says. "I'll make a deal with you."

Tyrone walks back and says, "Anyway you can help me will be greatly appreciated."

"Entertain the last customer over there, and I'll give you twenty percent of tonight's cut. The rest of the girls are beat and he's the only one left."

"20 percent?" he repeats. "Are you serious?"

"You heard me right."

Tyrone looks at the thug trade sitting on the sofa and says, "Make me a drink and I'll do it."

Immediately Tyrone knew something was different about the last trade. Although he was a thug, his eyebrows were slightly arched and he could tell he got his nails done on regular. Wearing a pair of Rock and Republic jeans, a white t-shirt and white Louis Vuitton shoes, Tyrone smelled nothin' but money.

Walking over to the trade Tyrone says, "I'm Sweet Ty, please come with me."

When they get to his bedroom door, Adrian walks out with the whip he asked to borrow in his hand. "Thanks, Ty. I'll bring it back when I'm done."

When Adrian leaves, they walk inside Tyrone's room and he nonchalantly asks, "So what are you lookin' for tonight? Are you a top or bottom?"

"Right now I just want some conversation and we'll see where the night leads us."

This irritated Tyrone because he wasn't feeling the romance scenario. He wanted to fuck this nigga and come up on twenty percent of Wayne's profits, nothing more, nothing less. Now he was realizing he'd have to put in more work than he planned.

"So what do you want to talk about?" Tyrone sighs.

"I'm not sure. I mean, it depends."

The more Tyrone looked into his face, the more he believed he seemed out of place. He could easily see him dressing in drag. Not only that, he didn't look like he was from anywhere near D.C.

"What does it depend on?"

"On how versed you are."

Tyrone rolls his eyes and says, "Look, are we fuckin' or not? I'm not tryin' to hear all that college talk and shit."

"I already told you what I want…conversation. And if you can't give it to me, then maybe somebody else will. I will tell you this though, I had plans to tip real good."

Realizing he was about to lose his cut of the profits and a tip he says, "If you ask, me there isn't a whole lot to say. You like men and I am one. You want to have fun and I want to please you."

"Here's your drink, Ty," Adrian says walking into the room.

"What?"

"I'm sorry, I didn't mean to interrupt but Wayne told me you asked for a drink earlier. So here it is."

"Oh…yeah…thanks." Tyrone downs the tall glass of his favorite poison, Vodka and OJ mixed, and says, "So let's speed this up a little. I have some other things going on tonight."

"Fine…so let me start then," the stranger smiles. "I finally figured out what I want to talk about."

"And what's that?"

"I want to talk about how I've been waiting for you all night." He says smiling into his eyes. "And that I asked for you by name."

"Oh really? And why is that?"

"Because somebody out there is playing matchmaker. They happen to believe that you're a perfect fit for me. What do you think about that?"

Tyrone yawns and says, "We won't know unless we get this over with."

"I'm serious…they think you and I deserve each other."

"You must really be confused now." Tyrone swallows the rest of the liquor in the glass. "Because ain't nobody out there looking out for me or you."

"Then you don't know your friends very well. Anytime Wayne brings me all the way from LA, to put in work for him, I take it that the offense is warranted."

Tyrone eyes widen and he tries to move…but suddenly his arms and legs feel limp and he knows immediately that he'd been drugged. He was familiar because of all those times his uncle would drug him to use his body for sexual pleasures.

"What are you going to do to me?" Tyrone tries to move again but it doesn't work.

Without answering, the stranger cocks back and steals Tyrone in the face so hard he passes out cold.

◆ •••••••••••••••••••••••••••••••••••••••••••••••••••• ◆

## *An Hour Later*

When Tyrone awakens, he is hog tied to the bed, lying on his stomach, naked from the waist down. When he looks around, he's able to see a table full of items that scare the hell out of him. On top of the table were five dildos as long as the length of a forearm and a box of saltine crackers.

"Can...can you please tell me why you're doing this?" Tyrone moans.

"Great! You're up! I need you awake for what I have planned for you. I was thinkin' to myself, SELF, there is no way on earth we're going to allow him to sleep through the party." He says, his voice more feminine than before. Tyrone knew immediately that he was a queen.

"Wayne!!!! Adrian!!!!!! Help me!!!!" Tyrone screams.

He waits for a second and no one comes to the rescue.

"Awe come on...you're being ungrateful and I didn't even start yet. Relax because we're going to be together for a while. And trust me when I say, even if someone was here, they wouldn't come to your rescue."

"What is this about?"

"Well, for starters you raped our house mother, Wayne. Didn't you, Tyrone?"

*How could he know that shit?* Tyrone thought. He never told anybody about that night and he felt if Wayne remembered, that he would have said something to him a long time ago.

"What are you talkin' about? I didn't rape anybody."

"Let me tell you how this is going to go down…you can be honest and take two of these up the ass ten times each or I can put all five in your ass until I get tired. Your call."

"Please," Tyrone sobs. "Don't do this to me. I didn't do anything to Wayne!"

"I'm going to ask you one last time, and you better think carefully, did you rape my house mother, Wayne?" This time he picked up one of the dildos and shook it a little…he wanted him to see that it barely moved.

"Can you call Wayne first? Maybe we can talk about this and clear things up."

"Bitch, I'm done playin' games with you! Now you're wastin' fuckin' time and I hate my time wasted! Answer my question!"

Tyrone knows now that everything that happened earlier that night was a set up. From Wayne saying that one trade was left, to Adrian coming into his room to borrow a whip.

"So Wayne put somethin' in my drink?"

"What do you think?" the stranger laughs. "Let's just say that it's the same shit you've put in everybody else's drink. Adrian's included." He smiles. "What kind of man are you? To rape mothafuckas?"

She knew then that there was nothing else he could do but come clean about everything.

"I…I did it, rape Wayne." He says with optimism. "But I thought he wanted it at first. I didn't know he was too high to remember."

"You are the worse human being I've ever met in my life," the stranger says, "next to me."

When the stranger walks up to him, and stuffs five saltine crackers in his mouth, he waits for him to chew them all. After he's done, he stuff five more down his throat."

"P...Please, can I have some water."

The stranger laughs and says, "People in hell want water, but they don't always get what they want do they? I wonder how many people wanted you *not* rape them? Yet you did anyway." Then he takes a dildo off the table and puts it in Tyrone's hand. "Touch this. I want you to see that this shit ain't hardly rubber."

He touches it and says, "Why does it feel gritty and hard?"

"Because it's gonna rip your ass in two. Unless," he pauses, "we have some KY Jelly over here on this table." He scans his table. "That way it'll go in smoother because I know you would like that wouldn't you?"

Tyrone looks at the table and cries harder. "But you ain't got nothin' over there do you?"

"Awe damn," he jokes, "I sure don't. But you know what, we can use spit. Every little bit helps."

"But my mouth is dry because of the crackers you made me eat."

"All I can say is, the wetter it is, the less damage to your ass hole. You make the call."

"Somebody help me!!!!"

"You tried screaming already." He laughs. "Now do you wanna lick this...or are you gonna be hard and take the tough route?"

"Fuck you!"

"That's what I'm about to do," he says parting his ass cheeks before ramming the extra large dildo in his ass with extreme force.

Tyrone felt all kinds of cramps in his lower stomach and he didn't know how much longer he'd be able to take the pain.

"Ahhhhh!!!!" The roughness of it going in and out of his anus causes it to bleed heavily. "Please...please stop."

"We have a long way to go before we even get to stop, buddy," he tells him. "You're in for the long haul. I want you to remember this, in case you decide to rape anybody else in the near future."

Over and over the stranger raped and tortured Tyrone until he got tired. By the end of the night, he had caused so much damage that his anus was ripped three inches wider. After awhile, Tyrone didn't feel the pain anymore. And a little after that, he passed out cold.

# *Hospital Break*

## ☙MISS WAYNE❧

Miss Tyrone was lying in a hospital bed suffering from severe anal fissures and incontinence.

As I look at her, with her ass up in the air, as she's lying face down in some type of gurney due to the stitches in her rear end, I wonder why I don't feel remorse. A machine linked to her body catches every heartbeat, and I can't help but feel pleased. He's an awful person and awful people deserve to be dealt with violently. Plain and simple.

So why did I call the ambulance when I came home and saw the work Romeo, my daughter from the House of Dreams in LA, put in? Because I didn't want him bleeding to death in my house. Two deaths were plenty.

When his eyes open slowly, he look confused when he sees me there, wiggling my black Christian louboutins pumps while eating a fresh apple.

"What are you doin' here?" he says so low I can barely hear him.

"Well let's see, you've already met the ghosts of evils past and present. And I represent the ghost of evils yet to come." I laugh.

"What are you talkin' about?" He coughs.

"All the shit you've done has caught up with your ass…literally."

"I can't believe you did somethin' like this to me, Wayne. We were supposed to be friends."

"Really? Is that what you call it? Because what I remember is an event in which my fake ass friend raped me after puttin' some shit in my drink."

He laughs and says, "You know what, I'm through lyin', so I wouldn't take a mothafuckin' thing back I did to you. Your ass was nice, soft and wet, just like Adrian's."

"Were you really raped as a child? Because it's obvious that somethin' fucked up happened to your sick ass."

"And what about you, Wayne? You don't think this shit you did to me qualifies as sick? You gonna get everything you deserve too…watch. You and me are the same, 'cept you like to hide behind the word *hero*. But I'm not gonna let you. You're just as fucked up as me."

"I did the world a favor! You're sick, Tyrone."

"Maybe. But maybe not." He smiles. "Let's think about it for a moment, I take what I want like the people around me have always done to me. Does that make me really wrong?"

"Worse than wrong, rapist!"

"All I know is, when I get out of here, I'm comin' after you, Adrian and whoever that was who did this shit me. Oh…and your precious little Parade is on my list too," he laughs. "You'll wish you never fucked with me after I get through with her."

"Number one you ain't goin' nowhere and number two you ain't doin' shit even if you could."

"And why is that?"

"Because I know about the murders, Tyrone. Notice there's an S at the end of the word."

"Who are you talking about? That stupid ass kid who died in *your* house? Because if it's that, I might as well tell you that I called Garisha and told him to let a detective know that *you* were the one who killed that boy not me. You're a day late and a dollar short if you think about snitchin'," he laughs.

"You are so stupid! Garisha sold you out for her own ugly freedom. She's gonna testify under oath that you and you alone did them procedures in my house, without my knowing and that you even did her face recently causing her disfigurement."

"Bullshit! Garisha is my friend."

"Tyrone, how can you expect loyalty when you've never given it?"

"I don't believe you."

"Well it's true...and as far as being short or late...never. Especially after the five thousand dollars you gave me."

"What you talkin' about, Wayne?"

"Why do you think I asked you how much money you made from those injections?"

Silence.

"Because I was plottin' on how much to take. And when you thought you were giving Miss Rick a security deposit, it was really going straight to me. And to make sure you were broke and busted, I sent a fake ass uncle to check you about the nephew you murdered. After splitting the money in half with everybody involved, I'm still up about five thousand. Thanks, Ty."

The look on his face was priceless.

"So what bitch...you actually makin' me feel better now."

"And how is that?"

"Because now I don't have to worry about lookin' over my shoulders wonderin' if his uncle will snitch on me or not. In my opinion, the ten thousand dollars I gave ya'll to leave me the fuck alone was worth it."

"Oh I'm sorry...I forgot to tell you about the signed confessions you gave me."

"I didn't confess to shit."

"Tyrone, you not smarter than me and you could never be. I set shit up to perfection. When you signed them papers Miss Rick gave you, they weren't for a lease, you were signing two confessions to murders."

"Wayne, stop playin', 'Cause for real, I'm payin' you no mind. Plus Miss Adrian ain't say shit when I asked her if the paperwork was good."

"Bitch I know you know by now that Aid and Day are in on all this shit with me. That little fight we had in the living room was all staged. Think about last night. Who gave you the liquor?" I laugh. "And as far as the murders, let's see. For starters you murdered that kid you injected with that bullshit. Oh…and then there are the keys I found under your bed."

"What keys?"

"The keys that must've fallen out of his pocket when he died. I remember when I walked into the bedroom and saw them on the floor, I knew they would come in handy later and I was right. So I kicked them under your bed and came back later to get them."

"So what you have the keys."

"Tyrone, we wiped my fingerprints off those keys and gave them to you the day you signed the lease. I know you remember asking Miss Rick to pass them over in a napkin, since you hate snot so much." I laugh. "Now the only prints on them keys are yours. I took them out of your room right before I called the ambulance for you last night."

Silence.

"Wow, Tyrone, I haven't heard you this quiet in a minute. So let me continue to burst your bubble. Ryan followed you the night of the murder and took pictures of you disposing the body in a park in Baltimore. What was it? Druid Hill Park? I gotta give it to you though…you and Garisha went pretty far to hide your shit.

"So let's see…I have the boy's keys with your prints on them, pictures of you disposing of a body and two signed confessions. You know what, Miss Tyrone…you're federally fucked. "

Tears were streaming down his face and I could care less. He wipes them away and says, "Why do you keep saying two signed confessions?"

"Because I know, Tyrone. I know about the man you burned alive in the alley when you were younger too. And how you did it just to have fun."

"That wasn't me, bitch! That was Miss Dayshawn! You ain't 'bout to pin none of that shit on me!"

"Yes the fuck I am too! One of the two confessions you signed admitted to all that shit. And it's our word against a sneaky murderer, who hid the body of a child as if he were trash. Who do you think they gonna believe?"

"Wayne," he pauses, "please don't do this to me. I'll do anything you want. I'll move out and you'll never see me again. Please, Wayne."

"All that's too late," I say, "But I did forget one last thing…Big Boody Brandy wrote me a letter before she died." I dig in my purse and pull it out. "Now I also know about the football player you and Garisha were last seen with before he got missing. And if you don't cop to them other murders, and let shit ride, I'll add this to the rest of your problems too," I say, "You hung yourself fuckin' wit' me. So tell me again Tyrone, was my ass really worth it?" I say getting up.

"Wayne please."

"You're through…Tyrone. It's over for you. I'm not hatin', I'm just statin'."

As I'm leaving, an officer walks in to formally read him his rights and Ryan calls for the third time that day.

But now I'm feeling good and for some reason I accept his offer for lunch and agree to a cup of coffee. After all, he has earned it.

# *Ball*

## MISS WAYNE

The ball was off the hook! I worked the hell out of my walk and my gown stunned everybody. Finally, after so many years, I was awarded the category I always deserved! I'm finally legendary bitches!

After I accepted my crown and check, I hug Adrian and Dayshawn. We're jumping up and down like I just won Prom Queen!

"You did it, Miss Wayne! You finally did it!" Miss Adrian says.

I'm on cloud nine and couldn't believe we also won the 'Best House' category thanks to my LA chapter. Those queens came out here and killed the walk, bitch! Do you hear me? They worked it! Twerked it and twisted it in so many ways, I wonder if they still got bones. Miss Dayshawn and Adrian did their thing too and together we showed that the House of Dreams is here to stay!

In my excitement, I was really surprised when Queen Ocean walked up to me to give her congratulations. "Congrats, diva! You killed it." She gave me one air kiss on each side of my face.

"Thank you honey," I say giving him the fake hug we passed out so many times *just because* at these balls. "The House of Diamonds represented too."

"That may be true but the real diva and the real house won. I never saw you walk like that before…you really did burn down the competition, me included."

When I look into his eyes, I know he's serious.

"I appreciate it, Ocean. I thank you for the letter too, that shit came in handy."

"To tell you the truth I don't even know what it says...I didn't open it, out of respect for Big Boody."

I smile and I say, "Well take care. Let me go celebrate with my girls. You know how it is, the party's really just beginning."

When Ocean left, I couldn't get over how much respect I was getting from the other houses. It was very surprising. Because trust me when I say fights usually break out quicker than pimples on a teenagers face at these things. It can get real ugly and queens have been murdered fucking around in the ball circuit.

As I get myself together preparing to leave, I smile when I see Miss Dayshawn walking toward me with Adrian directly behind him.

"We're on our way to the after party at the Embassy Suites in DC. You going right?" Miss Day asks.

"Yeah, but I'ma stop by the house first. I gotta change clothes."

"Wear what you have on."

"Naw...I wanna be comfortable."

"Okay..." he says looking at me longer than usual. "I just want to say, thank you for taking that murder shit off my hands. I can't tell you how much happier I am now that I don't have to worry about it. What did you do to get Tyrone to take the rap?"

I never told Miss Dayshawn about the football player or what was in the letter Brandy gave me. Some things a girl has to keep to herself.

I look around me and say, "Remember when I said don't bring that shit up ever again, I mean it Day. It's over and you were never there as far as we're concerned."

I can't lie; he's making me mad a little. He's talking more about the murder than he did before I knew about it. I wish he just dropped it.

"You're right...but thank you again." He says hugging me. "I'm gonna repay you for this shit one day watch. You'll see."

"Bye, Day!"

Adrian walks up to me and hugs me one last time before yelling at Dayshawn, "Let's go! I want to shake me chi-chi-ka-ka tonight honey! Chris is meeting me there too and I can't wait to get some dick finally."

"I'm glad to see ya'll back together...go head. I'll meet you there."

I'm still smiling until I see the handsome face of the next person who embraces me. In fact, I believe I feel my heart flutter.

"I know I should have asked first...but can I get a hug too?"

He was someone I hadn't seen in a long time...Mr. Officer D. Hurts. Back in the day, he was investigating the murder of a girl my best friend Sky killed at this party we all went to. Me and the officer had a thing on the side, fucked a few times and even grabbed a few bites to eat...but in the end, the flames died. To tell you the truth, I can't remember which one of us caused the split. It could've been me because after Sky's murder, I was depressed. Or maybe he had a wife or a girlfriend! Who knows...and better yet...who cares?! He's here in front of me right now looking like a million bucks and that's all that mattered.

"Wayne...damn you look sexy. How have you been, baby?"

"I'm good," I smile happy he saw me on the most beautiful night of my life. Honey the face is beat, my gown is stunning and thanks to Adrian keeping the drinks flowing, I feel on top of the world.

"Well I think you are better than good. But that's just my opinion."

I blush. "What are you doing here? Mr. Officer D. Hurts."

"I'm doing security for the event. Basically making a little money on the side. It's tough livin' on a cop's salary alone."

Aww shit. This nigga's broke and that's my cue to not even be bothered. Gone are the days in which I take care of a grown ass man.

"So I started my own security company." He continues. "And we've been pretty successful ever since. It's just a matter of time before I leave the police department to run my business full time."

Scratch that…he's got it goin' on and I love it.

"Well, you look good too," I say observing the black slacks he wore with his powder blue v-neck cashmere sweater. "I'm glad to see you didn't let yourself go."

"Thanks, beautiful. But I could say the same about you."

I blush.

The chemistry between us is on crazy and I haven't felt this way in a long time.

"Look, what are you about to do? I mean, you mind if I take you to get a bite to eat? That is if you don't have plans with anyone else." He pauses and says, "Fuck that…I know somethin' as fine as you not goin' home alone tonight. So cancel plans with him and get with me. Cool?"

Up until that moment I forgot all about Ryan. You see, we were supposed to hook up at the after party. Now all I'm thinking is…FUCK RYAN!

"You're right, I don't have any plans I can't change," I say. "But let me step to the side and make a quick phone call."

"I'll be waiting over there," he says touching the small of my back. "But don't keep me waiting too long."

He did it! The one thing I love a man to do and he did it. I quickly dial Ryan's number. "Ryan...where are you?" I ask hearing a bunch of noise in the background.

"Waiting on you. You ready to come celebrate with me? I heard you won the ball and before you say anything, I'm sorry I couldn't make it."

*It figures.* I thought.

"Actually I'm calling to tell you I can't see you tonight. I'm kinda tired and want to go home and rest. I'm sorry."

"Why...is everything okay?" He asks angrily. "Is it something I did?"

"No...just tired with everything that has been goin' on in my life lately. You know how it is."

"Well let me come over to take care of you. Cook you some dinner or somethin'."

"Ryan...I can't. Okay? I'll call you later."

"Well...I guess I'll get up with you later then." I hit the end button so quickly I forget who I was even talking to.

"I'm ready," I say to Officer D. Hurts. Damn do I love a man in a uniform. "You don't mind me wearing this for the rest of the night do you? I have my coat in my car if you don't want people knowin' you hangin' out with a drag queen."

"To me you couldn't be more sexy. Just the way that you are," he continues.

I didn't think it was possible for me to have more fun than I already had tonight. What a perfect ending to an amazing night. For some reason I think that it will be a night that I will never forget.

◆ ⋯⋯⋯⋯⋯⋯⋯⋯⋯⋯⋯⋯⋯⋯ ◆

# *Across The Room*

Wayne unknowingly walks out of the ball and past Ryan who is standing in the corner with a bouquet of flowers. His feelings were beyond hurt when he saw him leave with another man. To say he was enraged was an understatement. Ryan didn't want Wayne to know that he'd seen the entire ball and wanted to surprise him. Now it looked as if he would never get his chance to show him how much he cared.

"Well hello there," a queen says walking up to Ryan, who turned around to see Wayne all hugged up on Officer D. Hurts. "Are those flowers for me?"

Ryan staring at the Wayne doesn't hear the queen at first.

"I said are those for me?" The queen persists.

"What?!" he screams looking at the pretty drag queen for the first time.

"Oooo, a rude boy? You just my type. Mean and fine!"

When he says that, Ryan cocks his fist back and steals him in the face so hard, he passes out.

"Fuckin' faggots! Love playing games!" he says rubbing his knuckles. He throws the flowers on him and spits in his face. "You lucky I don't take you out of here and gag you wit' my dick like I do the rest of 'em. Consider yourself lucky."

Ryan didn't care if anyone saw him. He had one thing on his mind, making Wayne pay for hurting his feelings. And he wouldn't stop until he had done just that.

# *Attempted Murder*

## ⊛MISS WAYNE⊛

When I got home, it was about 3:00 in the morning and the house was completely empty. Tyrone was in the hospital and Adrian and Day were at the after party so I was all alone.

And all I could think was that I never felt more attractive than I did with Officer D. Hurts. In my entire life. He took me to dinner, sexed me in the car, took me to eat again and kissed me passionately for ten minutes before I left him. If you had been a fly on the window, you would've thought we were lovers all our lives. I hadn't even made it to my room before he was calling my phone.

"You safe?" Officer D. Hurts asks when I walk into the house. The living room is still dark and I flop on my couch.

"Why...you gonna come save me or somethin'?"

"I want to do more than just save you, Wayne. I'm ready to be serious about you. Only when you're ready though."

I laugh. "We'll see how you act in the morning. I know how you guys are at night when passion runs deep."

"The morning? I already fucked that pretty ass of yours and I'm still saying the same thing I said in your ear. I want you to be mine. I'm tired of fuckin' around with you."

My stomach flutters again and I wish he stops driving me crazy.

"Well you keep treatin' me the way that you did tonight and we'll see."

"I can show you better than I can tell you," he says.

"I don't know about all that, Officer. But I do know I'm about to get in bed. Call me tomorrow?"

"No doubt. And make sure you're thinking of me while you're resting that pretty little head of yours."

"I will."

"Bye, beautiful."

When I walk into the hallway, I lean against the wall with the phone pressed to my chest. I swear I feel like a teenage girl right now. That man thrills me!

I was just about to turn my cell phone off, when I see a voicemail from an unknown caller. The time shows that the call came in when I was at the ball so I see how I missed it. Still, I was curious so I hit the playback button.

*"Mr. Peterson, I really needed you to answer the phone tonight. First off I want to thank you for your help in the case of Juan Anders. His family is indebted to you. However, when we finally got the warrant to exhume the body at the location given to us in Baltimore, the body wasn't there. Now I hate to involve you in this case again but since Tyrone isn't talking or even willing to help, we need you. Please call me or Officer Adesene soon as possible. You have my number."*

When I hang up, for some reason I feel eerie and bumps rise on the back of my neck. Thinking my uncomfortable feeling was because of the call, I walk deeper into my dark house. And when I enter my room, I hear an inner voice. I know it's crazy but I swear it sounded like Miss Daffany saying, *'Please leave, Miss Wayne! Leave now! You're not safe here.'*

*"Girl, relax!"* I say to myself.

"I'm sure there's a perfectly good reason why the body wasn't where it should've been. And in the morning I can help them find out why."

When I first came home I was still going to the after party at the Embassy Suites. But I decide against it because I'm drained. Instead, I get into bed without washing up, something I never do.

"Don't worry, Wayne, you'll take a nice long bath first thing in the morning." I say.

I'm under the covers for five minutes before I remember all the nasty things I did tonight. And how Officer D. Hurts bent me over the edge of the car, and pumped himself in and out of my warm, waiting body. Then I think about how I dropped to my knees and sucked his dick dry.

So I hop out of bed, take my clothes off and take a nice long bath. I'm a freak but I'm not trying to sleep in my shame either. When I'm clean, I slide into a white teddy with matching silk panties. Once under the covers, I feel something cold and hairy next to my leg. Pushing the covers off my body, I gasp when I see the decapitated head of the boy who had died in my house earlier that the week.

"Ahhhhhhhh!" I scream jumping out of bed.

Then I see Ryan walk through my bedroom door, his white t-shirt covered in brown dirt. His eyes are bugged out and he looks like a zombie. When he runs up to me and places his entire weight on my body, he knocks me to the floor. I try my hardest to fight him off but he's overpowering me, and considering how strong I am, this is no easy feat.

"What are you doing?!" I scream hitting him wildly. "Why are you in my fuckin' house?!"

"Shut up you fuckin' tease!" he says stealing me in my throat so hard, I'm no longer able to make a sound.

"You wanna play games with me, huh?" He asks pulling my hair and throwing me on the only chair in my room. On some sort of sick ass mission, he ties my arms and legs to the body of the chair. "After all the shit I did for you...you give somebody else what belongs to me. This is why I can't stand fuckin' faggies! You play too many games!"

He rips my satin nightgown off, pushes my panties to the side and rams four fingers in my ass. My legs tense up and sweat pours down my face. For some reason, I wonder if this is how Tyrone felt when I sent someone to take care of him. I guess I should've thought about how I treated people, good, bad or indifferent before I dished it out.

"You fuckin' whore!" he continues ramming his fingers in and out of my body. Fingernails scrapping my inside. Nervous and scared, I partially release my bowels and feces cover his hands. Crazed and insane, he licks the shit off his fingers and stares at me wildly.

"You had him inside of you, didn't you? I can taste him." When I don't speak he says, "Answer the fuckin' question!"

Again I try to speak, but soon realize he may have crushed my windpipe from when he hit me the first time. I only pray that I will be able to continue to breathe. Feeling my breaths go shallow, I inhale and exhale very slowly while trying my damndest to remain calm.

"Why you make me add you to the list of faggies I hate huh?" he asks walking around the chair. "Why you make me do this to you even though I didn't want to?"

"Please don't kill me," I mouth, no sound leaving my lips. "Please."

Tears run down my face and he uses his soiled hand to wipe them away. I smell my own bowel on my face and I feel nauseous.

Reaching behind his back, he removes a metal ball hooked to a strap from his pants then jams it into my mouth, shattering a few of my teeth. I immediately piss myself.

"You're not going to believe the things I'm going to do to you. First I'm going to fuck you like I know you want to be fucked. Then I'm going to decide if I'm gonna keep you around as my slave or kill you like I did the others. They gave me the name the Drag Queen Slayer, when I should've been called Justice Slayer. I think that would have been a better fit don't you?"

Oh my, God! He's the person who's been running around murdering gay men. It wasn't Queen Paul after all. They arrested the wrong man for some shit he did.

"Look at your thick pretty legs…I wonder how they'll taste if I eat them."

I never imagined this happening. I don't want to die like this…not when I have so much to live for. My mind races and I look up at the ceiling so I won't have to see the horror in his eyes in my last minutes alive.

When out of nowhere, he hits me in the face so hard, blood fills my mouth and I start choking. Trying to breathe, I swallow my blood and choke wildly.

"What the fuck were you just thinking about when you were looking up there? Are you trying to hatch some fuckin' plan to escape? Don't fuck with me, Wayne! You got a better chance of doing what I tell you to do and living, than anything else."

I start coughing and he pulls the ball from my mouth to allow the blood to pour out. I bend down and cough harder to clear my throat. When he the thinks I'm fine, he slams the ball back into my mouth shattering more of my teeth.

"Now I can't have you dying on me now can I? I need you to stay around, Wayne. Don't you want to stay with me?"

Tears run down my face but I know they are useless. The only thing I can do is make peace with my fate. And for some reason, when I close my eyes, I see Miss Daffany and Miss Sky smiling at me. They are waiting on me and I feel a sense of peace knowing that I have angels waiting in heaven. I guess I'm not alone even in my darkest hour after all.

"It's okay, Miss Wayne. Everything is okay." Says Miss Daffany.

"We love you and want you to know that everything will work out at the right time." Says Sky. "Trust in God and remember your faith."

The moment she says that, I'm struck over the head with an iron baseball bat.

◆ • • • • • • • • • • • • • • • • • • • • • • • • • • • • • • • • ◆

## *Two Hours Later*

When I come back to consciousness, I see that he placed the dead boy's head on my bedroom dresser, his body on the floor directly below it. I close my eyes and cry silently.

Lying flat on my stomach and I can feel Ryan behind me pounding in and out of my body. And the panties I slipped into after my bath, which are covered in feces, sit next to my face. The leather strap, which is connected to the ball in my mouth is so tightly bound, it burns my skin.

"You feel so good," Ryan says. "Just like I like it.

In that moment mentally, I go somewhere else. I remember the time my mama bought my first pair of heels and I think about not being able to see her before she dies. After that I think about being with my friends on the steps when we were kids and how close we were. What I wouldn't give to go back to those days.

"Uhhhhh," Ryan moans loudly into my ear as he raises himself up off my body, and releases warm sperm onto my back. Then he turns me over, looks at my battered face and jerks himself into another thickness. I know now that he gets off on the pain and conquest more than anything else. "You look beautiful. Just like I like 'em. You wanna taste it don't you, Wayne? You wanna suck my dick?"

I turn my head to the side and he turns it back.

"Look at you...even now you still want me. After all this shit I did to you, you still want to be with me don't you? You like to be beat. Yeah I know it...that's how all you faggies are and if I'm ever caught I'm gonna tell them the same thing."

When he's hard again, he removes the ball from my mouth and rams his dick in and out my throat. I want to bite him but all of my teeth in my mouth are gone. When he cums again, he turns me over and starts all over fucking me again...this continues for more than two hours. And when he's had his fill, he gets up and says, "I'm gonna make us somethin' to eat, baby. You hungry?"

The tone he uses sounds like it did when I first met him. It was as if nothing terrorizing just happened.

I nod yes.

When he disappears into the kitchen I try to move. And then I realize my right arm is broken or dislocated because I can't move my fingers. I try again to move...and nothing.

That's when I give up.

I let go.

I accept my fate and pray it will all be over soon.

The moment I surrender all, I hear my mother.

*"You're strong, Wayne. You can do anything in Christ who strengthens you."*

Then I think about Shantay, Miss Parade and not being able to say goodbye to any of them. So I force myself to move until I'm out of the bed and on my feet. Since my ankles are tied, I hop toward the bedroom door and I can hear him moving pots and pans in the kitchen.

I knew then that one of two things were going to happen …either he was going to kill me or I was going to leave with my life. Nothing in between. One thing was certain, I wasn't going to allow him to rape me any longer.

Moving slowly into the hallway…I hop as lightly as I can toward the front door so I don't make a sound. My heart races when I see I'm only ten feet away from escaping. So I hop faster, making more noise than I wanted to now.

When I reach the front door, I turn around so that my left hand, which is still tied behind my back, is on the doorknob. I turn the knob slightly but realize the lock, which is further up on the door, prevents me from opening it up. So I turn around, put my mouth on the lock and twist it. It's open. When I turn back around to turn the knob Ryan is standing there, looking at me. He hits me in the face so hard I fall to the ground like I had so many times that day. This is it babies. It's over for me. I'm dead I just know it

"I see you gonna make me kill you earlier than I wanted to." He says staring down at me. "I shoulda killed your ass after you acted up at the airport. I wanted to! But I'm not gonna make the same mistake and let you live again."

When I hit the floor, I keep my gaze on the sunlight that is shining through the window next to the front door. And then I see two figures coming through the door. Am I seeing things? Am I losing my mind?

As he drags me by my hair toward the bedroom, I believe I see Adrian and Dayshawn walk in the house. On a mission, Ryan pays no attention to the door opening. But I see their faces as they gasp quietly and cover their mouths in horror.

For some reason I think back to the question Ryan asked me earlier in the week. He wanted to know if I lived by myself.

That little lie may very well be the same lie to save my life.

Maybe.

# The Eyes of a Madman

## QUEEN DAYSHAWN AND ADRIAN

After a long night of partying, Adrian and Dayshawn finally made it home to find Wayne being drug by his hair at the hands of Ryan. At first they thought it was some kind of freaky sex game until they saw Wayne's blood splattered alongside the door. Quickly, Dayshawn walks back out the front door, pushing Adrian back outside with him. The nickname he earned as sneaky Dayshawn came in handy once again.

"Oh my God," Adrian whispers. "Did you see that shit? What's goin' on?"

"I don't know, Aid," Dayshawn whispers. "But you go call the cops. I'm going to go help him."

"No! He'll kill you!" He says loudly.

"Look, stop bein' so fuckin' loud!" Dayshawn mutters heavily. "Now, I'm not leaving Wayne in there by himself. Now go call the fuckin' cops, Aid and stop bein' cunt! I'll be fine!"

Dayshawn carefully reopens the front door and enters the house slowly. Grabbing the bat they call the 'The Long Arm Of the Law', which sits in the corner, he creeps toward Wayne's room.

Ryan, believing Wayne when he told him he lived alone, was not counting on anyone catching him for the

first time ever in the act of a crime. For real he believed
he was going to get away with all of the crimes after
Queen Paul was arrested. After all, who knew Paul would
kill Big Boody in the same fashion Ryan would commit a
murder?

Sure Ryan didn't want the shoddy work Paul did on
Ryan to be classified as his own. In the end Paul leaving
his fingerprints at the scene made everyone believe he
was the Drag Queen Slayer. No one knew that if he got
away with murder, that he had plans to kill Tyrone, Dayshawn and Wayne in same fashion. Given the sick gift
Paul had given him, Ryan made a promise to never kill
again, but in the end he couldn't fight his own sick desire
to conquer and murder.

In the bedroom, Ryan releases Wayne's hair and allows him to fall back to the floor. Then he hits him so
hard in the face with a porcelain blue flowerpot, that he
passes out cold again. Blue pieces shatter everywhere
throughout the room.

Ryan steps back and takes a look at what he'd done,
knowing all the while that he wasn't hardly finished. But
the moment he turns around, Dayshawn hits him so hard
with the bat that the flesh on his forehead splits wide
open. So much blood leaves his body that when it spills
out, it's hard to tell if it's Ryan's or Wayne's.

Ryan falls back on the floor and jumps up to lunge at
Dayshawn. But Day knew what he was fighting for...life
or death. There was no way he was going to give up that
easy, knowing he could be laying on the floor next to
Wayne if he gave up.

Seeing the condition Wayne was in, Dayshawn held
on to the bat tighter than Sammy Sosa and hit him in the
head again. There was no getting up from that. Even after
Ryan's body dropped and remained motionless on the

floor, Dayshawn gave him ten more blows to the face for safety's sake.

For whatever reason, he gets confused and spins around the room. The grim condition shocks him. And when he sees the boy's head and body he screams, "Oh, my God! What the fuck is goin' on around here!" Mommy! I want my mommy!"

It took everything in him to calm down and tend to Wayne.

When Dayshawn was sure Ryan was either knocked out or dead, he walks over to his friend who was near death.

Dropping the bat to the floor he says, "Wayne...can you hear me?"

Police sirens blare in the background.

"Please, Wayne! Talk to me."

Lifting his head slightly, Wayne tried to pull his bloody pasted eyes open. When he realized he couldn't, he drops his head back on the floor as the smell of feces and urine wafted heavily within his breathing space.

"Wayne! Wayne!" Dayshawn calls above him. "Are you still alive?"

Finding not the energy to answer, Wayne felt as if the room was spinning. And as he had several times that day, he drifted out of consciousness.

# *Epilogue*

It was a beautiful sunny day when Wayne, with the help of Parade and a cane, walked into the hospice center to see his mother for the first time in years. He would have come earlier, but it took two weeks in a hospital bed just to recuperate from Ryan's violence. He suffered five fractures in his face, a broken arm, a torn rectum and two broken ankles. And with Jay's blessing, Parade spent each day by his side.

"Wayne," a kind white nurse says approaching him, "what happened to you, honey? I haven't seen you in such a long time. Are you okay?"

"It's a long story," he smiles. "Let's just say I'm older, wiser and stronger despite this cane right here."

"Well I'm glad you're here now and your mother will be too. She's over there by the window." She points.

Before they reach her the nurse says, "I want to let you know that her condition has worsened, Wayne. Be prepared, son. She's in the latest stage of Alzheimer's."

Wayne nods his head although nothing could prepare him for dealing with the fact that his mother was dying.

As Wayne and Parade approach Marbel, she has her back toward them and is looking out of a large window. The view shows a beautiful garden filled with colorful flowers and large oak trees. It looks like a scene from a beautiful Picasso painting.

The nurse says, "Marbel, your son Wayne is here." Then she takes the wheel chair she's sitting in, and turns her around to face him. Her head remains down. "Look, Marbel. It's your only son."

Silence.

"Well, I'll leave you all alone. But will be right over there if you need me," says the nurse before walking away.

Wayne's heart races because he can't believe how much older she looks. More silver hairs fill her mane and a few more wrinkles found their way upon her beautiful face. Sure it had been a few years, but he never would've thought that time could move so fast. Still, when he laid eyes on her, he realized that he loved her even more.

"Wayne, sit right here," Parade says helping him into a chair near Marbel who still hadn't acknowledged him. When he sits Parade says, "I'll be back when you're ready. I want to give you some time alone."

When Parade leaves, he feels alone. When Marble finally lifts her head, and looks into Wayne's eyes, she sobs heavily. Wayne touches her gently on the hand concerned she was in some sort of pain.

"Are you okay, mama? Are you in pain?"

Her sobs are heavier and she doesn't stop.

Seeing this Wayne breaks down also. "Mama, why are you crying?"

Being in the last stages of her illness, she can't speak. But she does place her soft hand on his face and continues to wail. And Wayne knows then, that despite her condition, something in her spirit recognizes her only son. And more than anything, she had been waiting on him.

"Mama, you see me don't you? You see me," he cries wrapping his arms around her body. Pulling himself together he continues. "I don't know if you know who I am, but my heart tells me you do. And mama, I just want you to know how much you mean to me. You are the best mother a son could ever have. And had it not been for my memories of you, I don't think I would have made it through the most difficult time in my life."

She looks at him as if she understands and tears continue to stream down her face.

"I just want you to know…" he sobs heavier, "I just want you to know…that it's okay to go home, mama. It's okay to let go and be with grandma. I'm strong enough to take care of myself, mama. I have loving friends and a little girl who needs me just as much as I need her. And I'm going to lavish all of the love I have for you on to her. You did a good job of raising me and you…you…need to let go. I don't want you in pain anymore." He says his body jerking forcefully from crying. "It's okay to rest now, mama. I'm strong now. It's okay to let go."

He hugged her as tightly as he could without hurting her frail body. And later that night, she died peacefully in her sleep.

◆ •••••••••••••••••••••••••••••••••••••••••• ◆

# *After The Death of the Original Queen, Marbel Peterson*

Wayne moved back to LA after all, but in a twist of events, Dayshawn, Adrian and Chris went with him. Together they ran a little restaurant that catered to the gay community and Adrian and Dayshawn also became honorary members of the House of Dreams in the LA chapter. The DC chapter was no more.

Wayne purchased a big home and the three of them, with Parade's help raised Shantay to be a beautiful little girl. Although some looked at their lifestyle as being rad and over the top, nobody in Shantay's school had more love than she did. She had three men who loved her to death and who kept her fresh and dressed in the latest gear. But being the gay men that they were, they always made sure she had a little twist to her fashion statements. Whether it was a feather boa or a pair of sneakers with rhinestones embedded in them, Miss Shantay was always fab!

Miss Wayne was so happy that he didn't think his life could get any better. And then a year later, Officer D. Hurts retired and moved to LA to be with him too. Before that they maintained a long distance relationship flying to see each other four times a month. After some time had passed, they decided to make it official. And with his love, Wayne couldn't feel more complete.

Once a year, Wayne visited his mother's grave back home. But instead of crying over her death, he celebrated her life. He felt proud to have a mother who stood by him no matter what, and he was happy to share the memories and her legacy with Shantay. He figured if she could be half as strong as his mother, she would be better for it. He could feel her guidance when it came to raising Shantay and that put him at peace.

Parade, along with her husband Jay by her side, finally confronted her father about his sexual abuse. Instead of denying what he'd done, he begged for her forgiveness. Parade forgave him, but chose not to forget or maintain a relationship with him any longer.

Mrs. Knight refused to acknowledge that she knew about the sexual abuse and after some time grew sickly. She eventually took ill and died six months later. At the funeral Parade said her goodbyes to her family and never saw her father again. She moved on with her life and didn't look back. Jay and Parade raised their three children in peace and a year later renewed their vows. They couldn't be more in love.

Ryan Carter, the Drag Queen Slayer, didn't die. Instead he was convicted and sentenced to death. The media went crazy over the case and every lawyer who wanted to be in the spotlight, tried to defend him. Movie deals were in the works along with books. This bothered Wayne because he wanted the entire thing to go away…it didn't.

Tyrone was imprisoned for both the murders of Juan and the man he burned alive in the alley, and was given life in prison. After a year in jail, he had someone write apology letters to Adrian and Wayne. When they didn't respond, he tried to get his sentence appealed by saying he was wrongfully convicted and that it was Dayshawn who committed the murders and not him. Hearing this, Wayne eventually wrote him and when Tyrone opened it, he asked his cellmate to read what it said.

"It's just one word."

"Well what does it say?" Tyrone asked.

"Football. There's only one word on this paper and it says football."

Tyrone knowing what the word meant snatched the letter and threw it in trash. He also dropped his foolishness and did his time without another mumbling word. He felt bitter, especially since his best friend Garisha didn't even answer the phone for him when he called from jail.

Paul tried to get his sentence overturned after learning the real Drag Queen Slayer was caught. And although most of the charges went back to Ryan, his attorneys were able to prove that he was nowhere near Brandon Bar the night he was murdered, and that charge remained on Paul's record as a copycat crime. He is currently doing his time in a federal prison. Although Kevin snitched on Paul about the murder, he was also charged with being an accessory, but his sentence was reduced due to his cooperation.

Wayne continues to live to be what he was born to be. A great son, friend, lover, mother and fabulous queen of LA. As far as he was concerned, nothing could stop him now.

Note to my readers....

Most of the time I know if a sequel is in order after I write a book. But, this time I'm going to leave it to my fans. If you want a sequel to this book titled, Miss Wayne and the Queens of LA, let me know. What I do I do for you.

Love *T. Styles*

Send responses to:
www.facebook.com/author.t.styles
www.thecartelpublications.com
www.ustream.tv/channel/tstyles/v3
www.youtube.com/user/tstyles74
www.twitter.com/AuthorTStyles

THE
CARTEL
street team
makin' this shit look too good...
Wanna earn some extra cash?
Join our street team and find out how?
Visit: www.thecartelpublications.com for more information.